# PRAISE FOR THE DESROSIERS DIASPORA SERIES

The empathy and tenderness that Tremblay has for his characters are evident on every page.  —*Le Devoir*

Few men write about women with his empathetic immediacy and emotional acuity. The way they talk to each other, the various masks and voices they adopt according to the needs of the moment, their deep reserves of humour and compassion – the Desrosiers sisters, and indeed the young Nana, are so alive on the page that you all but hear them speaking.  —*Montreal Gazette*

One of the most poignant novel cycles in contemporary Québec literature, shedding new light on a gallery of characters increasingly inseparable from our collective imagination.  —Voir.ca

Tremblay ... sets the groundwork for understanding that the world and the people in it are Janus-like. Good and bad, French and English, country and city, moral and immoral, brave and scared, everything is all rolled up into this thing called life.  —*Globe and Mail*

It would be unforgivable not to highlight the mastery with which the author depicts the social context of the time and, in particular, the injustice experienced daily by the working class and, more generally, by women. It is undoubtedly one of Tremblay's great strengths to be able to re-enact whole societies and families, portrayals in which the personal and the intimate forcefully unite with great social movements.  —fugues.com

## FOR MORE ABOUT THE DESROSIERS DIAS~~PORA SERIES~~ PLEASE SEE ~~...~~

# ALSO BY MICHEL TREMBLAY

All published by Talonbooks

THE DESROSIERS DIASPORA
BOOK V

# THE GRAND MELEE

## MICHEL TREMBLAY
Translated by Sheila Fischman

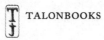 TALONBOOKS

Talonbooks
9259 Shaughnessy Street, Vancouver, British Columbia, Canada v6p 6r4
talonbooks.com

Talonbooks is located on xʷməθkʷəy̓əm, Sḵwx̱wú7mesh, Stó:lō, and səl̓ilwətaʔɬ Lands.

First printing: 2021

Typeset in Caslon
Printed and bound in Canada on 100% post-consumer recycled paper

Cover design by andrea bennett. Interior design by Typesmith
Cover illustration by Brad Collins

Talonbooks acknowledges the financial support of the Canada Council for the Arts, the Government of Canada through the Canada Book Fund, and the Province of British Columbia through the British Columbia Arts Council and the Book Publishing Tax Credit.

This work was originally published in French as *La grande mêlée* by Leméac Éditeur, Montréal, Québec, and Actes Sud, Arles, France, in 2011. We acknowledge the financial support of the Government of Canada through the National Translation Program for Book Publishing, an initiative of the *Roadmap for Canada's Official Languages 2013–2018: Education, Immigration, Communities*, for our translation activities.

LIBRARY AND ARCHIVES CANADA CATALOGUING IN PUBLICATION

Title: The grand melee / Michel Tremblay ; translated by Sheila Fischman.
Other titles: Grande mêlée. English
Names: Tremblay, Michel, 1942– author. | Fischman, Sheila, translator.
Description: Series statement: The Desrosiers diaspora ; book v |
    Translation of: La grande mêlée.
Identifiers: Canadiana 202102390oX | ISBN 9781772012613 (softcover)
Classification: LCC PS8539.R47 G7213 2021 | DDC c843/.54—dc23

*For Hélène Stevens, Roland Laroche,*
*Robert Asselin, and Norbert Boudreau*

*The past is never dead. It's not even past.*

—WILLIAM FAULKNER
*Requiem for a Nun* (1951)

# THE ART OF THE CHRONICLE

When *The Fat Woman Next Door Is Pregnant* was published in 1978, Michel Tremblay was unaware that he was embarking on the immense project that would become the *Chronicles of the Plateau-Mont-Royal*. The cycle – which would later amount to six volumes published over the next two decades and become a staple of francophone literature – was immediately adopted by thousands of readers. Anthologized in 2000 in Éditions Leméac's prestigious Thesaurus series (and individually published in English by Talonbooks in the 1980s and 1990s), the six volumes of Tremblay's *Chronicles* (*The Fat Woman Next Door Is Pregnant, Thérèse and Pierrette and the Little Hanging Angel, The Duchess and the Commoner, News from Édouard, The First Quarter of the Moon*, and *A Thing of Beauty*) have continued to gain new aficionados in both French and English.

Himself an avid reader of chronicles and literary sagas of all kinds – Balzac's *La Comédie humaine*, Zola's *Les Rougon-Macquart*, Proust's *In Search of Lost Time*, Sartre's *The Roads to Freedom*, Asimov's *Foundation* series, Herbert's *Dune* novels, Simmons's *Hyperion Cantos*, and, more recently, Follett's *Century Trilogy* – Michel Tremblay had already staged in his theatrical works several hundred characters, both real and fictional, when he began the writing of the *Chronicles of the Plateau-Mont-Royal*. Many of these characters at one point left the theatrical stage and moved into novel territory, a passage that allows readers to trace their evolution. And so the *Chronicles*, set between 1942 and 1963 and taking up more than a thousand pages, are the sum of several entwined stories forming a coherent narrative whole. Contemporary writers capable of creating a family tree of characters of such magnitude are rare. In fifty years of writing, Tremblay has given life to more than three thousand characters; they circulate in an oeuvre that celebrates their deeds, their youth and old age, their joys and sorrows, their freedom and *mal de vivre* – that indefinable virus always so impermeable to happiness.

Twenty years after the publication of the last book of the *Chronicles*, the nine volumes of the second of Michel Tremblay's great sagas, *The Desrosiers Diaspora*, have also been anthologized in a fourteen-hundred-page Thesaurus edition by Leméac, and are in the process of being translated into English by Talonbooks (*Crossing the Continent*, 2011; *Crossing the City*, 2014; *A Crossing of Hearts*, 2017; *Rite of Passage*, 2019; *The Grand Melee*, 2021; *Twists of Fate*, forthcoming 2021). The *Diaspora* follows the lives of hundreds of Felliniesque new characters – pragmatists, dreamers, poor souls, frolickers, inconsolable or unrepentant, but always bolstered by the natural resilience of ordinary people – who mingle with the old ones by getting off trains, checking into hotels, walking up and down avenues, visiting shops, entering train stations, boarding trams, exiting kitchens, setting foot in clubs. They end up piecing together the great puzzle of a clan scattered across North America, from Sainte-Maria-de-Saskatchewan to Providence, Rhode Island, to Regina, Winnipeg, Ottawa, Montréal, and Duhamel, in the Laurentians. The Desrosiers move a lot, eager to believe that happiness is (always) elsewhere – but they all have a lump in their throats and a weight on their hearts.

Rhéauna, nicknamed Nana – the "fat woman next door" who will give birth to Jean-Marc, the author's alter ego – is undeniably the central figure of Michel Tremblay's fictional universe. But the story of the artist's origins, his childhood and love stories, the household of his youth and the women who helped him grow through the joys and sorrows of his destiny – his great-grandmother Joséphine and his grandmother Maria, his great-aunts Tititte and Teena, his heroic cousin Ti-Lou, a.k.a. the She-Wolf of Ottàwa – all remained to be written. Starting with *Crossing the Continent*, the first volume of the *Desrosiers Diaspora*, Tremblay has listened to the gentle stream of maternal memories and begun to narrate, sometimes by way of invention, the incredible adventures of the Desrosiers family.

He has started to unearth the treasures of his own family's maternal side. This grand story, unfolding from one novel to the next, takes on fantastical accents, to re-enact the real and the marvellous, the comic and the tragic, the faded romances and the impossible ones, to weave the personal and collective memories.

The art of the chronicle consists of staging real or fictional characters, all the while evoking authentic social and historical facts, and respecting the chronology of their unfolding. However the art of the chronicler is to blend the true and the false, the intimate and the social, the near and the far, the grand design and the modest story, all with their different lineages and their chance occurrences, so as to snatch a little more meaning from flowing, tranquil, impetuous life.

The art of the chronicle, of course – but the art of the chronicler, especially.

—PIERRE FILION, JUNE 2017
translated by Charles Simard

This is a work of fiction. The names of some characters are real, but everything else is made up.

—M.T.

# PROLOGUE

It took them a while to locate Josaphat.

You can't say that they were desperate, or even anxious, especially in the beginning; after all there was no rush. They knew – Florence often told her daughters – that the time would come, when they were walking on the street or leaving a store or a movie, when he would introduce himself to them, his fiddle under his arm or not, a little older maybe, but just as sharp, just as charming as before, with those eyes that transfix you, his supple walk, his casual manner of an independent man. How would he greet them? Ignore them? Walk by as if he didn't even see them because he felt he no longer needed them now that he was making a life for himself in the big city? Or on the contrary, would he throw himself into their arms, saying that he'd been waiting for so long that he'd despaired of ever seeing them again? And above all, that he'd been bored out of his mind? Wanting conversation over slices of bread with molasses, knitting baby booties, and music, music most of all, the music that had filled and lulled so many afternoons that otherwise, without them, without the piano, without the fiddle, would have been desperately dull. And that he hoped to start everything anew here, now that they'd found one another.

They knew that he was there, however, that he hadn't disappeared, hadn't been swallowed, digested or destroyed by this hostile environment that had been imposed on him, far from the gentleness of the Laurentians, and that he was ever vigilant because every month, year in, year out, the moon rose full and white and regal, without one spot of blood on its wrinkled surface. No trace either of the horses struck down by pain. The sky owed Josaphat nights of tremendous

3

calm, and on nights when the moon was full, when the sky turned stormy or there was a threat of a blizzard, only nature's disorders were responsible. He hadn't once forgotten his duty since the birth of his son, a sign that he was taking his task seriously and that he still accepted the huge responsibility incumbent upon him. Wherever he was and whatever he was doing, he would take his fiddle from its case and send into the icy or the sticky night his jig or his ballad. To save the moon.

Rose, Violette, Mauve, and their mother Florence criss-crossed the streets of the metropolis in search of the man who made the moon rise whom they'd brought into the world and who had broken away from them by following his sister into the city.

At first they had been disconcerted by the commotion of the city. Having taken refuge for so long on the outskirts of a remote little village on the border of the Gatineau, they had eventually forgotten the clatter and roar of large centres and the constant hum of cars. The smell of gasoline too, to these women who till then had known only the piquant scent of horse manure, had been unsettling. But finally they'd come to enjoy the great intermingling of humanity in perpetual movement, excited as little girls by the variety of clothing, colours, odours, the comings and goings that didn't stop till nightfall, by the vivid conversations they overheard. The Montréal language astonished them with its residues of old French and the constant presence of English words translated by sound, genuine neologisms born from the fact that the men who worked for English companies brought home English expressions, while the women wanted to go on speaking French.

They had criss-crossed the city streets from north to south, from east to west, sloshing through slush in the spring and stirring up dust in the summer, kicking up piles of dead leaves in the autumn and creaking across the snow in the winter. They had walked along the last orchards on avenue Laurier and crossed the depressing business sections, visited the nightclubs on boulevard Saint-Laurent and wandered along the paths in parc La Fontaine. They came to know a good number of the boutiques and department stores on rue

Sainte-Catherine, they'd even gone all the way to Longue-Pointe at the very end of the Island of Montréal in the east, and they had ventured to Verdun in the southwest.

And so, the weeks became months, the months, years.

Had they been visible, one could have asked who were these ladies from another age, dressed as if in the last century; squeezed into impressive outfits cinched at the waist; gloved summer and winter; wearing broad, sophisticated hats when for some time now fashion had dictated narrow, shortish dresses and cloche hats. But they were strolling through the city where no one could ever see them. People passed through them unawares, without detecting any sort of perfume along the way. Now and then, though, someone would turn their head or break off a conversation: something, there, had brushed against them, a vague scent of roses or violets had gone by or a voice out of nowhere had spoken a word or two.

When that happened, Florence would say to her daughters: "That might be a candidate for us ..."

Or:

"If we had time to look after ..."

They continued on their way, though, their task being to find Josaphat, not to look for recruits. So far their protege hadn't failed at his task – who knows what can happen in a big city where temptations are many and transgressions easy? Especially when you're dealing with a moony type like Josaphat? But it was not yet time to look for a replacement and they continued their systematic exploration of the city.

They lived in empty houses or apartments they'd found during their strolls. For more than a year, they'd haunted a huge six-room apartment at the Château on rue Sherbrooke Ouest, until it was rented to a wealthy engineer with the department of roads whose arrogance they'd hated at first sight and they had moved out without further ado, then a number of smaller places in the vicinity of avenue du Mont-Royal, which they liked because the population reminded them of the people in Duhamel with whom they'd rubbed shoulders for so long. Most of them, who'd moved to the city to earn a living, came from the nearby or more distant countryside, weren't very happy in the big city, and held on to their provincial attitudes, which Florence and her daughters appreciated.

They moved into these places without giving them much thought: an apartment around the corner would be free, they just had to open the door and all their possessions would already be there. They would settle in for an undetermined period, unquestioning, switch on the stove, the electricity – an amazing but invaluable invention – without even bothering to see if food was waiting in the cupboards. They knew that there would be and that nothing would be missing. It didn't matter to them anyway, their quest was more important than their personal well-being, and they'd have been content with a simple room with two double beds if by mischance it had come to that.

No matter where they settled, the pregnant women in the neighbourhood received a pair of baby booties (blue or pink) the day after giving birth because Florence's daughters went on knitting – it had always been their main task – when they came back from their wandering. The long evenings – with or without the gramophone, another fascinating novelty for them – were spent amid the click of their needles and the innocuous remarks that they exchanged. A teapot would be keeping warm inside a cretonne cozy, Florence would be tinkling on the piano, or the gramophone would be filling the room with music that seemed to come from another planet, so muffled was the sound, the evening would pass with a slowness that without being altogether unpleasant, left the four women with a sense of incompleteness.

And they set out again every day in search of Josaphat – or of Victoire, because they knew she would lead them to him – indifferent to snowstorms or rain, weaving through cars on the main streets, making haste through disreputable neighbourhoods, slowing down when one piqued their curiosity. They went so far as to laze on park benches for long hours. Just in case. You never knew when good luck would appear out of the blue and it was most important not to miss it, Josaphat could show up at any moment and it was most important that they did not miss him. But still he did not appear and Florence had to talk to her daughters more and more often about patience and trust when she herself, after all this time, was starting to doubt the appropriateness of her decision to leave Duhamel for this life of wandering through a hectic city looking for a musician-poet, vigilant to date but who could at any moment break his word and set off a disaster. It was their role to avoid that disaster and to see to it that Josaphat didn't falter, didn't give in to his natural laziness, his dangerous daydreams, on condition that they could find the man so as to protect him. Meanwhile Florence had to encourage her daughters to continue this adventure of which she herself was beginning to sense the conclusion.

One damp summer day as they were strolling along Mont-Royal listening to the conversations of passersby, the odd remark anyway, which amused them, they stopped in front of a window of the L.N. Messier department store, between rue Fabre and rue Marquette on the south side, with its offerings of the loose and pretty well shapeless sack dresses which they thought were hideous and would never wear.

Rose (or Violette or Mauve) had shrugged.

"Is that what we'll see on the streets this fall? Poor women!"

Florence had tugged at her veil, which had slipped aside in the slight breeze.

"Maybe it's handier for walking on the streets, but it sure is ugly!"

"Handier? What d'you mean, handier?"

"At least it won't drag in the mud ... It's modern."

"Maybe it is, Moman, but they don't have to show so much leg!"

"You just see a little bit above the shoes ..."

"Even that is too much!"

Florence had hidden her smile behind her glove.

"We've seen so many things, we've been around for so long, nothing should surprise us, it seems to me."

"I still think they're going too far!"

"You said the same thing when plunging necklines came in, long ago ..."

"And I was right!"

"You have to keep up with the times."

"We don't have to say yes to everything."

"Maybe what's coming will be worse."

"Then I'll criticize it when it comes!"

Florence had laid her hand on the shoulder of Rose (or Violette or Mauve).

"You don't like things to change, do you?"

Her daughter had pointed to the dresses in the window.

"No. But I guess that doesn't mean anything. I'll just have to get used to them. And so will you. 'Specially in the city where everything changes so fast."

Her mother had laughed.

"We've been here for a while now. If you still aren't used to ..."

Absorbed as they were by their study of the style they thought was ridiculous in the dresses displayed in the window – slightly loose at the waist, the top drooping, the shapeless sleeves that hung every which way – they didn't hear the fiddle music coming through the open doors of the department store right away.

Florence reacted first.

She was about to reply to a remark by one of her daughters when a familiar sensation, a sense of déjà vu, like the recurrence of a long-sought state of grace thought to be lost, the perfect note of a favourite perfume, made her look up. It took her a moment to understand what was going on.

The note was stretched out, melancholy, a single note on a fiddle that held all the nostalgia in the world, a caress at the level of the heart that, though not painful, nonetheless stirred up a whiff of concern, of doubt and languor in which one could have let oneself drown. It made you want to cry without being really sad. And to experience terrible ordeals.

A lady leaving the store had turned around on hearing it and she'd hesitated for a few seconds before continuing on her way. She had glanced inside the establishment as she went past the second door but didn't decide to go in and see who was playing. After taking a handkerchief from her purse, she'd gone into the shop next door, a shoe store.

Florence had pressed her hand on the glass when a second note, just as devastating, replaced the first one. At the third, she recognized the beginning of a tune she had often listened to with her eyes closed, head thrown back, hands on the armrests of her chair. A melody born in the soul of a budding great musician who expressed with his instrument things that he couldn't share with other people.

"I think we've finally found what we've been looking for."

All four looked at each other, astonished, before joy and relief took hold of them.

After so many years. All that fruitless wandering, the futile exploration of a teeming city, mistaken hopes when a scrap of music emerged from a tavern or a restaurant, had nonetheless brought them here, in front of a display of dresses too modern for their taste, just when they were beginning to despair. Had they not stopped to pass judgment on what women's fashion had in store come autumn, they'd have once again gone home – an attractive apartment facing a park – weary and on the verge of dejection. Had it happened before? And how many times?

So they stepped inside L.N. Messier with hope in their hearts.

He was standing erect, legs apart and head high, at the end of the central aisle of the department store. He had closed his eyes as he so often did when playing one of his favourite pieces. His body was swaying slowly to the rhythm of the music. His left hand was stroking the cords without seeming to touch them, while the bow, held firmly in the right, rose and fell, producing extraordinary sounds.

Some women had stopped to listen after setting their packages on the polished wood floor or a nearby counter. It was not the sort of music they were used to, nothing to do with folklore or facile romance, but its hold on them was obvious: they were listening, necks craned, bodies leaning forward as if they wanted to get closer to the musician and his instrument; some had their hands at their hearts, others had taken out a handkerchief. It made listeners want to cry, yet go on living in spite of everything. It was a balm for unconfessed ills, a welcome distraction, a ray of hope in the middle of a far-too-ordinary afternoon.

An old lady who seemed to know more about music than the others had leaned across to her neighbour, most likely her daughter, murmuring:

"What's he doing playing the fiddle at the back of a store, he oughtta be in a concert hall! Poor man!"

Florence and her daughters hadn't dared get too close for fear that he would sense their presence, which would unnerve him. They occupied the centre of the main aisle with no one aware of them. And a great sadness was already beginning to change the happiness they'd felt at finding him again.

He had aged. In Duhamel they'd have said that he'd put on years. His complexion was yellow, his hair – his pride and joy in the past – was dull, turning grey in spots and thin as well, wrinkles crossed his forehead, a harsh line marked his mouth in spite of the beauty of what he was playing. Everything that mattered to him, they realized, was summed up in the melodic line that was rising at this very moment in a store smelling of dust, yard goods, the metal of household appliances, and the cheap perfume that was given away to customers. As soon as he opened his eyes at the end of his serenade, the magical world of music, his reason for being, his refuge, would vanish and he would be once again deep in the sad reality of his present-day existence: a great talent wasted, an exceptional musician doomed to make his living at the back of department stores, an artist humiliated, a poet rejected. His whole body, despite the beauty of what he was playing, cried out his distress. And his defeat.

Where was the enthusiasm of his youth, his passion for Victoire, his great love for his son? Had he lost all of that? Had the big city in the end swallowed him up, even if every month he still found the courage to take out his instrument to help the full moon rise? And even that, did it still matter to him? Wasn't he really doing it now out of habit? Because of an old promise? Were they seeing merely the empty shell of what at another time had been a receptacle of urges, of enthusiasms and hopes?

At the end of his piece, he had kept his eyes closed as if he were refusing to leave the world he'd been plunged into.

Some women had applauded. The saleswomen, accustomed to hearing him play and a little exasperated by the diversion of each of his performances – one in the morning, the other in the afternoon – had just folded their arms and waited for customers to come back and lean across the counters or ask for their advice. Among the staff, word was getting around, though of course no one knew the source, that this fiddler brought bad luck, and they did what they could to avoid him. Once his fifteen minutes were up, the clients retrieved their rolls of yard goods and kitchen utensils, he went back down the central aisle amid general indifference and left without saying goodbye. The managers kept him on because customers liked listening to him play. If it was up to the saleswomen, though, he wouldn't have lasted long. Even if some of them found him attractive despite his haggard look and his downcast expression of a lost man.

The old woman had come up to him, touched the edge of his threadbare jacket sleeve.

"You play too well to stay here ..."

A sad smile formed on his lips.

"I don't always play good like that, you know."

Then he opened his eyes.

He recognized them right away but he knew that he mustn't react because he was the only one who could see them. He couldn't cry happily, throw himself into their arms, embrace them, and tell them that he thought about them every day in his exile, that hundreds of times he had dreamed about boarding the train to join them and lose himself in their universe where all that existed was the love of music and bread and molasses. And the full moon, once every month. All he could do was smile.

And the smile he gave them, so glorious after the sorrow contained in the answer he'd just given her, the old woman took for herself.

"You must've been some looker when you were young."

He answered without looking at her.

"I'm still young, Madame. What's old is the life I live."

The old woman had moved away, brushed against Florence without realizing it, and walked out of L.N. Messier, humming the beautiful melody she'd just listened to, which would haunt the rest of her day. And her night. She was already planning to come back and listen to him the next morning.

In fact that was one of the main reasons the store management was determined to keep him on.

He had walked through his friends, telling them very quietly to follow him. He'd even touched Florence's sleeve to convince himself that he wasn't mistaken, that they really were there.

A saleswoman who'd heard him had called out:

"You've got some nerve! No way I'd follow you! Anywhere! I'm gonna complain and you'll have to put on your silly show some-where else, let me tell you! Cheeky!"

As soon as he was out on the sidewalk he'd leaned against one of the display windows.

"It's like that all the time. Every single day."

He held his fiddle case close to him.

"If people walking by hear me talking to you they'll think I'm crazy. Mind you, it wouldn't change much. They already think that."

Florence came up to him, ran her hand over his forehead.

"I'm glad I found you again, Josaphat."

He had bent double, at the risk of dropping his fiddle onto the sidewalk.

"Don't make me cry. Don't make me cry right now. Follow me, we'll find a place where we can talk."

The lady who had gone into the shoe store earlier had come out onto the sidewalk when she saw him pass by.

"Was that you playing the fiddle just now? I saw you getting ready but I didn't know you were so good! I didn't have time to stay but … I'm going to come back and listen to you."

He answered a hasty thanks, without stopping.

"Are you there every day?"

This time he turned around. And spoke to her as he was backing up.

"Twice a day, Madame. From ten o'clock to ten-fifteen, then three o'clock till three-fifteen."

She gestured to him.

"I'll be there! And you'll play the same thing as this morning! I want to hear the whole piece this time. And … I don't know but it seems to me I know you."

A voice had come from the back of the store:

"There's customers waiting, Mademoiselle Desrosiers …"

Josaphat had turned south on rue Fabre.

"We'll go to parc La Fontaine. There's not many people at this time of day."

As he had predicted, the park was nearly empty. Most of the people who crossed it at this time of day were going to the work site of Hôpital Notre-Dame, one of the biggest in the city, or coming back from there. Josaphat had settled on one of the first benches, near rue Rachel.

"Nobody but police around now. If one comes by I'll stop talking to you, then I'll start again after he goes … I just hope he won't ask me too many questions. Sometimes they take me for a lush and I have a hard time proving that I'm not."

He looked at them for a long moment, hugging his fiddle case.

They wore the same clothes as when he used to take refuge at their place to play music with Florence while her three daughters knitted in silence or chatted quietly. They hadn't aged one day whereas he, he was aware of it, had deteriorated over the years because of how he'd abused his body: drink, too many rough nights, easy women, laudanum, even a little absinthe, the poets' poison, in fact everything the big city can offer a man who's suffering and who wants to forget. He was a young old man, while they would be forever ageless, impervious to the ravages of time, eternal consolers of those they chose to help or who were sent to them. The four faces, so kind, looked at him with the same indulgence, the affection he could read there, as in the past, making him forget the troubles, the embarrassment, the torments. Their mere presence wiped out everything that was negative and painful in his life.

"You aren't talking. Want me to go first?"

Florence had sat next to him while Rose, Violette, and Mauve, whom he still couldn't tell apart, settled at his feet on the clay path with their dresses spread around them like petals. He had thought, as in the past, about their names of colours and flowers, and tears had finally sprung to his eyes.

"Oh boy, does that ever feel good. To cry. I haven't been able to for so long."

Florence had pulled up her veil.

"We've been looking for you for years."

"Years? You've been in Montréal for years?"

She then told him a shortened version of the attempts she and her daughters had made to find him. He'd cried even harder, saying that they shouldn't have, that he wasn't worth it, that he didn't deserve so much attention, but soon a hint of aggressiveness tinged his remarks.

"I made you a promise when I was young and never, you hear me, *never* would I dare to not respect it! Even dead drunk, even sick, and that happened, believe me. If you'd looked for me to waylay me, if you came here to spy on me, let me tell you, you could've not bothered and stayed in your fancy transparent castle on the shores of Lac Long. I don't need you to tell me what I gotta do!"

Florence had placed her hand on his knee.

"We aren't spying, Josaphat, and we don't lack confidence in you either."

"What is it then?"

"We've just found each other after years, Josaphat, if you ask me this is no time to squabble. Two minutes ago you were crying tears of joy, then all of a sudden …"

He'd calmed down, apologized.

"I was mad at you for letting me leave without following me. After that I was glad to be free. But finally I was desperate because I was too lonesome. I'm so lonesome, if you only knew! I let Victoire live her life, I didn't have the right to get involved with her business, she's the one who chose to marry Télesphore to give Gabriel an official father, and I knew she was right ... She was real lucky to find a guy who agreed to marry her with her kid ... Seems Télesphore can't have children and he was ready to adopt Gabriel ... But me, I couldn't stay in Duhamel, so far away from them! They were everything I had in this world! My sister and our child. I'd rather be unhappy close to them than happy but far away! I started by playing the funny uncle with Gabriel, I wanted to be serious about my new role so I'd get used to it, I told myself that eventually I'd accept it all ... Him, the child I loved so much, at first he didn't really understand what was going on but Télesphore was real good with him and he finally got attached to him. Him, he saw every day but me, it was only now and then ... I don't think he even remembers I'm his father! I don't think he remembers!"

He'd taken out a big checkered handkerchief, wiped his eyes, then blown his nose with it.

"So when I found out ... When I found out Victoire was pregnant when we left Duhamel, that we were going to have a second child ... I decided not to see them anymore, none of them, I yelled at Victoire, then I went through a really bad period, heavy drinking and living on the street like a homeless beggar. I didn't even try to earn a living with my fiddle, I ate whatever, whenever. There was just the promise I made to you, the only thing I never forgot. Not once! I could be in a tavern, drunk as a skunk or in a club looking at a beautiful woman who wanted nothing to do with me, I could've had an aching skull or been sick as a dog, I could'a stunk like a skunk or vomited down a hole, I never forgot my promise, not once. Not one single time. True, I sometimes cursed the moon, I was pissed off 'cause she depended on me, just like that, I felt like ... like her slave or her servant, but I never would'a let myself abandon her. That's all that was left of my old life! If I'd disappeared, if I'd jumped in the river like I often thought of doing, who'd'a looked after her? Who? I did it out of love for you. Because you gave me the gift of music. Because you'd saved me. Even if you'd condemned me to do the very same thing every month for the rest of my life to avoid some terrible tragedy."

He'd gotten up, walked away a few steps. He had gone on talking as if he'd reached the crucial part of what he had to say, that he was a little ashamed of.

"Albertine. That's her name, Albertine. Our second child. And she's the very opposite of her brother. As much as Gabriel was a peaceful, quiet child, she was ... I don't know ... Victoire says it comes from our mother's side, and it's true they were a weird bunch. Tough, stupid, mean. I don't know ... Maybe because I don't see her very often, but ... I've hardly ever seen that child smile, I don't think. She's always hidden away in some corner, moping, always looks like she's mad at us, always fighting with her mother. It's as if ... She's just a child but it seems like already she doesn't think much of life. I'm scared for her. I try to picture her in ten years' time, twenty years, and I'm scared of how she'll take everything she'll have to live."

He'd turned towards Florence and her daughters.

"Sorry to be talking about all that. But I'm on my own and I never talk to nobody. Maybe I do in a tavern when I'm pie-eyed or lying in bed in a cathouse, but I don't remember that afterwards and it doesn't make me feel any better."

He coughed into his fist, then came back and sat down.

"What do we do now we've found each other again?"

Florence pulled down her veil and stood up.

"We're here so you'll tell us about those things, Josaphat. We were too far away to protect you anymore but when you feel the need to say things like that or if you're in the mood to do something stupid, as of now you can do like you used to, you can come and see us, that's what we're here for."

"Are you going away? But we just found each other ..."

"No, we aren't going away. I'd like you to show us where you're staying. We'll try and find something nearby."

"I'm on rue Amherst, corner of De Montigny. It's over a passage that leads to the back of the house, so it can't be heated in winter but it doesn't cost much. And by chance, there's an empty house right next door."

"It's not by chance, Josaphat ..."

Before getting to his feet, he'd stared at them, one after the other, frowning.

"You're really there, eh? You exist for real? It's not just 'cause I'm crazy? Comfort me. Put my mind at rest, I honestly don't know ..."

That morning the few people who'd seen a fiddler in parc La Fontaine had not seen the four women who were following him, smiling.

And as of that day, lights shone every evening in the empty apartment next door to where Josaphat-le-Violon was living; people even claimed to have heard music, piano and fiddle, on nights when the moon was full.

PART ONE

# AN IRRESISTIBLE
# INVITATION

# MONTRÉAL, MAY 1922

## *Rhéauna*

She should go and wake up the girls. But this morning she'll give them the gift of a few minutes more sleep. They'll just have to eat breakfast faster. Or spend less time primping. Especially Alice, who at sixteen is a little too aware that she is turning into a magnificent creature and spends hours admiring herself in the mirror, trying out new hairstyles and unlikely colours of rouge and lipstick. Béa, always a bit overweight – that's been a problem for her since childhood – has trouble shrugging off her natural laziness and would gladly spend all day lolling on a sofa eating chocolates and reading fashion magazines. She can't follow fashions; nothing suits her, practically nothing about this new way of dressing which tends to show what used to be hidden, but she devours anything that's printed about new styles and encourages her sister in her delusions of grandeur, her desire for extravagant dresses and storybook adventures. Through Alice she lives the dreams that she won't indulge in herself, which annoys Rhéauna who thinks Béa is beautiful in spite of and maybe even because of her stoutness; she's convinced that her sister could find a good match if only she'd take the trouble. If she has seen some boys hang around Béa, mainly she has sensed her sister stiffen at their advances, as if she can't believe that anyone would take an interest in her or find her attractive.

Béa often tells her sisters that those boys think she's "delectable," while she'd like a man who would love her for something other than her generous curves, her intelligence for instance, her sense of humour, her conversation. Rhéauna is well aware that's not true, that Béa dreams of men looking at her the way they look at Alice, that they'd find her more than delectable, go into raptures over the narrow waist she doesn't have and the lightness of movement that she'll never be able to mimic, and it infuriates her. She wishes that her sister would accept her physique; in spite of everything she senses Béa getting stuck in a kind of self-hatred that she finds shocking.

All right. Time to shake them up in their beds. Another session of grunts and protests and expletives, too, from Alice who, ever since she's been working as a leaf shaker at Macdonald Tobacco, has been using language that would make your hair stand on end.

She brings the mirror up to her face, plucks a flake of dry skin off her nose, spreads a little rouge on her cheeks. She thinks that she's not so ugly this morning. She'd slept all night though she'd been expecting nightmares because of the tiresome day ahead of her – buying a wedding gown can't be easy – and thinks about the third of June with some excitement instead of the usual anxiety.

On the third of June she will marry Gabriel at the Church of Saint-Pierre-Apôtre on Dorchester, two minutes from the apartment on Montcalm, and for the first time since he popped the question – which she'd been anticipating, of course, and had been a long time coming because of her prospective husband's terrible shyness – she doesn't sense the little shadow of doubt that until then had been clouding her heart. Not that she was questioning her love for Gabriel, no, of that she is certain, she wants to spend the rest of her life with him, she's known that ever since she started spending time with him. Something else is troubling her, a sense of uncertainty regarding this definitive choice, the loss of her childhood dreams with no appeal perhaps, or the avenue that she's about to take which will change her life forever. She will go on working when they are first married, but as soon as she's in the family way she'll have no choice but to do like all other women and shut herself away to bring up her offspring.

It's been a long time since she dreamed of becoming the greatest writer in Canada, she knows that was childish, and she smiles now when she thinks of it. The great leap that she's going to take, however, that plunge into the world outside the family, the world unlike that in which her mother, whom she admires so much, has been living for so long, her new world where the woman stays at home while the husband, the chief, the provider, earns their sustenance, makes her dizzy because she doesn't know if she will be able to endure it for very long. For her husband, for their children, yes – she wants several and she will love them as very few children have ever been loved – but deep down, in the very depths of herself, will she ever accept that loss of independence, that tremendous sacrifice? She realizes that she won't be able to do otherwise, that the world is made that way, that she can't do anything about it, but … It's strange, though, sitting at her vanity this morning, it no longer bothers her. And instead of relief, she feels anxiety.

She gets up, puts on her new dress that her sisters envy and that cost a good chunk of her weekly salary. She won't go to work today, she has an appointment at the Salon de la Mariée at Dupuis Frères with her mother and her two aunts, Tititte and Teena. She would have liked to choose her wedding gown in total peace, perhaps with her mother who would have let her make her own choice all alone, but Maria had insisted that Tititte, the family's fashion expert, always dressed to kill and the height of elegance despite her more-than-limited budget, had to be there. Tititte had flawless taste, she claimed, even though she was also a bit too inclined to impose it on everyone else. Then Maria had added that if ma tante Teena discovered that they'd gone without her to buy something so important, she'd have a fit that could go on for weeks. So Teena had been invited to join the group.

Putting on her shoes, Rhéauna wonders why she has gotten ready so early: the appointment is for the afternoon, she could have spent the morning in her housecoat, reading magazines or the rest of

Colette's novel *Chéri*, which she'd started a few days earlier and is particularly interested in because it's on the Index, in any case, waited till the last minute to get dolled up. Most likely she'll have to do everything over before they leave. She thinks that she's ridiculous when she leaves her room. She's not fourteen any more, she should be able to employ patience, better control herself.

She is attracted by a sound from the back of the apartment. And strangely enough it smells of coffee when she's the one who makes it every morning.

She finds her mother and her little brother sitting at the kitchen table. Théo is eating a bowl of oatmeal. Rhéauna can't remember ever seeing her mother fix the morning meal for her children and tries to hide her surprise by blowing a kiss to her brother. Théo, as Béa had shown him years before, has poured a huge pile of brown sugar onto his porridge and poured milk over it all. The milk has penetrated under the cereal and raised it, hence the name "floating island" for the dish, at least according to Béa who claims that she invented it and is quick to take credit for it.

Maria scrutinizes her daughter from head to toe.

"Where d'you think you're going, all dolled up first thing in the morning?"

Rhéauna pours herself a coffee, sits down beside Théo, and ruffles his hair. He jerks his head away, grumbling. He's nine now, not a baby, he hates it when his sisters cuddle him. Being spoiled, receiving presents or devouring what's cooked for him, so be it, but caresses and childish things get on his nerves. He's independent now and he wants people to know it.

"I know I'm silly, Moman, but I couldn't wait to get dressed for the appointment this afternoon."

"Poor you, you'll have to do it all over again. You know you can't go that long without getting dirty, you know what you're like."

"That's exactly what I was telling myself on my way out of my bedroom. If it happens, I'll just start over. I've got other dresses."

"But that one's the new one."

"So…"

"You don't want to put on an old dress to go out and buy a

wedding gown. It doesn't make sense! You have to show you've got good taste or else the salesgirl's gonna try to sell you any old thing!"

"I don't know her but when she finds out that I work at Dupuis Frères, so I'm her colleague, she won't try and sell me any old thing. Besides, ma tante Tititte will be there, there's no danger."

"As far as that's concerned ..."

Maria gets up to put two slices of bread on the old wood stove.

"Go put your nightie back on while I make your toast."

Rhéauna sticks her finger in the lukewarm oatmeal and Théo lets out a cry of protest.

"Hands off my porridge!"

Maria turns towards her children, arms akimbo.

"That's enough, you two! And Nana, I told you to change! I don't want you to shame me in front of your aunt Tititte!"

Rhéauna, who has no intention of going back to her room to get into her nightie, tries to create a diversion by changing the subject.

"They aren't awake yet? I'll go and shake 'em up."

She plants a kiss on her mother's neck before she exits the kitchen.

"And what're you doing up so early? I heard you come in around 1 a.m., as usual. You'll be tired when you go to work tonight."

Maria turns the slices of bread on the stove burner.

"Your toast's nearly done and you're still in the kitchen!"

"You didn't answer my question, Moman ..."

Maria takes the butter out of the icebox.

"Okay, I'll eat that toast myself."

Rhéauna leans against the door frame.

"Moman, I asked you a question."

Briskly, Maria slaps the toast onto a plate, then seats herself across from Théo.

"I'm allowed to have a date in the morning, aren't I?"

Rhéauna shrugs.

"Sure. With Monsieur Rambert?"

Maria spreads too much butter on her bread, tries to scrape off the excess.

"Hardly."

"So you don't want to tell me with who?"

"No, I don't want to tell you with who. D'you understand? Now go wake up your sisters."

Opening their bedroom door, Rhéauna finds Béa and Alice already up. Their work clothes are scattered over the beds, shoes are strewn on the floor, there's a smell of cheap perfume, and the girls are bustling around for fear of being late.

"How come you didn't wake us up?"

"D'you know it takes me an hour on the streetcar to get to work?"

"All I know is Mademoiselle doesn't give a hoot about us, Mademoiselle's going to buy her wedding gown!"

Rhéauna merely smiles.

"You aren't one minute late. Neither one of you. And you, Alice, you've just got half an hour on the streetcar, don't exaggerate! If I'd come to wake you, you wouldn't've gotten up any earlier, I know you! I have to threaten you every morning before you move your big toe! You got up at the same time as usual, late, as usual, but it's easier for you to pin it on me!"

Béa, already hot, wipes her face before putting on her dress, a threadbare old peacock-blue thing that she wears as a last resort when she hasn't anything clean to put on.

"I can't understand why that cookie factory opens an hour before the other stores!"

Alice's makeup never looks good because she puts it on too fast; she shrugs and makes a face.

"It's so greedy guts like you can start overeating earlier than the others. Is there already a lineup of fat women at the door when you get there in the morning?"

Béa gives her a smack upside the head.

"Aren't you funny! Instead of playing the clown you ought to check your hose. There's a great big run in the left one!"

Alice lets out an oath, gets up, tossing her lipstick onto the vanity, turns around at the mirror hanging behind the door.

"That's not even true!"

"Scared you, eh?"

"How'd you like to sell cookies by the pound with a black eye, Béa? Just say the word and …"

Rhéauna remembers their arrival in town six years earlier. Her sisters' panic at the hustle and bustle of the city – they'd known nothing but Sainte-Maria-de-Saskatchewan; their reluctance – which had lasted for quite a long time – to go out, even just to the wooden sidewalk on rue Montcalm; their consternation at the sight of streetcars and the number of automobiles criss-crossing rue Sainte-Catherine; their astonishment, too, at the size of their new school and the fear inspired at first by the overly strict nuns who demanded of them a discipline they'd never imagined could exist.

Everything has changed. They quickly became real urbanites: bold, especially Alice, who wasn't easily scared, and they learned a little more every day about living at the rhythm of a metropolis. School hadn't lasted long: the appetite for independence, the need to acquire by themselves the things essential for city life, had won out over education and, to the dismay of Rhéauna, who regretted having had to leave school too soon, they'd found jobs. As for their mother, who in any event had always hated school, she'd looked favourably at the money – little though it was – that the two younger girls brought home every week. She had quickly agreed then to let them take the plunge onto the job market.

Alice smells of tobacco when she comes home from the factory at the end of the afternoon, Béa of vanilla and ginger. They eat whatever Rhéauna has prepared for them while their mother gets ready to go to the Paradise, and during the week they go to bed early because they're exhausted. They never complain, though, they like this life a hundred times more than the boring study of grammatical rules and the strict religious laws they think will be useless once they're married.

As for Rhéauna, she only works afternoons in the bookkeeping department of Dupuis Frères, where she is heading, in fact, to buy her wedding dress, taking advantage of the 10 percent discount granted to store employees.

"Get ready for a surprise: Moman's up already. And she made porridge for Théo."

The two girls freeze.

"She's already up?"

"She made breakfast?"

"Is she sick?"

"Is there something the matter?"

Rhéauna opens the door which she had closed behind her.

"I don't know. She says she's got a rendezvous."

"A rendezvous! In the morning! Something's wrong, for sure."

Alice studies Rhéauna from head to toe before leaving the room.

"How come you're all dolled up at this hour of the day?"

"Don't you go to work at Dupuis Frères just in the afternoon?"

Maria is stacking the dirty dishes in the sink when her three daughters emerge from the corridor into the kitchen.

"Nana often says that you get up at the last possible minute but today you're going too far."

Alice snatches an orange from the fruit bowl on the table before she heads to the door.

Maria grabs her by the arm.

"It's easier for Béa because she works nearby but you, Alice ..."

"I won't be late, Moman, don't worry."

"No, but you'll have an empty stomach ... An orange isn't enough."

"I'll eat more at noon."

"That's no answer."

"Moman, please, you're gonna make me late ..."

"That's right, it's always my fault ..."

She slips a banana into her hand.

"Eat that on the streetcar at least, it's good for you ... I spend a fortune on fresh fruit, take advantage of it! And I don't want Madame Desbaillets to come and say she saw you throw a banana in the garbage ... It's nutritious, a banana, and you need to put some meat on your bones! You look like a walking skeleton! And take your raincoat, it's freezing!"

"Good grief, Moman, why're you such a mother hen this morning? Is there something you need to be forgiven for?"

She stuffs the banana into her raincoat pocket, runs outside.

"What're we having for supper tonight, Nana?"

And races down the wooden stairs without waiting for the answer.

Maria shrugs.

"I don't know why she always goes out the back way, she has to go all the way around the house ... We've got stairs out front!"

Béa is already sitting over a floating island of steaming oatmeal.

"Do you talk with Madame Desbaillets now, Moman? Seems to me you two always used to be fighting."

"Well, we're still fighting! The old shrew! Anyway, I just said it to scare Alice!"

Rhéauna pours three cups of coffee, sets them on the table.

"If you think that'll stop her from throwing the banana in the first garbage can she runs into ..."

Béa swallows a mouthful, then adds:

"Besides, she doesn't like bananas."

That simple remark makes Maria jump, then blush.

Her daughters look at her.

"What? Why're you looking at me like that?"

Béa sips some coffee.

"You didn't know Alice doesn't like bananas?"

Her mother pulls out a chair, sits, leans towards her.

"You think I'm a bad mother, is that it?"

"I didn't say that."

"But you think it ..."

"I do not ..."

"I can hear you thinking, Béa! Your face is like an open book with illustrations in colour! A good mother isn't somebody who knows that her daughter doesn't like bananas, a good mother doesn't give a damn if her daughter likes bananas or not, she's a responsible person that knows what's good for her daughter and makes her eat a banana when she leaves for work in the morning without eating even if by chance she doesn't like it! That's what a good mother is and nothing else!"

Aware of how ridiculous her remarks are and unable to think of anything else, she gets up from the table, takes off the apron that she'd tied around her waist, tosses it onto the counter, and leaves the kitchen.

Rhéauna gives her sister a slap upside the head as she gets up.

"You could've just left it alone, honestly!"

"What? Now what have I done? I was surprised that Moman didn't know that Alice doesn't like bananas and I said so, that's all!"

"How d'you think she felt?"

"If she got up at the same time as the rest of us, she'd know those things."

"She comes home after midnight every night, Béa!"

"Then she can just get another job!"

"She comes home after midnight every night so you've got porridge in your bowl every morning, Béa! And if she got another job, if she had to take a job that hardly pays, like yours for instance, if she had to sell cookies by the pound on rue Ontario, maybe we wouldn't have porridge to eat in the morning. Or fresh fruit! We may be the only family on the street that eats fresh fruit, because it costs so much! Moman may not know if we like bananas or not, but at least she can afford to buy them. She's got a job that pays, Béa, thank the Lord."

Béa gets up from her place, bumps into Théo on her way out of the kitchen.

A few seconds later, Rhéauna hears the front door slam.

Théo frowns. He hates it when his sisters fight.

"What's wrong with Béa? Did you tell her that she eats too much again?"

"Hardly, that's not what we were talking about … Want some toast?"

"No, I'm not hungry. I just ate."

He kisses her cheek, grabs an orange, and runs out.

"For later on. In case I get hungry at recess."

Rhéauna gets up, heads for the sink.

"I'm not doing the dishes decked out like this! Great, here I am talking to myself first thing in the morning! Boy, this day's getting off to a bad start!"

# Maria

The cold washcloth she'd put on her forehead feels good. She is breathing better, the seething anger is being resorbed little by little, the migraine she thought at first was inevitable doesn't seem to have been triggered. She takes long breaths, tries to calm down by emptying her head of any negative thought but can't do it. The anger will pass, but she won't be able to stop herself from seeking its causes and being upset about it.

She wonders if her urge to hit Alice because she'd dared to stand up to her was really a roundabout way she'd devised to react beforehand to the fearsome day that lay ahead. Especially the two appointments she'd made for this morning, each of which in its own way terrorized her. Had she come close to expressing, before she even had a legitimate reason, the frustration she saw as inevitable, because either of those two appointments might very well not happen? To the detriment of her daughter Alice in whom she's been seeing a little too much of herself and who is getting on her nerves. Probably as much as she herself had got on the nerves of her own parents when she was Alice's age and they'd seemed to her so ridiculous, so narrow-minded, which she showed with all the cruelty of a spoiled brat? Had she wanted to punish herself through Alice for having asked to meet those two individuals whom she had no desire to see?

Anxiously, she feels that soon the moment will come when

she'll hear from her daughter's mouth the arguments she'd served up to her own parents twenty-two years before. The reproaches, the recriminations, the accusations. It's not a small village in Saskatchewan that Alice wants out of, she's already far away and she didn't have to ask. No, like most girls of her age, it's from the influence of the family, of what she believes is the yoke of her mother and her older sister that she wants to free herself. To fly with her own wings. To prove that she can get somewhere on her own. So young. So fragile. So unintelligent ... Because she leaves the house every morning and goes to stir tobacco leaves in an overheated factory for a ridiculous salary, she thinks she's strong and ready for independence when she is still just a child who needs to be told what to do.

Should she react as her parents had done back then? Has she already arrived, so soon, good Lord, so soon to advise one of her own children to avoid making the same stupid mistake she'd made herself? Talk about mistakes, experience, wisdom, caution, when Alice only wants to rebel? Like her? Like when the prospect of burying herself deep in the prairies with a beer-drinking husband and producing a series of children drove her crazy? Is she about to see herself in the role of the woman who advises her daughter to accept the things that she herself had wanted to avoid?

The other one, the cookie seller, the limp noodle with no personality whom she despairs of seeing settle down some day ... She pictures herself already urging one to react while trying to hold the other one back ... And Rhéauna, for so long her right-hand person, who is leaving to make her life with a fine young man who's half-deaf and none too bright, what will become of her? Not to mention the youngest who can't take a step without the help of his big sister, all the time maintaining the opposite?

She takes off the cool cloth, carefully sets it next to her glass of water on the bedside table. A totally ordinary act, the arm that unfolds, the hand that opens as it approaches the dust-covered varnished wood table which she follows attentively as if it were the most important thing in the world, perhaps to avoid – in vain, needless to say – thinking about the fate of her four children and in particular, about the two chores, closer and hence more dangerous, that she has imposed on herself and that she'll have to carry out in the next few hours.

One is quite close to her place on rue Sainte-Catherine, the other in the old city, at the back of a godforsaken place called the ruelle des Fortifications, which she has never heard of.

Even the timing of these appointments annoys her. First, she'll have to go to nearby rue Sainte-Catherine, then cross the city. But no, she has to first run to the other end of the world to be humiliated for the first time, then come back, most likely already discouraged, play beggar in front of a man who'll most likely laugh at her.

A knock on the door.

"Is that you, Nana?"

"Yes. Is everything all right? Need anything?"

"No, I'm all right. I'm getting dressed. Gotta leave right away."

"You don't want to talk about your rendezvous?"

"For sure not with a closed door between us! But no, it's okay, we'll talk afterwards. Maybe."

"What d'you mean, maybe?"

Maria gets up, crosses the room, opens the door.

"Listen, Nana ... You've got secrets, right? Well so do I! It's simple, it isn't complicated: I've got two rendezvous this morning, not one, two! True, I'm not crazy about either one, but I don't want to talk about them just now, and maybe I never will! Get it? So go and change 'cause I've got tons of things to keep me busy before we go to the Salon de la Mariée at Dupuis Frères and you've got plenty of time to get your new dress dirty!"

She turns around and opens the closet door.

"Now let me get dressed!"

Before she leaves, Rhéauna leans against the door frame.

"Those two rendezvous, have they got anything to do with my wedding, Moman?"

Maria turns towards her, arms already full of clothes.

"Not everything's about you, Nana. Not everything's about you and your damn wedding!"

# Alice

It doesn't smell good in the streetcar. Luckily the windows are wide open. It smells of a lack of personal hygiene, of clothes that aren't washed very often, of rollies made from cheap tobacco – in fact it reeks of poverty. And that's the smell that Alice wants to get rid of. She's convinced – even though deep down she knows that it's not true – that poverty has a smell, that you know a person is poor because, in addition to their clothes and the shame you can read in their eyes, their skin gives off a slight stench. Though you try to hide it under a layer of perfume, it's always there, it follows you everywhere, it betrays you, announces you.

She lowers her head, sniffs the collar of her raincoat.

There is no doubt that it's less perceptible with her because she uses all kinds of ploys to conceal it – though she didn't have time to wash this morning, so she keeps her elbows close to her body, just in case – perfumes a bit too expensive; long baths afloat with exotically named oils; fragrant bath salts that took time to dissolve and smelled of roses, jasmine, or gardenias. Or so they claimed on the flasks or the cardboard boxes, even if it wasn't always obvious. But she's afraid that the fundamental stench of poverty is indelible and she thinks about it ten times a day, especially at the factory when it's very hot and sweat runs down her forehead and her back.

She remembers her grandmother Joséphine in Saskatchewan

who always said: "We may be poor, but we're clean!" She got them – her sisters and herself – used to never neglecting themselves, never to show up anywhere at all without being sure that everything they had on was clean and that they gave off no body odour. She showed them how to wash themselves parish by parish every morning, with a wet facecloth, not neglecting any strategic place. The obligatory bath was weekly but the wash with soap and water happened every day. And if they often suffered from the bad smells that filled the air in the single classroom of the grade school, especially in winter, at least they knew they weren't responsible.

An elderly man comes to sit beside her on the woven straw seat. He gnaws on a bit of bread, which reminds Alice that she's hungry and that she still has a banana in her raincoat pocket. She takes it out, peels it, and starts to eat. It's good. And it's true that it's nutritious. She'd have had trouble waiting until noon. She'd never have admitted to her mother that she was right, though. The old man, with a grimace and slightly crazy eyes, leans over her, just a little, just enough for their shoulders to touch.

"You like to eat bananas, Mademoiselle?"

She pretends not to understand the allusion and replies without turning towards him.

"What I like most of all is punching old pigs like you that talk to me in the streetcar."

Laughter rises up around them.

The old gentleman seems more amused than shocked by her reply.

"How about that, a woman who can answer back!"

That too, she'd like to get rid of forever. Being gawked at by the poor, by men with nothing but lousy jobs, who stare at her every morning because she's always the prettiest girl on the Papineau streetcar. Without expecting Prince Charming, Alice still hopes that one day a different race of man, one not wearing overalls and workers' caps, from somewhere else, where apartments have hot water all year long and where the heat doesn't smell of coal, not a gorgeous one, no – though that would be nothing to sneeze at – but someone who was always clean, with a job that paid and the means to spoil her, a real *Monsieur*, in other words, a real *Monsieur* who'd be interested in her.

Is that too much to ask for?

The old pig keeps talking to her but she's not listening. She knows the type. He won't be easily discouraged, he'll insist, keep up his smutty innuendo, try to make her blush by making his insinuations more and more precise.

She sighs, closes her eyes.

All she sees is her mother yelling at her once again because she came home late or she's wearing too much makeup. She calls her a child, the thing that Alice hates more than anything, orders her to come home earlier, and holds out her hand for the five dollars board that her three daughters have been paying since they started working.

My God, to get away from that, go somewhere else, anywhere at all but far from here! Like a real Desrosiers.

A powerful smell comes to her nose, she doesn't know if it's real or if she's imagining it, but it's strong, it stings her eyes, makes her want to vomit. She realizes that it's coming from the banana peel. She throws it out the window, screaming at the top of her lungs:

"It stinks in here, it stinks, it stinks!"

The old man, thinking that she's talking about him, falls silent all at once in mid-sentence while the other passengers on the streetcar laugh harder than ever.

# OTTAWA, MAY 1922

## Ti-Lou

The address reads:

Mademoiselle Louise Wilson
Château Laurier
Ottawa, Ont.
Canada

Ti-Lou tears open the envelope after checking to see that it had
been postmarked in Montréal. She doesn't know many people in
that city, which she had actually visited only rarely and always in
the company of individuals more or less important in Ottawa who
wanted to be seen with a beautiful woman on their arms, old bachelors wanting to hide their true sexuality or businessmen enjoying
a night on the town and hoping to forget their worries – and their
families – during a weekend.

She was charmed by the nightlife in Canada's metropolis, which
has the reputation, well deserved, of being a little wild and very
open-minded – if you could ignore the yoke of the Catholic Church

on the francophone population: jazz clubs open all night, attended by the best Black American musicians; fashionable restaurants; the famous blind pigs where money was so unimportant that some gamblers used ten-dollar bills to light their cigars – even if they were sorry when Lady Luck didn't smile at them – but like a real tourist she knew nothing about everyday life. She would have liked to escape for a few hours from the arms of the men who paid for her trips and sometimes turned out to be too demanding and often spineless and contemptible, leave the chic hotel for an afternoon stroll along rue Sainte-Catherine, the most famous commercial street in the country, looking for outfits that were not to be found in Ottawa because the wives of cabinet ministers or government employees dress rather conservatively; climb to the summit of Mount Royal which is said to be one of the most beautiful parks in the world; visit her Desrosiers cousins, especially Maria whom she hasn't heard from in ages and who seemed so frail the last time she'd visited, six years earlier.

Six years.

Immediately she looks at her hands. It's been an obsession for some months now. Despite her relative youth – she's not yet fifty – brown spots have started to appear during the winter – death spots, as they've always been called by courtesans who see them as a forerunner of the beginning of the end of their reign. She has done everything to conceal them, using exorbitantly costly creams that have turned out to be ineffective even though they promised clear and silky skin; she has tried in vain to launch a fashion among Ottawa prostitutes: gloves to be worn all day long, even while eating, even while making love – she has tried to show her clients only the palms of her hands, but hands on their backs are ridiculous and that would only bring her embarrassing questions.

"Hiding something, Ti-Lou?"

How to reply? That you have age spots? That you're an aging prostitute? That it might be time to retire?

She filches a chocolate from the enormous box that Senator Dumont had brought her the night before. Her favourites, Cherry Delights, sold exclusively, it seems, at the souvenir shop in the hotel lobby. The manager, a Mrs. Carlyle, orders several boxes every month, knowing that she'll sell them. They're for the suitors of Mademoiselle Wilson, Ti-Lou to her closest friends. The She-Wolf of Ottawa. *La louve d'Ottawa.* The shame of the Château Laurier. Mrs. Carlyle never greets Ti-Lou when she runs into her in the lobby, though she's perfectly happy to sell Cherry Delights to the She-Wolf's regulars.

Ti-Lou breaks the chocolate envelope with her tongue, lets the cherry juice run into her mouth, bites into the candied fruit, and chews it at length before swallowing.

She calls it her *fatal consolation*: true, it does console her for everything, at least as long as the exquisite flavours combine on her tongue; for one brief moment it lets her forget the ugliness of some of her clients, their vulgarity – but it's also true that it's dangerous for her. She decides to ignore danger, though, and closes her eyes after she has popped a second Cherry Delight into her mouth.

Dr. McKenny – who so often has come to her aid when one of those nasty diseases of "scarlet women" struck her – had told her a year earlier that she had diabetes and that she had to cut all sugars and as much fat as possible from her diet. She'd laughed, running her hand through his hair. Then she added that without her Cherry Delights, existence would be unbearable. And that she would give up her profession before she'd cut them out of her life. Along with all the other desserts that she devoured, the rum babas, the mille feuilles, the maple sugar pies that numbed her while making more bearable the humiliating and at times grotesque sessions heralded by lavish meals in a restaurant or in her suite at the Château Laurier.

And when he had added in a scolding tone that it was serious, that it could kill her eventually if she refused to take care of herself, that she was liable to lose her eyesight, that gangrene threatened her, she had merely added, as she got up to leave his office:

"The Dame aux camélias had consumption, me, it's diabetes. She died coughing, I'll die eating chocolate. I'd rather have my condition than hers. Do you want me to pay you in kind or will you send your bill to the hotel?"

Never mind the appearance of brown age spots, along with the goddamn diabetes that will do her in sooner or later (even though she's decided to ignore it), by blocking her arteries, attacking her eyesight, or blackening the tips of her toes, those spots have come to sow a big doubt in her vision of the future. A courtesan who's diabetic, maybe even obese – because she has also put on weight – and covered with age spots? No.

No.

Better to escape while there's still time. Flee Ottawa and its hypocrisy, take refuge some place where no one knows her, Montréal maybe, yes, why not, retire – she can afford it if she pays a little attention to her expenses – in a city that she'll be able to love, live her final years without men, commit suicide by sugar, in any event quit her profession before she's too old and becomes the laughing stock of a city where they already give her the cold shoulder.

And allow the threat – that'll teach them – of an autobiography, even if she never intended to carry it out, hang over her. Her entire life. Uncensored. Deserving no doubt to be placed on the Index and terrorizing the whole city. Naming all the politicians, all the professionals, all the members of the clergy – Catholic or Anglican – with whom she kept company and whose most shameful secrets she knew. And their measurements.

She rests her head against the back of her armchair, laughs that wonderful dirty laugh that still makes so many men shiver.

*The She-Wolf of Ottawa* by Louise Wilson. Or maybe *Ti-Lou's Revenge*. Available at all good bookstores. But under the counter.

She wipes the tears that are running down her cheeks.

All right. Now the invitation.

She takes a poor-quality card from the envelope, puts on her glasses – another incontrovertible proof of the progress of her diabetes.

*Madame Maria Rathier*
*is pleased to invite you to the marriage of her daughter,*
*Rhéauna, to Mr. ....*

Little Rhéauna getting married! The overwrought, fearful little girl with such intelligent eyes, who'd spent a night with her during her journey east from Saskatchewan a few years ago, the child, so beautiful, who had broken her heart with her account of her hesitation between her yearning to see her mother again and her desire to stay with her sisters and grandparents in the small village deep in the prairies where she'd grown up, is now a woman ready to settle down. No, it's not possible that so much time has passed since her stop in Ottawa! That would be what – eight years, nine? Already! Yes, it's true, Maria had also come to see her some years later, after she'd taken her children back to Saskatchewan ... Maybe she's confusing the two visits.

She looks again at her hands. Along with brown age spots, for a while now there have been ugly blue veins bulging under the skin. Every prostitute knows that you can disguise anything but your hands. The hands condemn women whose job it is to seduce and who have reached the threshold of physical decline. How can you think about seduction with hands like that? She gets up, strides across the room, settles in front of the huge mirror in which she has checked so many times how a gown falls or the effect of a new hairstyle. She leans in towards her reflection, looks herself straight in the eyes. Still beautiful. But that may not make up for the aging of the hands. In fact the whole face is still beautiful. More so even. Radiant. She has been told so often that she was radiant. If she tried to remember the last time, though ...

She closes her eyes, rests her forehead against the mirror.

"Okay, old girl, it's time, right? Now listen. You've had a fine career ..."

She's surprised not to feel the slightest regret. None. She understands all at once that, even today, she could leave her lavish way of living – the suite at the Château Laurier, the outfits, the parties, the perpetual light-headedness, without turning her head and with a light heart – when the thought had never yet occurred to her. A real Desrosiers whim from the side of her mother, Gertrude, who all her life had controlled the natural impulses towards self-reliance that haunted her family and had died of sadness and frustration.

To retire with no warning, disappear from Ottawa with no fare-wells to her clients who scorned her as much as she had scorned them. One last blaze of independence ...

Because, come to think of it, she has also lived under the yoke of men and wouldn't be unhappy to be free of them. True, she hasn't depended on one man only, true, she didn't devote herself to a husband who'd have had all rights over her, but what she took for freedom, that life of dissipation and fake ease, was nonetheless associated with men's desire for her and to which she had submitted. Hadn't she in spite of everything been an oppressed woman too?

She raises her head.

No. All the same.

She has to avoid taking that dangerous road. All her life she has boasted of being a free woman, she's not about to start doubting ...

She goes back to her easy chair, picks up the invitation.

No doubt it was Maria who put her on the guest list. She wonders what the other members of the Desrosiers family – her cousins, Ernest, Tititte, Teena – will think when they see her turn up at Rhéauna's wedding. The whore coming to celebrate the sacred union of marriage!

She smiles.

Why not? A little trip to the big city alone for once, with no ties, wouldn't hurt her. She could even start prospecting, visiting apartments, seeing if the cost of living there would be too high for her.

She checks the date of the wedding. It gives her a few weeks to think about her plans.

The phone rings, once, then stops. A warning that a client is on his way up, that he may already be in the elevator.

She looks at her watch.

So early in the day.

Another federal government big shot coming to relieve an unexpected rush of blood who certainly doesn't want to ask his wife for anything.

## Maria, Victoire

"It's really nice of you to come and meet me ..."

"I'm glad to do it. We've always met when there were loads of people ... This way we can get to know each other better ..."

The woman's gaze is so consuming that Maria feels as if she can see past her face, that she can read her thoughts, that she may already have guessed what Maria has come to tell her. It's a gaze that is more than inquisitive, intimidating, one from which you'd like to shield yourself because it's so intense.

"I had a little trouble finding your street ..."

"Say it, Madame Rathier, it doesn't bother me: it's not a street, it's an alley. You're not the first person to have trouble finding it, either. And on top of it all we live in the last house in the back."

She hasn't lost the country accent. An accent not so definable, so marked as that from Charlevoix, for example, or Gaspésie, but Maria recognizes the very distinctive sounds that she'd heard during her visit to Duhamel some year earlier. The *r*'s are rolled – not like Montrealers', though – the *t*'s are clearer too, they don't sound so much like *t*'s.

"Rhéauna tells me you're from Duhamel."

"That's right. And she tells me you spent a week there a few years ago."

"Right, at my sister's place. She bought a house there."

"Do you sometimes want to go back?"

"Oh yes, it's so lovely."

"Me, I think about it all the time."

"And the house is in such a good location ..."

"Oh yes? Ours was too ... Outside the village."

"Ours too."

Obviously, they don't realize that they're talking about the same house.

"Pardon me for asking, but how come you moved to the city?"

"I got married."

"It's true, that's a good reason ... Did you come here with your husband?"

"Oh no, my husband's from here. I came and joined him after he proposed."

A kind of self-consciousness settles between them. Her hostess looks away. Maria is convinced that she's hiding something, that her decision to leave Duhamel was difficult, that she might even have been forced to leave the Gatineau. A marriage of convenience? Or on the rebound after a breakup?

Victoire gets out of her chair all at once and is still talking as she practically runs towards the living-room door.

"Good grief, what a bad hostess I am! I didn't even ask if you wanted something to drink. I've got tea, coffee ..."

While she's off fixing the tea, Maria takes the time to look around her.

Everything is heartbreakingly poor, from the old furniture, most likely picked up here and there, at auctions or department store clearance sales, to the threadbare rugs that don't really cover the wood floors and mended curtains. As the apartment is in a sub-basement, the windows are small and high up, which explains why even at 10 a.m., the lamps are lit. A meticulous cleanliness, though, prevails in the room.

It smells of more than poverty, it smells of bad luck. And it was here that Gabriel, Nana's fiancé, was brought up.

Rhéauna had told her that Gabriel's father was the janitor of the building and that his wife gave him a hand with the thankless tasks for which he was responsible. She'd also confided that her fiancé had left home a few months earlier to live in a room near carré Saint-Louis while still paying board to his parents. Because he was tired of living in a sub-basement at the end of a dark alley, he needed light, he wanted to be away from his father who, apparently, was no treat.

Maria had seen the coal chute right next to the front door and wondered how everything in the apartment wasn't covered with dust. Gabriel's mother, besides all the rest of her work, must be constantly fighting it.

A little girl comes into the room, coughing, and Maria thinks to herself that the lungs of the occupants of this apartment most likely are not sheltered from coal dust. And that Gabriel was right to get away before he came down with some disease. The little girl stops at the sight of her. She has the same piercing eyes as her mother. She too seems to see farther than what the person she's talking to wants her to see. Something else can be seen, too, in those black eyes, a kind of questioning, as if the little girl, even while she can imagine what the other person is hiding, is at the same time asking if she too could read what her soul is hiding. It resembles a call for help: Help me, I can't give words to my unhappiness, and it's killing me.

Her mother arrives nearly at the same moment with a tray laden with teapot, cups, and cookies.

"Did you say *bonjour* to Madame Rathier, Albertine? Her daughter is the lovely Rhéauna. This is the older of my two daughters, Madame Rathier. She stayed away from school this morning on account of she had a cough. My other daughter, Madeleine, is nine. She's in grade four. Then there's another boy, Édouard, he's ten. But Gabriel must've already told you all that. Or maybe I did it myself, the first time we met."

She runs her hand through Albertine's hair but the girl pulls away, making a face.

"Albertine's in grade six … But she's not crazy about it. Say hello to Madame Rathier, Bartine."

Instead of answering, Albertine turns and runs out of the room.

Her mother sets the tray on a rickety little occasional table that stands between the couch and the armchair.

"They're not very sociable at that age. Frankly, you could say that Bartine's never very sociable ... Anyway, she's got a nasty little temper, let me tell you. Milk in your tea?"

Maria asks herself how she's going to bring up the matter she wants to talk about with Gabriel's mother. Getting straight to the point would be most logical, but she doesn't know where to start.

Her hostess sets down her cup, coughs into her fist.

"You want to talk about something in particular, eh? I could feel it ever since you got here. Go ahead now, don't be afraid. Maybe it'd be easier if we stopped saying Madame. I'm Victoire."

Relieved, Maria holds out her hand, then realizes it's ridiculous. "And I'm Maria."

Then she launches right into the speech she'd prepared the night before.

"I came to ask you to pardon me."

"Pardon you? What for? We don't even know each other."

"I want to ask you to pardon me because I probably won't be able to give my daughter and your son the kind of wedding they deserve, and I'm ashamed ... I didn't know how much a wedding costs. When I got married myself I was far from home and it was my husband's parents that took care of it ... Usually the bride's father pays for everything but Rhéauna hasn't got a father and me, well, even if I make a decent living, I'm on my own, I've got nobody to help me, and I make less than a man with a good trade would make ... I've got four children to support, a house to run ... You'll see, when it comes time to marry off Albertine ... The church, the flowers, the new clothes for everybody, and the Pâtisserie Paris- ienne in our case, they'll be making the lunch for fifty people ... Oh, it's fine to want little fancy sandwiches in different colours but you have to be able to pay for them! I guess I was thinking too big. I invited some Desrosiers, my side of the family, from the other end of Canada, I didn't know if they'd come but if they come what'll I do with them? On top of everything else will I have to put them up? The Rathiers, we've been out of touch for too long to invite them ... I wanted to have a big family reunion around my daughter's wedding – me who's always hated family – because I know it matters to Nana. I wanted to have visitors from Manitoba and Saskatchewan, a bit of her childhood, I wanted Nana to remember it her whole life, but what will happen is that if she does remember it all her life, it'll just be because it's a failure... I've done some calculations... It can cost up to five hundred dollars, a wedding like that, and those five hundred smackers I haven't got, so what I did was I started cutting down. The invitations are in the mail, everything's been ordered, and I don't know how I'm going to pay!"

Victoire cuts her off by raising her hand as if to protest.

"I hope you didn't come to ask me to contribute to the wedding, Maria..."

"No, no, it's not that, absolutely not, don't worry..."

"... Because money, I'm pretty sure I haven't even got as much as you, dear child..."

"I'm telling you, that's not it... But there was no one else for me to talk to... I couldn't tell my sisters, they're even bigger drama queens than me! I told myself maybe you and me, we'd understand each other, we're both mothers... And then I want to ask you to forgive me. Because Gabriel deserves a nice wedding ceremony and a nice party, too. The worst thing is, they might have it but never know it'll never be paid for, that I might end up in jail like a thief because I just wanted to give my daughter a nice wedding!"

"Don't exaggerate, Maria, that's going too far."

"Maybe the part about jail, but the rest..."

"What about your gentleman friend, Monsieur Rambert, can't he help you out? He looks like somebody quite well off."

Maria takes her last sip before replying. If only Victoire's eyes weren't so inquisitive. What does she know, or guess, about her relationship with Monsieur Rambert, who asks her to marry him ten times a year and whom she turns down strictly out of pride, even though he's the father of her youngest child? She doesn't want to depend on him or risk getting caught up in a second marriage as miserable as the first. Of course he would help her out, but she doesn't want her daughter to owe her wedding to a man who's not even her official stepfather. After all, she isn't going to promise Monsieur Rambert she'll marry him just so he'll pay for Nana's wedding.

"I don't want to ask him for anything."

"Why?"

"It's hard to explain … I don't want … I don't want to owe him anything … I'd feel like I was putting myself in his hands … I don't know how to put it … I don't want to depend on him. For any-thing."

"Is he the type of man that insists?"

"No, but I'm the type who'd think about it for years and make myself sick from thinking about it too much. I'm like … I'm like a prisoner, and I don't know how to get out of my situation. I'm so ashamed!"

Victoire sinks deeper into her chair. Lets a long moment pass before she speaks.

"Can I ask you something, Maria?"

"Sure."

"Is your own pride more important to you than your child's hap-piness?"

Maria gets up, takes a few steps in the small room. Victoire thinks that she's gone too far, that her visitor is going to leave and they won't see each other again until the day of the wedding. No, Maria sits down again after hesitating at the doorstep. She too lets a moment pass before she speaks.

"You're going to see that it's not like that: when I leave here I've got an appointment at a finance company that's just opened not far from our place. I'm going to have to borrow to pay for the wedding. That too I'm ashamed of."

"But not as ashamed as borrowing from somebody you know? Who maybe wouldn't charge you any interest? Who might even make you a gift of it?"

"You're right when you say that it's a matter of pride. The money I borrow, nobody's going to know about it. Not even Monsieur

Rambert. Just you will know about it. I'll arrange things so if he asks me where I got the money, I'll tell him I'd put it aside."

She takes a handkerchief folded in four from her purse.

"I'll pay till the end of my days if I have to, but nobody'll ever know a thing."

"Why'd you come here and tell me?"

Maria blows her nose noisily, apologizes.

"I told you just now because you're the mother of the man my daughter's going to marry! Because I was scared you'd think that the wedding I can afford for Nana and Gabriel isn't worthy of them, and you'd think I was a penny-pincher. I'm not a penny-pincher, I'm poor! I'm going to have to cut some things and I'm afraid it'll show, do you understand?"

"The other guests will realize it too."

"Yes, but you, Victoire, you can forgive me *in advance.*"

"I've got nothing to forgive you for, Maria. You'll do your best, I know that. When Albertine gets married, which will happen sooner than you think, I won't even be able to borrow the money because I won't be able to pay it back! Even if I paid for the rest of my life, as you say you're going to be obliged to do ... The main thing is our children's marriage, not the coloured sandwiches from the Pâtisserie Parisienne!"

"But I want those coloured sandwiches from the Pâtisserie Parisienne! And a chicken vol-au-vent! And a cake with four layers! And flowers from Mademoiselle Gerney! I might have to drop one layer of the cake and a few bouquets but there'll still be a big cake and lots of flowers! I want my daughter to remember her wedding for the rest of her life! Poor child, after all I've put her through ..."

Victoire leans over to her, places a hand on her knee.

"If you've got serious things to be pardoned for, coloured sandwiches and three- or four-layer cakes aren't going to help ... Talk to her, poor little girl, ask her to forgive you, not me ..."

Maria gets up again, straightens her hat, heads for the living-room door. This time, she's going to leave. Victoire follows her.

"Leaving already? But you've hardly arrived ..."

"As you know, I've got another appointment now. I've got papers to sign that are going to bleed me dry for the rest of my life. Thanks for listening to me. After the wedding I hope we'll see more of each other … Maybe to play cards. Gabriel says you really like that … Me and my sisters, sometimes we'd like to be four, so we can play canasta or five hundred …"

Before leaving the apartment, she turns towards Victoire.

"There's important things I couldn't bring up with Nana. That's what I'm like. Most of the time I've got a big mouth for giving orders, but when it's time to talk about important things … Nana thinks I've got the means to pay for a nice wedding and I want it to stay like that."

She glances at the coal chute before starting up the stairs to the main floor.

Victoire turns red.

"You aren't the only one that's ashamed, you know."

Then she closes the door.

In the lobby of the building, Maria leans against the wall, wondering if her second visit will be as pointless as the first. Because she doesn't feel any relief. And she suspects that if ever she has the money to pay for the wedding expenses in her hand, she won't feel any better.

## *Victoire*

"I know you could've gone to school this morning, Bartine."

"I was coughing."

"You're always coughing."

"I was coughing more than usual."

"Oh no you weren't! You don't like going to school so you go out of your way to stay home."

"You can just take me out of it then."

"I told you there's no question of that till you're at least fifteen! You can't go out to work at your age, what're you thinking? What could you do?"

"I could help you here ... Poppa can hardly ever do his janitor work ... You do it all, everybody knows that. Have you ever heard of a woman janitor? 'Cause that's what you are!"

"I've told you before, don't judge your father! And if there's anything wrong, you're just as lazy as him so you've got nothing to say!"

"I am not lazy!"

"So prove it to me and go back to school."

"School's boring."

"And you think it's more interesting here? My darling child, if you only knew ..."

"I don't learn nothing in school anyways."

"Force yourself."

"I forced myself. It didn't help."

"Force yourself some more!"

"What good is it to force myself to learn stuff that I'll never use! When you're scrubbing floors do you ever use stuff you learned in school?"

"At least I know it! I had to leave school when I was young and I've always regretted it!"

"Yeah right, you've said that a thousand times. I don't want to know stuff, Moman! It doesn't matter."

"Bartine! Children go to school, period! You're a child? So go to school like everybody else, it's not you that decides! I'll never believe that I'm going to bring up a girl that's ignorant on top of everything else!"

That child is going to drive her crazy. Always the same subjects, always the same arguments, always the same stubborn look, the same stupid expression!

Victoire pulls the plug in the sink, shakes her hands before wiping them dry on a rag. The water makes a sucking noise as it drains away and she has to put her fingers back in to unblock the pipe.

"I've told them a hundred times they have to put toast crusts in the garbage before they put dishes in the sink! But I'm wasting my breath! We'll end up blocking the pipe and we'll have to bring in a plumber. As if we could afford it!"

Albertine has collapsed onto a kitchen chair, head thrown back, looking at the ceiling.

"Do something, Bartine! Come here and give me a hand! Quit talking nonsense, talking about helping me, and do it for once!"

Albertine gets up, dragging her feet, takes the rag her mother dried her hands on, runs it without much conviction over the oil-cloth covering the table.

"Quit yelling like that, you'll wake Poppa!"

Victoire yanks the cloth from her hands.

"I've told you not to judge. Don't judge your father!"

"I wasn't judging him!"

"Oh yes you were! There was judgment in your tone of voice!"

Albertine goes back to her place on the chair.

"Moman! Poppa's still in bed at 10 a.m. because he came home drunk at dawn! How could we not judge him! We can hear him snoring all the way out here."

"Don't say *we*. It's you that judges him, not the others!"

"Come on! D'you think I'm the only one? Why d'you think Gabriel left? Before he got married! Because he couldn't take it anymore!"

"Bartine! Watch what you say!"

"If we watch what we say we'll go on letting him do what he wants and he'll end up taking us all down with him!"

Victoire brings her hands to her mouth. She nearly said it. Once again – it happens more and more often – she has nearly said the words that she'd promised to keep to herself. The fateful words which would show that Albertine and Gabriel were right. If they learned the truth.

"Meanwhile, go and dust the living room."

"It's clean."

"Do it anyway."

"It's clean! Why should I dust a living room that's already clean?"

"Bartine, get out of the kitchen! Now! Go back to bed if you want, behave like your father, but get out of here!"

Albertine knows that when her mother uses that tone of voice she has to obey. If not, the argument will last all day and she'll nearly be sorry she didn't go to school to learn some useless things.

"All right, all right, good Lord, no need to get your shirt in a knot!"

She pushes her chair under the table.

"I can't wait to be old enough to get married! Believe me, I'll be out of here like a shot."

"If you find somebody stupid enough to marry you!"

Victoire immediately regrets her words.

Albertine, pretending she didn't hear, walks out.

Her mother clenches her fists, sits on a chair, puts her forehead on the kitchen table.

Once again, her secret is choking her. It will kill her if she doesn't confide in someone, anyone, even a stranger on the street whom she'll never see again. Who cares if they think she's crazy, if they point at her, it has to come out, the words have to form in her mouth, gush out like something repulsive, she has to unburden herself, maybe when you're unburdened you don't suffer anymore!

Once she had confessed to a priest and what he said in reply had been so cruel that it had left her sick for months. Instead of helping her, which was his role, instead of consoling her, of granting her forgiveness, he had let out a torrent of abuse, condemned her, saying that she was guilty, that she had seduced her own brother, that it was all her fault, that there was no absolution for women like her, and that she would pay in hell for all eternity for what she had dared to do on earth, because there was no atonement for that filthy sin that had reddened the forehead of God and of the Blessed Virgin. She had pressed both hands against the grille that separated them and told the priest that she knew that if Josaphat were to confess the same sin, he would grant him absolution immediately, that Christian charity existed only for men between themselves, that women are only forgiven for trivial things, and then she'd left the confessional, slamming the door.

And had never gone back to the church.

She raises her head towards the window that's close to the ceiling. For several minutes she looks at the legs of passersby. Hems of trousers and skirts – that's all she has seen from her window for years.

She takes a deep breath, shuts her eyes.

For some time now, to calm down after a row with Albertine or one of her own rages against Télesphore who's recited poems while drunk again or neglected his janitorial duties, she cranes her neck towards the window, shuts her eyes – and flies up into the sky over the city itself. A vulture. Not a beautiful bird that sings and turns somersaults to the great delight of those who see it, but a raptor that soars above the ruelle des Fortifications and, should he want to, could plunge towards the last house before the dead end, and to keep from destroying everything, use his beak along with his claws to tear the face of Albertine or Télesphore, or to prevent himself from suffocating under the weight of his terrible secret, throw himself at the basement window. To put an end to it all. A raptor who kills himself so as not to kill.

They would pick him up on the sidewalk, toss him in the garbage, and he'd atone for his sins in birds' hell. So he wouldn't have to confront the reddened face of God. And of the Blessed Virgin.

Sometimes, the raptor does it. Other times, no.

Today, however, it's not working. She sits there, motionless, no wing pushes her, no claw, she doesn't see the sidewalk on the ruelle des Fortifications move away, the house shrink, the steeple of Notre-Dame Church outlined right next door, she doesn't soar above her misery before she plunges into death, she is still sitting in her kitchen, helpless and overwhelmed.

Now she can't even dream.

## Béa

Her big sister has already explained that eventually you forget smells. When a chicken is roasting in the oven, for instance, or a big roast beef, you go into raptures for a few minutes, you cry out how good it smells, that you can't wait to eat it, then maybe – again according to Nana, because the nose stops working, or something like that – you realize that you have to go outside or take refuge in a closed room for a few minutes and come out again if you want to enjoy again the scents that are drifting around the kitchen. In any case, it's true that they talk about the turkey for a month, they can't wait for it to be Christmas, not just because of the presents but also because of the excitement that will make everyone shiver when the first aromas of roasting flesh emerge from the kitchen and take over the house. Everyone will howl with delight, Béa will say that it smells so good, she has tears in her eyes. What's true, though, is that in half an hour they won't talk about it so much, and an hour later they'll have almost forgotten it. Maria will complain that the children go out too often to "wash their noses," that it cools down the house when they open the door, that they can simply escape to the bathroom for two minutes to experience the same effect. And Béa, to defuse a row in the middle of Christmas afternoon, will make them all laugh by saying that she's going to lie down in the oven next to the turkey so that her nose won't go to sleep.

Alice, on the other hand, doesn't miss a chance to declare that she would never forget what the bathroom smells like in the morning after everyone has finished washing and getting ready, and her mother tells her not to talk about such things.

If Béa thinks about all that behind her cash register, it's because there's been a weird phenomenon ever since she's been working at the Biscuiterie Ontario: never, ever, can she forget that she's surrounded by cookies. And not just because she can always see them. Nana's theory doesn't apply at all, then. There are some things that always smell. Or noses that don't get used to certain odours. In any event, hers is constantly tantalized by the aromas of vanilla, chocolate, coconut, ginger, and cinnamon that emanate from the dozens of glass-covered wooden racks that line three of the four walls in the cookie shop. If she had thought on the first days that it was because of her excitement at having found a job as difficult as Alice's, who all day long shakes and stirs up tobacco leaves in an overheated room – she says, and everyone at home believes her, that she doesn't smell the scent she transports with her when she comes home from work – Béa finally realizes that the exciting blend of scents never leaves her, that it smells as strong at four in the afternoon as at nine in the morning. That in particular, it was as tempting at 4 p.m. as at 9 a.m.

Moreover, that is the heart of the problem: temptation.

When she spotted the ad in the window: *Experienced Saleswoman Wanted*, she hadn't hesitated for a second. She had pushed open the door and in fewer than ten minutes she had convinced the owner, Madame Guillemette, a powerful woman corseted to the neck and made up like a burlesque dancer, that even with no experience she was capable of selling cookies better than anyone else. Lots of them, too.

"Look at me, Madame Guillemette, it's obvious that I like cookies! Put me behind the counter, let me praise the quality of your products to the customers, give me permission to taste the cookies that interest me and I swear, you won't regret it! I'm convincing when I want, and let me tell you, customers will leave here with more cookies than they intended to buy when they came in!"

And she was right. Over the slightly more than a year since she had hired Béa as a saleswoman, Madame Guillemette didn't regret having hired her, even though she suspects that the girl dips into the cookie jars more liberally than allowed. She is a conscientious employee, honest, clean, and always cheerful when she should be. That is, in front of the clientele. The owner of the cookie factory has noticed, though, bouts of sadness – face sombre, brow furrowed – when Béa is alone behind the counter and thinks no one can see her. She suspects that a dark stain is hidden behind Béa's smiles and kindness, but has never dared to bring it up. Her stoutness, most likely.

And so this is how Béa ends up every day, for several hours, deep in temptation. Madame Guillemette has told her she can sample the new products – she serves in a way as a tester – so Béa tastes everything. And when the owner is out at the bank or shopping, she fixes what she calls a *plate of sweet treats* and for long minutes, eyes wide open, concentrating happily, munching royal cakes, lemon squares, nuns' buns with coconut. She tries not to overdo it, doesn't always succeed, and often feels slightly sick to her stomach when Madame Guillemette comes back and asks if there've been a lot of customers.

She is standing as it happens over one of those plates of sweet treats. All that's left is a royal cake, her favourite treat – rectangular wafers interspersed with butter cream and milk chocolate frosting – and wonders if she should wait and savour it during the afternoon break. Madame Guillemette has been gone for a good half-hour, she mustn't catch her over an empty plate with a few lingering cookie crumbs.

The bell above the front door dings. Béa looks up with a start. Customers enjoy watching her eat. They often tell her that it reassures them to see that she likes what she sells. Béa, though, is afraid that they'll tell Madame Guillemette about it, indeed that they'll denounce her, without knowing it, for taking too much.

But the man who has just come in isn't liable to run away from Madame Guillemette. Because two or three times a week he takes advantage of Béa's generosity. She gives him cookies that are starting to dry out in their box or new sorts that aren't selling, and to thank her, he plays a piece on his violin, anything at all, whatever comes into his head. And it's always wonderful.

He lives nearby, at the corner of De Montigny and Amherst. He plays the violin every day in a department store on Mont-Royal, or so he claims, and stops at the cookie factory several times a week not to ask for charity, he's way too proud for that, but to help Béa – and at the same time, Madame Guillemette – to get rid of what he calls the *old stock*, emphasizing the expression with a wink and a quizzical smile. Béa adores him and awaits his arrival every day, impatiently. If he doesn't stop, if he goes right past without saying hello, without even looking up, she knows that it's one of his bad days and puts a couple of cookies aside for the next day.

"Monsieur Josaphat! Have you finished your work for the morning? Seems to me I haven't seen you for a while! Don't you like my cookies anymore? Have you found better ones somewhere else?"

"There aren't any better ones anywhere else! As you know perfectly well."

"You're just saying that to make me happy."

"Sure I'm saying it to make you happy."

The old man – in his fifties, though he looks at least ten years older – lays his violin case on the counter.

"Well, sweetheart, I guess I had other things to do than come here and eat cookies with you!"

He turns around and looks behind him, as if he thought that someone was standing near the door listening to him.

"Let's say I saw some people I hadn't seen for ages and that's kept me pretty busy..."

"People in your family?"

"I guess I could say that, yes. People in my family. Actually, no. But just about."

He turns around again.

Béa cranes her neck.

"Are you expecting somebody? Is it them that you're looking for? Did you arrange to meet here?"

"Nope, no, I'm not waiting for nobody."

"So why are you always looking behind you?"

"An old habit."

"I never noticed it till today."

"There's lots that you don't know about me, sweetheart."

Béa picks up the royal cake she hasn't yet eaten, grabs a few cookies from the display under the counter, especially some of the tea biscuits Monsieur Josaphat adores, puts them all in a paper bag.

"Here, take this. No music for today. Madame Guillemette will be back any minute."

Josaphat starts to protest, opens his violin case.

"I don't mind. I've got the right to play for my favourite saleslady, haven't I? She doesn't know I never buy anything. And if she thinks I'm courting you, let her think!"

He turns a little towards the window to play.

"I'd say you aren't playing just for me today, Monsieur Josaphat!"

And what he plays this morning is so beautiful that Béa feels like running to the door, opening it so passersby can enjoy what flows from the instrument, inviting them inside the cookie factory. You never know, it could help sales ...

# Gabriel

He's a fat, jovial man who reeks of cigar. His hands are on either side of the telephone which he has set down right in front of him, in the very middle of his desk, as if he were expecting an important call at any moment.

Gabriel, relegated to a straight chair on the other side of the massive desk – the side for employees, insignificant individuals – wonders how Monsieur Asselin used to spend his days before he had the telephone installed. You'd swear that if he could, he'd plug it into himself and transport it with him everywhere. Does he always have so many essential things to say that he doesn't want to take his eyes off the phone? Is it his new toy, his new god? The telephone's not that recent an invention. More and more Montrealers have one. He himself can now call his mother – the janitor's apartment is equipped with a telephone – though Victoire is wary of this modern invention ... Anyway, she claims she has no one to talk to except tenants when they have complaints, that the whole thing is a waste of time.

But all the time they are talking, the telephone doesn't ring even once and it's not till the end of the interview that Gabriel will understand why it's always there in front of Monsieur Asselin.

While he waits, the man takes his eyes off the telephone for a few seconds and looks at Gabriel.

"You're wasting your time, my boy. You should've realized before you came in that I couldn't give you a job ..."

"No, I didn't suspect a thing. And I still don't get it."

Monsieur Asselin takes a puff of cigar and blows the smoke in the direction of the open window that looks out on rue Sainte-Catherine where a streetcar is clattering along. A horse neighs, scared. Monsieur Asselin shrugs.

"Let 'em get rid of one or get rid of the other, they can't put the streetcars and the horses on the street at the same time! Makes no sense! Any idiot can see that, seems to me!"

He looks down at his silent telephone.

"To get back to where we were, this here's an institute for people that can't talk or hear anything, we only hire people like that and you can hear a little ... It's run by nuns, see, and I gotta go by their rules, understand? True, you could be an interesting candidate, you look like you know your trade, your letter says you're a real good pressman, but what can I say, my hands are tied!"

"You yourself can talk and hear!"

"Me, I'm the boss, that's different! I deal with all kinds of representatives and salesmen ... They don't all know sign language and I can't expect them to learn it ... It's inside the institute that there's rules ... Remember, it's called the Institut des sourds-muets ..."

"I know it."

"You know what?"

"Sign language. I learned it as soon as I knew I was gonna lose the hearing in my right ear. Maybe the other one too, on account of some infections that the doctors can't control."

The boss places his cigar in the ashtray, glances again at the telephone.

"*You* know sign language?"

"To my fingertips."

Gabriel laughs at his witticism which Monsieur Asselin doesn't seem to appreciate. Or didn't get.

"You need somebody that's responsible on the floor, Monsieur Asselin, somebody you can talk to without just using your hands."

"It's in the bylaws of the establishment!"

"But if it can save you from some problems? If it could prevent accidents?"

"Don't try to bamboozle me, I told you I couldn't do nothing for you."

"If I'm trying to bamboozle you, it's to convince you that you need me, Monsieur Asselin! I know that for sure! I been working on presses since I was twelve years old, I've probably got more experience than all your employees together."

"Don't try fooling me."

"Is it more important for you to hire somebody that can't hear or talk or somebody that knows his business?"

"They know their business!"

"I've seen the things you print, Monsieur Asselin, and I'm here to tell you they don't know their business, not all of them. It's okay, what you print here, but it could be a hundred times better. The school in Saint-Hyacinthe doesn't specialize in printing, the candidates they send you don't know hardly anything about how print works, and I could help the ones that come here to work while I'm doing my own work."

"The ad didn't say nothing about a supervisor..."

"I'm not asking to be a supervisor! I just want to give you a hand! In five years, ten years, I'll be as deaf as them but I'll be able to talk! That'll come in handy, won't it?"

For the first time, Monsieur Asselin can't come up with anything to say.

Gabriel takes the opportunity to slip into the gap he's just opened.

"I'm getting married on the third of June, Monsieur Asselin, to a girl I adore, and I'd give her the moon if I could... I want her to cook with butter, not lard! And when the little ones arrive I want them to eat good food and I want them to be well dressed. I want a roast beef on the table every Saturday night and I want to buy myself a beer at the tavern every afternoon after work. For newlyweds, a good job is like the moon. True, I've already got one, but my boss, when he saw your ad in the paper, because it was him that told me about the job, he right away said it was made for me and he offered to write me a letter of recommendation without me having to give my notice! That's something! Call him up, he'll tell you himself! He's right to be scared I'll go deaf and useless in his plant, or even dangerous, not you!"

"I don't doubt any of that but …"

"At least tell me that you'll think about it."

"I can't do that."

"So don't tell nobody I mentioned it, that's all. I'll wait till we're alone to talk to you. Anyways, I wouldn't need to talk to the other employees. I could be the best thing that could happen to the print shop at the Institut des sourds-muets! Because I can make your reputation! You'll be printing other things besides religious calendars and church pamphlets, I promise!"

Monsieur Asselin mashes his cigar in the ashtray.

"Let me think it over."

"No! Tell me yes or tell me no, but tell me now!"

The boss leans back in his chair, crosses his hands behind his head.

"I can't say I'm not tempted."

Just then a small red light comes on at the base of the telephone.

"Somebody needs me on the floor. Wants to talk to me … That's a new invention by Bell Telephone, you just have to dial my number and a little red light comes on. It's for the deaf. Isn't on the market yet, this is a trial … For sure I don't need it, I can hear it ring, but I wanted to have one like everybody else, just to see … But I'm not used to it yet and I've got a habit of always keeping my eye on the telephone in case somebody calls me. Wears me out. But I guess I'll get used to it eventually … The others too. Mustn't let it keep us from working, eh? Me, anyway, I don't dare to call them yet, I'm scared they'll waste their time, like me, always with their eye on it …"

He gets up, holds out his hand to Gabriel.

"I'll think about it. Seriously."

Gabriel gestures towards the telephone.

"If you hire me you won't need that any more … I'll be able to come and talk to you in person."

Before he leaves the office, Monsieur Asselin turns to Gabriel.

"Your future wife, does she know you're gonna go deaf?"

"Of course she knows. In fact that's how we met. She was a nurse and she looked after me when I had my accident."

"And ... It doesn't bother her?"

"Sure it bothers her. I mean ... It makes her sad. But she says she can put up with it. Out of love for me. That's something, eh?" A glimmer in Monsieur Asselin's eye suggests to Gabriel that he has won.

"I'm going to call your boss once I make up my mind. But don't dream too much! Don't say anything to your future bride!"

As he leaves the Insitut des sourds-muets, Gabriel walks down rue Saint-Denis towards the carré Saint-Louis where he rents a small room. He takes off his jacket, folds it over his shoulder. It was cool when he got up, nearly cold, but now there's a gentle mildness over the city, an end-of-spring warmth, though it'll be more than a month till summer arrives. The buds have finally opened and the sky is tinged with great patches of tender green. By tomorrow the leaves will have grown and from the sidewalk it will be possible to recognize their shapes. He goes for a walk, grabs a quick lunch in a tavern on rue Sainte-Catherine, and that afternoon he can afford to treat himself to a movie, *Pay Day* at the Loew's, for instance, a comedy by Charlie Chaplin, the man who makes him laugh more than anyone in the world.

The night before he had asked Rhéauna again, for maybe the hundredth time, if she was sure she wanted to spend the rest of her life with a man who was liable to gradually lose his hearing and she gave him the most wonderful reply you could imagine:

"If it lets me tell you louder that I love you, it doesn't bother me at all. And if it makes me repeat it, that's even better!"

He is well aware that's not true, that it worries her, that she'd said what she'd said to reassure him, but it was that proof of love that made him decide to go to the Insitut des sourds-muets with the letter of reference from his boss at *Le Devoir* where he's been working for eight years, nearly since the newspaper was founded. Monsieur Saint-Germain was honest enough to tell him, when Gabriel announced that he was getting married, that he wouldn't be able to offer him a significant raise for a long time because *Le Devoir* is not a wealthy newspaper, and that if he wanted to start a family he'd need a job that paid better.

A loving wife, an honest boss, the prospect of a new and better-paying job, most likely more interesting too, what more could he ask of life?

In one month's time he'll be married.

With the responsibilities of a married man, even if Rhéauna insisted on continuing to work at the beginning of their marriage. They have found an apartment on rue Papineau, a small two-bedroom that doesn't look like much but they'll have to be content with it at first, in fact until the second baby is on the way because after all there's enough room for the first. He smiles. A year from now, if he's not yet a father, Rhéauna will most likely be pregnant. She will be the most beautiful pregnant woman in the history of humankind.

Then, without really knowing why, he thinks about the cookies that Béa, Rhéauna's sister, sells somewhere on rue Ontario near Amherst.

## Victoire

He is sprawled on his back, arms outstretched, mouth open. Snoring. A sickening smell of ill-digested alcohol drifts in the room. She hadn't noticed it when she woke up because she'd been inhaling it for a good part of the night.

She had shaken him a couple of times. He grunted, turned over in the bed, then onto his back. He murmured a few words that she didn't understand – most likely a vague promise to get up soon – gestured to her to leave the room. He hates it when his wife waits for him to wake up before she leaves the bedroom; not that he's afraid of her reproaches, they're always the same and he's used to them, but it's her cold look, the contempt she can no longer disguise, that he wants to avoid. He doesn't want her to catch him in that position of weakness, hair unkempt, complexion grey, back hunched, hands on his temples trying to rub away the migraine that has him bent double and wanting to vomit.

*Lorsque avec ses enfants vêtus de peaux de bêtes, / Échevelé, livide au milieu des tempêtes, / Caïn se fut enfui de devant Jéhovah* ... As if the eye of God that follows you everywhere, even to the grave, could seduce a woman! – so much would he like to hide himself six feet underground when she comes to wake him up the next morning to tell him that the doorknob in apartment eight is broken or that the steps of the front staircase need washing. The time for poetry is over, the night – that great consoler, that final refuge where alcohol serves to knock you out – is over, day has dawned, dreaded reality lands on him. Every morning.

She is still sitting at the end of the bed, though. She knows that if she leaves before he sets foot out of it he'll go back to sleep and the morning will pass without her seeing him again. In a few minutes he'll sit up, yawn, cough into his fist, scratch his head, his armpits. He may try out a bad joke to lighten the atmosphere, realize it's impossible, and finally bow in the face of the overly heavy day ahead.

She will ask him if he wants to eat, he'll say he's not hungry, she'll add that she's made him a coffee anyway. Black. Strong.

And as she does every morning she stays frozen, sitting at the foot of the bed in the same position. Now and then, on some days when she puts more effort into understanding him a little, she strokes the calf of this man, her husband, whom she has so often felt like killing but for whom she still feels pity. Not this morning. Is it because her escape hatch hasn't worked, because the raptor hasn't criss-crossed the sky above the ruelle des Fortifications and she has not been able for a single moment to forget her frustrations? She only feels like beating him. Like a selfish spoiled child. Give him the spanking of his life. Hit him till her hands hurt. She'd like to hear him cry, beg for her pity. She'd like him to beg for her pardon – totally sober, not pissed like he is every night – when she owes him so much. Respectability. After the debasement of a great love. Who wasn't him.

He had asked her to marry him, even though she was an "unwed mother," a fallen woman, because he thought he was sterile and dreamed of having offspring. He'd heard about her – and about her bad luck – during summer holidays in Duhamel with his uncle who was then the village *curé*. He had approached her one day at the general store – after all, she wasn't married – and from their first conversation he had let Victoire know that he was aware of her situation and that if she wanted … And he'd repeated his request every summer, for years. He knew that she didn't love him, that she would never love him. He also knew that she was desperate, that the forbidden love she was living was slowly killing her and he thought he would save her by taking her to the city, far from Josaphat. Her brother.

They had agreed to tell his family she was a widow, with no family, no ties, that she came from far away, which was true, and he agreed to adopt Gabriel, her ten-year-old son. He hadn't flinched at the unexpected arrival of Albertine: Victoire had admitted that she was pregnant when she married him. After all, this second child could be his, on condition that they claim she was premature.

But Victoire had hidden the fact that Josaphat was in the city too, that she'd forbidden him to get in touch with them, and that he was no doubt roaming the city looking for work. What could a country fiddler do in a big city? She trembled for him when she thought of it.

Télesphore had been so kind at first. So thoughtful. So grateful.

He had greeted Albertine's arrival with great joy, even though he'd have preferred a boy. He said, laughing, that she had his smile although she never smiled. He called her his little princess and proudly carried her to church in his arms every Sunday.

When he arrived in town, he had told Gabriel, who missed the country and Josaphat, that they, Gabriel and his mother, had spent some years in Duhamel at his uncle's place because Victoire was sick and needed good fresh country air. That they'd come back when she was cured. That if the boy didn't remember him it was because he was too young when they left. And that from now on he would be living here, in the big city, where life would be a lot more interesting than it was in the Gatineau, in the middle of nowhere, and most important, full of opportunities for a smart boy like him.

Gabriel had resisted everything: the big city, his new father, and even his mother whom he criticized for letting him call Josaphat *Poppa*, when he was just his uncle. To Télesphore he often said:

"If you were my father, how come we never saw you in Duhamel? Did you forget about us?"

To which neither Télesphore nor Victoire had any acceptable answer: work couldn't explain everything.

Gabriel refused to call Télesphore *Poppa*, content with calling him *Monsieur*, with a striking note of contempt.

And at the age of twelve he'd found work as an apprentice in a print shop, with the hope of leaving the household where he was so unhappy as soon as possible. The pittance he brought home was very useful – Télesphore was a translator and proofreader for a publishing house, which paid very poorly – and his parents left him alone. After all, printing was an excellent profession.

Meanwhile, and to his great surprise, Télesphore had made two children, one after the other, with Victoire: Édouard, then Madeleine, who was born scarcely a year after her brother. At first he'd been overjoyed, but he never neglected Gabriel and Albertine, treating them like his own children, though already tending – he thought it was perfectly legitimate – to favour the other two. His own. He had showered Victoire with gifts, worthless trinkets because he wasn't rich, far from it, but they expressed his gratitude. He claimed that she had worked miracles, that he was the happiest man on earth, that she'd proved to him that the doctors had been wrong: he'd had scarlet fever at seventeen and the doctors – had they even bothered to check him out seriously? – had declared that the disease had left him sterile. Despite Gabriel's reservations towards him and the difficult character of Albertine who, no sooner born than she squirmed and cried nearly non-stop, as if to complain at being alive, life had been fairly pleasant for a while. In any case until Télesphore found out by chance – a tavern remark along the lines of: You never told me, Télesphore, you've got a brother-in-law that plays the fiddle – that goddamn Josaphat had been here since their marriage, that Victoire had hidden it and a sick, destructive jealousy began to gnaw at him.

For the first time, he had doubts about Victoire's honesty and, furious, he had challenged her to admit that his last two children had the same father as the first two.

Though Victoire protested, swore that she'd never seen her brother again, that she didn't know where he was, in the city or back in Duhamel, doubt stayed anchored in him, eating away like a strong acid, as it did, she could sense it, when he told her, drunk, that he believed her and begged her forgiveness, crying, for making her life impossible.

He already drank a lot, like most of the men in his family, like most of the men Victoire had known, in fact, but the obsessive fear of having perhaps been cheated on by the woman he had saved from opprobrium – his own words – had piqued his pride and cast Télesphore into excesses from which he'd never again been able to escape. He could have repudiated her, he would most likely have had the right, but how could he confess such horrors to his friends and family, to his parents, without being laughed at? A storybook cuckold!

And a storybook cuckold he remained. Allowing himself to sink into the only solace ever available to the men of his race. And without ever thinking about taking a second test that might have settled the whole matter if he had turned out not to be sterile after all. When Victoire dared talk to him about it, he walked out, slamming the door, and his wife had concluded that he preferred doubt to being told a second time that he was sterile. There was no way out and Victoire had no choice but to accept it.

Because of his drinking and skipped workdays, he had lost his job. Lacking the courage – booze again – to look for decent work in his field, he'd ended up here, on ruelle des Fortifications, janitor in an apartment block that was falling apart before your eyes, victim of the tenants' whims, the perfect water bearer, he who had always rubbed shoulders with poetry, great books, and produced translations that were precise, relevant, and faithful, appreciated by his bosses and their clients.

That too, the janitor's work, he ended up neglecting, and from then on it was Victoire who took care of certain tasks. But not the biggest ones that demand the strength of a man.

"I told you yesterday morning, now I'm telling you again, Télesphore. You've got to go see Madame Coutu on the third floor. She says her icebox is leaking … And I'll have you know it isn't me that's going to get down on my knees on her linoleum to see what the problem is!"

He lifts himself up on one elbow.

"Okay, okay, I'll go."

When Victoire goes back to the kitchen, Albertine is sitting over a slice of bread dripping with molasses.

"You don't know what to do so you eat, is that it?"

Her daughter doesn't bother to even raise her head to answer.

"It's boring here. Like school. There's nothing to do."

"First of all, it may be boring here, but that sure as heck doesn't mean there's nothing to do! Take one look at my hands and you'll see. And after that, I'll tell you yet again that if you bothered to listen a little to what the nuns at school have to say, if you tried to understand just a little bit of what they're trying to drill into your stubborn head, maybe you'd find it not so boring. And don't tell me that what you learn there will never be of any use, little girl, that'd just make me want to give you a spanking! Another one! When you choose to be ignorant, little girl, you mustn't expect a lot out of life!"

"I don't expect a lot, I just want to be left alone."

"If that's what you want, go eat your bread and molasses in the living room or your bedroom. When you want peace, you sentence yourself to being all alone in your corner!" said Victoire.

"I just finished ... Well, nearly ..."

"Your father's getting up and if he sees you here ..."

"I told you a while ago, I heard him coming in at dawn ..."

"How come you weren't asleep?"

"Aren't I allowed to pee?"

"Just go on in that tone of voice and you'll be *really* sorry you didn't go to school."

Albertine gets up, takes her plate and her empty glass of milk to the sink.

"He seemed to be in a pretty good mood."

"He's always in a good mood when he comes home in that state."

"That's why I like him better pissed than sober. He's easier to put up with."

Victoire watches her daughter leave the kitchen.

Her too? Is it the case for everybody in the house?

When he has not been drinking, Télesphore – especially in recent days, especially since Gabriel left home, slamming the door behind him – is crabby, grumpy, quick with an insult, and lobs frequent threats – luckily he never carries them out – to grab someone, anyone, the first male or female he can get his hands on, by the scruff of the neck and to hit until it hurts, until his own hand swells up like a boxer's mitt after a fight. His acts of intimidation – ultimatums of a non-violent man that go too far to hide his vulnerability – are often ridiculous, but the mere fact that they occur to him terrifies Victoire who sees with apprehension the day coming when he could lose control or take it out on himself instead of on the family.

When he's been drinking, on the other hand, when he comes home in the middle of the night singing or reciting his goddamn poems, when he forces Victoire to get up and behold the full moon or dance a waltz with him right there in the living room, all her indecision disappears, all her fears, her despair at being betrayed and her desire for revenge. He is no longer jealous, he is charming, mild, he asks Victoire to forgive him, cries like a baby for hours, swearing that he adores her, that he couldn't survive without her, that she's the most wonderful woman in the world, that he knows that their two youngest children are his, that he still loves Gabriel and Albertine like his own, he's going to change, he'll be cured, he'll consult a specialist: a month, let her give him one month, two at most, and she'll see the transformation. He swears oaths, he believes them, he laughs, he lifts her in his arms, spins her around.

Drink does not make him aggressive, it makes him gentle as a lamb, noisy, it's true, like a baby, and often too clingy, but when all's said and done, easier to put up with than when he terrifies the household because sober, he's too frustrated.

How many women can say that they prefer their husbands pissed than on the wagon?

And now his own daughter has just remarked on it. Even the children are aware of it.

Télesphore exits his room, scruffy, suspenders hanging down his back.

Victoire watches him take his place at the head of the kitchen table.

"You know something, Télesphore? I'd like it if you'd start drinking first thing when you get up in the morning ..."

## Aunt Alice

She doesn't need to understand French to know what's in the invitation.

The daughter of her sister-in-law Maria is getting married. She was still a teenager the last time she saw her, she doesn't remember much about her. She sees a pretty, animated face with the plump cheeks of a child from the countryside and the ironic smile just like her mother's, and that's about all. She still remembers, though, that Rhéauna was the only member of the family, aside from her husband, of course, who agreed to speak English with her. She said that it made her practise, that she was afraid of losing the small amount of English she'd learned at school in Saskatchewan. And now she's an adult. Time passes ... Often with exasperating slowness, but it passes.

She slips the card into the envelope, then places it on the end table next to her favourite armchair. Will she even show Ernest the invitation? Shouldn't she simply throw it in the garbage, act as if it doesn't exist? Ernest might never know about Rhéauna's wedding. What difference would knowing it make in his life anyway? Because it's obvious that he won't want to go to that wedding, any more than she will, that if she doesn't throw it out he'll do it himself. Will he even bother to read it?

She wonders why Maria is inviting her and her husband to the wedding. An attempt at a reconciliation? At a wedding? That doesn't sound much like her. Out of simple courtesy? Because she knows they won't go but that she'll never be able to reproach herself for not having invited the whole family? I invited you, you didn't come, don't complain? That sounds a little more like her.

The chill between Ernest and his three sisters goes on, they haven't seen one another for years. Ever since the horrible evening, in fact, when her husband gave Maria a piece of his mind. How many years ago was that? Five? Six?

Anyway you can't say that she has missed them: her sisters-in-law have always been hateful with her – her husband claimed it was all in her head, that his sisters didn't detest her, that she was imagining things – they were contemptuous towards her, rude, critical of whatever she served them when they came to her place for supper, making fun of her, especially that, making fun because of…

She rests her head against the white lace doily that was part of her wedding trousseau and that she'd crocheted so long ago, before she got married, before leaving Regina, before seeing the collapse of any hope of happiness. In exile.

She looks at the time. Too early. Another long half-hour…

She waits for noon. Noon and her first drink. She doesn't even think of the word *gin*, she merely imagines the glass in her hand, which is shaking a little, the spicy smell that it gives off, the first sip that will soothe her. And when she starts to see the bottom of the drink, that magic moment, that too-brief second when she feels reality topple, no, before that, just before reality topples, that warmth at the level of her neck, the throat, relaxing, the very first little shiver, a trembling in her brain, the warning, because it is one, that the tremendous healing and the wonderful silence, both momentary, yes, and always too short, are coming. And the dizziness, the lightness that will last only a few minutes before the drunkenness, the powerful drunkenness that's so repulsive, full of holes and weird ideas, hits her. It's that little quarter-hour between a quarter past and half past noon, that she anticipates every day. That sense of pure well-being. A knot in the fabric of time. An indescribable and irreplaceable sensation of floating. Afterwards, the flabbiness in her legs, the spinning head, the dislocated movements, the naps visited by nightmares, the endless afternoons, the glass refilled too often, and the attacks of rage, the attacks of despondency, every day, every goddamn day, it's the price to be paid for those magical minutes.

She looks towards the dark wood buffet. For once, just today, she could start a little earlier.

No. After all.

To busy herself she picks up the invitation, reads it several times.

Then, unable to take any more, she gets up and heads for the freedom she has earned so well.

# Gabriel

A gathering has formed across from the Biscuiterie Ontario.

Gabriel drops a cigarette on the brand-new cement sidewalk, stubs it out.

Some women have their foreheads against the window, others stand in the still-open doorway. Children pull at their skirts fretfully. The women brush them aside. There's no question of their missing out on what's going on inside. It's so rare that they have a chance to hear real music, and they want to take advantage of it now. And the fiddle tunes being played one after another inside the cookie factory for more than half an hour – sometimes gay, mostly sad – thrill them. They feel like singing, dancing, crying. All at the same time. It's more than beautiful, it makes you want to live. In spite of everything that's going badly.

Gabriel recognizes the tone of the violin right away and steps straight up to the cookie factory, smiling.

Only one fiddler in the world is capable of producing such sounds with a tired old instrument that he does so little to take care of: his uncle Josaphat.

He pulls himself up on tiptoe behind the group of women.

Josaphat is standing in the middle of the big room, eyes closed, the way he does when he's inspired. It's as if he is playing not for those who are listening but for himself, to make himself want to sing, to dance, to cry. And to go on living in spite of everything.

Madame Guillemette has pride of place behind the cash register, Béa is sitting on a little bench, one hand on her heart, her head resting against the counter. Gabriel, who knows the cookie-factory owner well, being one of her best customers, thinks that she must be salivating at the prospect of all the sales she'll make when the concert is over. All these women who will want to come inside to say hello and thank the musician ... Concentrating as she is, though, with a smile on her lips – a rare thing – he thinks to himself that she doesn't seem at all concerned with what will happen when Josaphat-le-Violon has finished his jigs and serenades. For once she doesn't seem to be thinking about money but is indulging in a moment of genuine emotion. With no self-interest.

When Josaphat finishes his last note – long, throbbing, nearly a sob – there is a brief silence in the cookie factory and on the sidewalk. Then all the women watching begin to applaud together. Madame Guillemette opens her eyes – an abrupt return to reality – stands up behind her cash register, and starts looking around the store for potential customers. Her moment of weakness was brief, the businesswoman quickly regains the upper hand.

"Ladies, ladies, in honour of Monsieur Josaphat who has given us such a lovely moment, I'm putting my cookies on sale!"

She leans over towards Béa who clearly doesn't want to come out of her languor.

"Béa, go get the old boxes of tea biscuits, I've been wondering what to do with them!"

Gabriel has cleared a path for himself through the admiring crowd and now goes up to his uncle.

"So you play in cookie factories now, you old devil? Department stores aren't good enough for you?"

Josaphat opens his arms, his violin in one hand, bow in the other. He looks as if he wants to throw them up to the ceiling.

"Gabriel! How's things, my boy? Haven't seen you for ages, thought you were dead!"

Béa, who was on her way to the back of the shop, stops and turns towards them.

"Is that your father, Gabriel?"

Josaphat turns red, backs up a few steps, coughs into his fist. Gabriel bursts out laughing.

"No, he's my mother's brother! The artist in the family!"

Josaphat looks at them.

"You know each other, you and Béa?"

Madame Guillemette taps Béa on the shoulder.

"Béa! It's for today, not tomorrow! Hurry up before they leave without buying!"

Béa replies to Josaphat while she is opening the door to the back of the shop.

"He's my future brother-in-law! He's getting married to my sister Nana. Don't tell me you didn't know! You're his uncle and you didn't know?"

"I knew he was getting married but I didn't know the bride-to-be was your sister."

And she disappears while her boss shoots her threatening looks.

A few women have left, others are poking around in the shop as they await the arrival of the reduced merchandise Madame Guillemette just announced. Some let themselves be tempted by the gingerbread men or the maple-leaf cookies their children adore.

Gabriel takes out his cigarettes, offers one to his uncle who shakes his head no.

Josaphat lays his violin in its case, takes out the hand-rolled that he'd slipped behind his ear.

"You don't want a good old Turret, mon oncle?"

"Last one you gave me, my throat was on fire for three days! How can you smoke that?"

"These're real cigarettes! For real men!"

"If that's what you need to feel like a man, my boy, I'll tell you one thing, you got problems!"

Gabriel guffaws and lights their cigarettes with a big Eddy match with its good smell of sulphur and burned wood.

"I never thought I'd see you here … Small world, eh mon oncle?"

Josaphat aims his first puff of smoke at the ceiling.

"Yup. And getting smaller every day!"

Gabriel has never known why his uncle Josaphat isn't welcome at his parents' house. When he'd started asking serious questions as a teenager, his mother had told him that his father and his uncle had never got along, they didn't see life in the same way, that Josaphat, actually, was too bohemian as far as Télesphore was concerned. She'd had to explain to her son what *bohemian* meant and he'd replied that he didn't see a big difference between his father's behaviour and his uncle's, except where the violin was concerned. One was a genuine artist, the other dreamed of being one while he drank and recited old poems. Télesphore was as irresponsible as Josaphat, more so, in fact, because he had married and made a whole family suffer while Josaphat had been considerate enough to remain a bachelor ... Victoire had maintained that it might, in fact, be their too-great resemblance that kept them apart: his father didn't like to see his own flaws in his uncle and kept away from him to avoid having to judge himself.

And in the end Gabriel had made his mother admit that she thought Josaphat was a better human being than Télesphore.

But he'd never been satisfied with those explanations. He'd asked Josaphat – his mother had made him swear not to tell his father that she'd allowed him to see his uncle – who'd turned out to be even more evasive than Victoire. Gabriel had asked him if something had happened when they were living in Duhamel, a family squabble for instance, and Josaphat had replied, laconically, that their time in Duhamel had been the most wonderful part of his life, which hadn't helped the poor boy who came out of those conversations confused and flustered.

"So you're getting married on the third of June?"

Gabriel looks around the cookie factory. Women bustling about or waiting impatiently at the cash because Béa is taking her time returning from the back of the shop, children running all over and shouting.

"Right, and I can't wait!"

"Anyways, she's one of a kind! You're lucky, my boy, enjoy it!"

"On top of that I think I've got a new job! More pay. More interesting. In the print shop at the Institut des sourds-muets. Oh, and speaking of the print shop, that reminds me ..."

He extricates a white envelope from his inside jacket pocket.

"Here, I've still got some invitations on me..."

Josaphat takes the envelope, opens it.

"Why're you giving me this?"

"To invite you, what d'you think?"

"You think I'm gonna show up there? Your father'd kill me!"

"Never mind my father! It's me that's inviting you!"

"And what's your mother gonna say? She'd have a hell of a day if she sees me there."

"Be discreet, hide if you want, fix it so nobody sees you, but I want you to be there!"

"You're sure?"

"Sure I'm sure! Here, I got an idea, let me hire you as a musician, then they can't say a thing! D'you still do weddings?"

"What d'you think? That's what pays the best!"

"You see? Everything's working out!"

"Make up your mind! Just now you wanted me to hide, now you're asking me to play my fiddle! What is it you want, you want people to see me or not?!"

Josaphat wipes a tear with his shirt collar.

"Hey, mon oncle, don't start crying!"

"If you only knew, my boy... But I won't charge you. For you I'll play for free!"

Exclamations rise up in the cookie factory.

Béa, bright red, sets the boxes of tea biscuits on the counter.

"Look here, Madame Guillemette, you had these cookies hidden. They were in next to the garbage cans. I looked all over – I never would've thought..."

Her boss pinches her upper arm.

"Be quiet, featherbrain! Those are boxes I was going to throw out! I sell them now and then, make a little money off them, don't spoil my fun!"

## Maria

She was expecting an impressive business that would look like a bank branch, with marble columns and gilt on the ceiling, but here she was in a rundown dispensary upstairs from a pharmacy. She spent fifteen minutes waiting on a straight chair that clearly hadn't seen a dust rag for a good long while, until a secretary, *the* secretary actually, came to tell her that Monsieur Laverdière would see her now in his office, a dingy little room that smelled of stale cigars and sweat. Monsieur Laverdière was huge, he talked loudly, his mood was too good to be genuine. He sported a predator's smile and appeared to be so condescending that Maria immediately wanted to slap him and felt discouraged in less than five minutes.

If she is haggling with him again, listening to him spout the same arguments, it's because she is desperate and badly needs the money.

"You've got your reasons for coming to see us, but you have to understand, Madame Rathier, this is the first time I've seen a woman wanting to take out so big a loan."

"There's a first time for everything, Monsieur Laverdière."

"It's not me that decides, you know."

"It's not true that you aren't the one that decides. It's you that asks questions so it's you that decides."

"What I decide is whether you're a good candidate, and then

like I've already explained to you three times, I make a report for my boss ..."

"But you don't think I'm a good candidate?"

"That's not what I said. I said I'd never seen a woman wanting to take out such a big loan."

"What difference does it make if I'm a man or a woman? You'll see your money again!"

"So you say."

"Damn right it's what I say. I can pay you back. Maybe it'll take me ten years, maybe I'll have to give you two bucks a week for the rest of my life but I'll pay you back."

"Ten years from now will you still be working at the Paradise on boulevard Saint-Laurent?"

"When a man comes in to borrow money d'you ask him where he'll be in ten years?"

"Men that come to borrow money, most of them they've got regular jobs."

"Me too, I've got one! It's been years now I've been working at the Paradise and I don't intend to quit!"

"Look, Madame Rathier ... Women who work are pretty rare and on top of that, you're a waitress in a nightclub that could go belly up tomorrow morning."

"The companies your clients work for, they could go belly up too, couldn't they? So if I was a waiter you'd say the same thing because I wouldn't have a steady job?"

He looks at her, flabbergasted, wipes his face with a handkerchief of doubtful cleanliness. "Some jobs are more reliable than others."

"And one sex is more reliable than the other one."

"That's not what I said."

She leans across the desk where along with the usual mess of papers are greasy containers that must have once held food.

"Just tell me right now that you don't want to lend me any money because I'm a woman and that'll be that. I'll get the hell out and you won't see me again ... But I want you to tell me ..."

Again he mops his forehead, his neck. His smell is stronger.

Maria shrinks back, leans into her chair. But Monsieur Laverdière doesn't lose control for very long, he gets his wits back fairly quickly.

"Look, women that come here for a loan, usually it's a secret from their husbands."

"I haven't got a husband, I told you I'm a widow!"

"Stop cutting me off, let me finish what I'm saying! They come and borrow ten or twenty bucks because they want to buy stuff and keep it secret from their husbands – a dress, a pair of shoes, a hat, I don't know, women's stuff … And they've got a tremendous problem reimbursing us. You, you turn up here and ask for three hundred to pay for your daughter's wedding …"

"… Because she hasn't got a father! Because the one that has to pay is me! It's always the father that pays for a wedding but this time there isn't a father!"

"I know that! You've told me twenty-five times! I'm not saying I don't understand you, that I don't understand your situation …"

He gives her his sympathetic number, frowns, there are wrinkles on his forehead. Maria would throw him out the window if it were open.

"I just want to tell you that generally the women that come to see us, most of them have a hard time paying back their twenty bucks. So just imagine three hundred!"

"What about the men, they don't have a hard time paying back their loan?"

"It's not the same thing …"

Maria stands up, drops her purse on the desk.

"I knew you'd say that. I'm sure I've got more money in my handbag than most of the men that come for a loan have got in their pockets. I earn a good living, Monsieur Laverdière, a *very* good living. My problem is, I don't get an advance. I'm a widow, I've got four children to bring up, there's no way I can put aside any money, you should be able to understand that! And now my daughter is getting married! And that costs money! And I'd like to be able to owe money to just one place instead of all over town! It would be more convenient, I wouldn't have to chase around like a lunatic to repay a bit every week! I'm going to Dupuis Frères after lunch to buy my daughter's wedding dress, then I have to order the cake, then I have to order the meal, then I have to pay for the church, then I have to pay the musicians ..."

"I know all that."

"If that's so, why won't you help me?"

"I didn't say I won't help you."

"You're blaming me for being a woman!"

"I'm not blaming you! The law's the law!"

"What d'you mean, the law's the law? Is it written in the law not to lend money to women? Where? I want to see it! I want proof! If I were a man the contract would already be signed and I'd be celebrating it at the tavern! Maybe along with you!"

"Watch what you say, Madame Rathier."

"Why should I watch what I say? I come here in good faith, I really do intend to pay you back your goddamn money, even if I have to bleed myself dry to do it, then you refuse to lend it because I'm a woman! You're there to make money, right? Whether I'm a man or a woman you'll make money off me! If it takes me ten years to pay it back you could even get twice what I borrow, with your interest rate so high! My money doesn't have a sex, Monsieur Laverdière, it's worth the same as a man's, and the day when you get that in your head you'll have come a good way along the road! And let me tell you something, a woman's thing, before I go! You ought to get some air in here now and then, it stinks to high heaven! And you ought to wash yourself too! If your smell doesn't bother the men that come here, it sure as heck must bother the women!"

She turns and exits the room, cursing.

Like a man.

## Alice

The heat is unbearable despite the enormous factory windows left open in the hope that at some point in the day a breeze will sweep in and cool the women who slave away from morning till night amid the unhealthy fumes from the tobacco leaves they process.

The workers Alice is part of are arranged in three groups around an immense table on which the tobacco travels along a conveyor that makes a deafening noise because it is poorly maintained. The first group prepares the tobacco. They unwrap it – it arrives from the United States in huge bundles – open it out, and place it on one end of the big table with shower heads fastened above that release bursts of steam. The second group, to ensure that the leaves won't stick together, moisten the tobacco leaves by exposing them to the bursts of steam. Finally, the third group, which includes Alice, dry it by stirring it as fast as possible under a burst of compressed air. These women are called the tobacco shakers. It is by far the most exhausting work because it demands a lot of physical strength.

When these three tasks are completed, the tobacco will be slashed, shredded, reduced to a kind of sawdust from which cigarettes will be made.

Mireille Surprenant, the clown in the group of shakers, has just shouted above the din of the machines that if the rate of humidity were just a bit higher, it would be raining, which got a good laugh from the fellow workers who could hear her.

Another girl, Pauline Petit, who tried to be just as funny but rarely succeeded, told her: "At least wait till August before you complain!"

The girls were mad at her. They had no desire to think about August, the worst month of the year, the one that was called the sacrifice because that was when a good many of them took sick, suffocated by the heat and exhausted by their labour.

Because their work was so harsh, the shakers were allowed to work in light clothing, winter and summer, and needless to say their supervisors – all men – took advantage of it to get an eyeful, make stupid jokes all week long and, in the case of fat Guy Gingras, the most hated foreman on the floor whom they called *Foie gras*, allowed himself more than remarks, fondling – sometimes furtively, often more insistently if the girl wasn't shy.

For several weeks now, he has set his sights on Alice Rathier, whom he'd taken a shine to and didn't stop bothering.

That morning he had started by remarking on her hair, which she had pulled up instead of letting it fall to her shoulders as she usually did.

"You should've showed me that little neck before, Alice."

She made as if she hadn't heard and went on stirring her tobacco leaves. Water was running down her neck but she didn't dare touch it for fear that Monsieur Gingras would take it for a provocation. Or worse, an invitation.

He had nonetheless put his mouth close to her ear.

"Pretty little necks like that, you mustn't just walk by them, you have to get close, smell them, kiss them."

She knew that he wouldn't have dared to kiss her neck in front of everyone, his advances instead took place under the table – a pinched bum, a lightly brushed thigh, a hand lingering on the lower back; yet she hadn't been able to hold back a shiver of disgust.

"You've got a short memory! We spend all summer with our hair pulled up because it's so goddamn hot!"

"It isn't summer yet."

"Maybe not, but it's still plenty hot! And will you leave me alone so I can work, Monsieur Gingras? Otherwise you'll say I don't work fast enough and I'm not doing my job!"

Just loud enough for her neighbours to hear her. And understand that she was refusing to play the game, which some of them occasionally went along with to get favours. A cigarette break disguised as a trip to the bathroom, for instance. Or a little longer for lunch.

He'd straightened up, smiling.

"You're pretty quarrelsome this morning, Alice Rathier!"

"I always am ..."

"We'll talk about that later ... I like unwilling women ... I like to tame them, humble them ..."

Then he walked away, whistling "La java bleue," which the girls had been singing around the table for some weeks now, to pass the time.

Alice had peace for a good hour. Monsieur Gingras didn't even show up again at their table, though it was one of his favourites because at it he had posted the youngest and prettiest workers in the factory.

But he came back. He is there, behind her, she can smell his cologne. A rather corpulent man, he perspires even more than the workers he's in charge of and sprays himself with cologne to mask the smell of sweat. Yardley Lotus. When the girls aren't calling him *Foie gras*, they call him *Skunky*.

He's not going to start again ...

Yes. His mouth is very close to her ear. This time it's his smoker's breath that tickles her nostrils.

"If you wore your hair like that all winter I wouldn't complain, Alice."

It all happens very fast.

Without taking time to think it over, she gets up, turns towards the foreman, pulls herself up on tiptoe, and brings her face close to his.

"Will you leave me alone! Leave me alone once and for all! Leave me the hell alone! The rest of us too! We're here to work, not get hassled by creeps like you! I'm fed up with your insinuations and your hands you can't keep to yourself! We're all fed up! The whole bunch of us! If the others are too scared to tell you, I'll say it: I'm fed up, pissed off, is that clear enough? We can't take it, none of us! We work hard enough, we don't need to be felt up by perverts like you! If you want a hooker, go look on Saint-Laurent, there's loads of them, and let us do our work in peace!"

Monsieur Gingras goes pale but his acne scars, the worst disgrace in his life, stay pinkish, drawing grotesque arabesques on his face.

"You watch out what you say, girl … You don't know what you're getting involved in …"

"I'm not scared of your threats!"

"No, eh? D'you know what happens to hardheads like you?"

"Yeah and there's times I envy them 'cause they don't work for lunatics like you guys!" This time he turns red. No one has ever used that tone of voice with him. He places a forefinger on her forehead.

"Who d'you think you are?"

"I think I'm somebody who wants to work in peace! To earn her pay even if it's not much, and not have to put up with you and the rest of the supervisors!"

"Who d'you think you are, lecturing me!"

"Leave us alone and we won't need to!"

He wipes his face with the rag he's holding.

"One more word outta you and you pack up your belongings and get off the floor, understand?"

"What the heck d'you want me to do? Apologize? Ask you to forgive me? Sit down as if nothing happened? Go back to my job and not say a word? Put up with your hands on my backside and the filthy words you say in my ear? Maybe the others can take it but I can't. Tough, but that's the way it is. And if it costs me my job I'll find another one somewhere else! There's lots that aren't as crappy as this, let me tell you!"

"You're gonna lose this job, that's for sure!"

"So what! At least I've said what I think! What the others think too. Maybe they're too chickenshit to do it, but they'll be real glad that another woman did! It doesn't make sense to put up with it all year long like we do! You haven't got the right to behave like you do! We aren't slaves so don't treat us as if we are!"

He brings up his hand to hit her. This time, she's the one who jabs his forehead.

"Don't touch me! Just try and you'll be dealing not with me, but my mother! And if you knew who she is, you wouldn't have that grin on your face! My mother's got connections on Saint-Laurent, she knows an awful lot of people, if you see what I mean, and believe me, you wouldn't want her to meet them. You could end up with no hands to squeeze our backsides and no tongue for saying obscenities!"

He steps back, getting redder and redder.

"You're threatening me! You, you think you can threaten me! You think I'm scared? You think your mother scares me?"

"I can see why you aren't scared of me. But her ..."

"Who's your mother anyways, with those connections? The Queen of the Main Mafia?"

"She may be the queen of nothing but she knows an awful lot of kings ..."

"And I'm not scared of people that know people that know people ..."

"You ought to be."

"Yeah, sure, okay, we'll drop your mother for now and come back to you ..."

"Don't worry about me. I won't give you the pleasure of kicking me out. I'm leaving. Keep your shitty job, I don't want it! And don't worry, I won't sic my mother on you, I'm gonna try and forget you as fast as I can, you and your stink of skunk! So long!"

She takes off, running, circles the table where all activity stopped when the altercation began.

"So long, everybody! You're great, the whole gang of you, but you shouldn't put up with that! He's got no right to treat you like he does and you haven't got the right to put up with it."

She races down the stairs and across the lobby, pushes the front door. She walks out into a sunny day in May. A glorious day! She leans against the cement wall and starts to laugh. From nerves as much as happiness.

"I couldn't take it, I couldn't take it, I couldn't take it."

What she doesn't know is that at the very moment she was yelling at her supervisor here at the plant, her mother was yelling at a man who was refusing to lend her money, at the other end of town.

# SAINT-BONIFACE, MANITOBA

## *Bebette*

"*Saperlipopette!*"

The scream can be heard all the way to the end of the street. Heads turn. She gestures to a lady she knows to reassure her that all is well, that it's a cry of joy that she had just sent out as she was picking up her mail on the doorstep.

An invitation to a wedding! In Montréal!

If it were a mourning card it would have a black border; her envelope is white, it can only be a wedding invitation ... It's too late in the school year to be a First Communion.

Only one of her nieces is old enough to get married ...

In her nervous state she tears open the envelope and drops it onto the balcony.

Just as she thought. Rhéauna is going to be married. Little Rhéauna, so delicate, who'd spent a night here years ago and for whom they'd given a wonderful birthday party, is now a woman. Bebette wonders what she looks like now. Surely she's a beautiful woman, she was such a pretty child. All the same, she hopes that the girl doesn't have her mother's character.

She goes into the vestibule, shuts the door. Her cup of tea and her morning paper are waiting in the kitchen.

Ever since the death of her brother, Méo, who'd come from Saskatchewan to live with her after the death of his wife, she has felt all alone in this big house that she ended up hating because it seems so dead, though for such a long time she'd been happy there. Busy, in any case. Her husband is dead, her children have gone to live their lives, her brother too has left her after some years of happy companionship. She volunteers at the cathedral in Saint-Boniface, is bored to tears there because she's never been very religious, and decorating altars is not, in her opinion, the most thrilling activity in the world. She goes to the movies several afternoons a week – she's seen *The Lotus Eater* with John Barrymore three times in the past week, and the actor's grimaces are starting to get on her nerves and he's a lot less appealing than he used to be. The rest of the time she spends at home, down in the dumps. She adores reading but there's a limit to how many hours she can sit in a chair ... She has too much energy to expend. Every ten minutes she looks at the grandfather clock whose tick-tock is driving her crazy. The mornings are endless. The afternoons stretch out. To busy herself she goes to the kitchen, she makes cups of Indian tea and lets them cool without touching them. She phones friends who are bored like her and who annoy her as much as she annoys them.

She has a little money set aside – living alone doesn't cost much and Rosaire's pension is enough for her, she could buy herself a nice dress, a hat, shoes, reserve a seat on the train, close up the house for an undetermined length of time ...

The big city!

She has been dreaming of it for years.

She rereads the invitation.

The great adventure that she and her husband were never to afford ... Cross part of the country by train, treat herself to a good hotel rather than impose on some family member, visit her nieces whom she hasn't seen for years, Maria, of course, but also Tititte and Teena, attend a wedding in a truly big city, maybe allow herself a few glasses of wine or a show in one of the numerous theatres ...

And above all, visit from Mount Royal to the Saint Lawrence River the city she's heard so much about, both good and bad!

She thinks that she's still entitled to a discount on train tickets as the widow of a CPR employee, maybe even in first class! She'll have to check.

A woman travelling alone, though, isn't that a little suspicious? Who, or what, would they think she is? All the same, she wouldn't want to come as a woman of disrepute …

She smiles. Pretentious! At your age!

Why not? A former woman of disrepute travelling for her own pleasure.

She has always gone unnoticed. Except for her resounding *saperlipopette!*, of course, that has made her famous in the neighbourhood. All her life she has presented an image of honesty and discretion – though discretion, with that voice of hers! – it could be fun to feel the enquiring glances of men wondering who that beautiful woman might be travelling in first class by herself …

She produces a second *saperlipopette!*

After all, she might not have to travel by herself!

She runs to the kitchen, rummages in the scattered papers in the first drawer under the counter, finds the notebook where she has jotted the telephone numbers of her acquaintances, few in number, who have a telephone.

She picks it up, shakes the hook, shouting in English:

"Miss! Miss! I would like to call Regina in Saskatchewan, please!"

# MONTRÉAL

## *Théo*

At half past eleven every morning after school Théo takes a fairly long detour to arrive at the Biscuiterie Ontario. Hidden from Madame Guillemette, his sister Béa gives him a small paper bag where she has put a handful of cookie crumbs. Most of the time they are real broken cookies that she's found at the bottom of boxes when she was cleaning up; it also happens that she'll sometimes break a few cookies herself if the harvest has been disappointing. Théo calls it his surprise bag. Béa makes him promise not to touch it before he's eaten lunch, though she knows full well that his hand will be in the bag as soon as he's out the door.

Rhéauna, who is fixing lunch before she leaves for work, often wonders why Théo eats so little at noon. He plays with his food, pushes it around with his fork, gets up from the table before dessert.

Théo, no fool, wipes his mouth on the sleeve of his shirt or his coat before stepping into the house, and to date he has never been caught.

That morning, though, Béa thinks he looks sad. He took the surprise bag without showing his usual enthusiasm, has not asked her what's in it, and is getting ready to leave the bakery without thanking her.

"What's the matter, Théo? You look glum."

"I don't look glum."

"Oh yes, you do! You look like Moman when she wakes up in a bad mood."

"That's a lie and you know it."

"Théo, quit sulking, you look like you're going to cry! Did something happen to you at school?"

He plunks his bag of cookies on the counter next to the cash register.

"Hide that in your school bag in case Madame Guillemette shows up. D'you want me to lose my job?"

He does as she asks, making a face.

"Did somebody upset you? Tell me! You mustn't keep those things inside."

He runs the tips of his thumb and index finger along the metal edge of the display case without answering. Something that he can't put into words is bothering him.

"You know, Théo, you can tell me anything."

"Yeah, and then you'll go and repeat it."

"No, I won't. What is it? If you don't tell me now you'll be late and Nana will worry."

He looks up when he hears the name of their beloved older sister and his eyes fill with tears.

"Is it true that Nana's going away? When she gets married?"

Béa is caught up short. Of course Rhéauna will leave the house after she's married; it's normal. She doesn't understand what Théo is getting at.

"Sure, it's true. She'll have her own house, with Gabriel. They'll be living together, Théo, they'll be married!"

"We'll never see her anymore?"

"Of course we will. She'll come and see us ... As often as she can, I imagine."

"But we won't see her every day."

"No, for sure we won't see her every day."

Théo backs up a few steps, hugging his school bag against his chest.

"I don't want her getting married, then!"

Suddenly Béa gets it.

It's Rhéauna who looks after him, she's the one who is bringing him up, sometimes Théo even makes a mistake and calls her *Moman*. She's the one who makes him do his homework, recite his lessons, take his bath every week and makes him wash his face every night before he goes to bed. She reads him a story before he falls asleep even if he's too old, and gets up in the middle of the night when he has a bad dream. Without a doubt she is the most important person in his life and he's going to lose her. He will be staying with a mother who goes off to work when he needs her and two sisters who don't know how to do anything around the house.

She hadn't thought about that: Who will wake them up in the morning, starting now? Who'll make their breakfast? Who'll yell at them so they won't be late? Who will make Théo's meals at noon and in the evening?

"What're we going to do, Béa, when she isn't there?"

She comes out from behind the counter, kneels in front of her brother, hugs him tight.

"We'll sort it out, Théo ... We'll talk about it with Moman and Alice ... We'll figure it out. Come on now, don't worry like that!"

He wets the top of her dress; she lets him.

A vise has just tightened around her heart, she feels slightly dizzy, and for the first time in her life, she feels the icy hand of anguish.

*Bebette, Régina-Cœli*

"I just went to get my mail off the balcony. There's nothing for me!"

"That's because Saskatchewan's farther away than Manitoba. It'll come tomorrow, you'll see."

"Or maybe they didn't invite me."

"Come on, why wouldn't they ask you?"

"Or maybe they were just being polite?"

"What d'you mean?"

"They sure don't think that at your age you'd hop on a train to go to a wedding on the other side of the world! Maybe it was just to let you know that Rhéauna's getting married ... Maybe the last thing they want is to see you there. Or me either."

"It wasn't a letter, Régina, it was an invitation! An invitation! On white cardboard with gold letters, a wreath of flowers, and two turtledoves kissing with a ribbon in their beaks! You're just saying that 'cause you're jealous."

"Why should I be jealous?"

"'Cause you didn't get an invitation, what'd you think!"

"Maybe they knew you'd call me so they didn't bother sending me one ... It was simpler for them to send you one invitation for the both of us!"

"Régina! Enough maybes! We've been talking for two minutes and you've said it twenty-five times!"

"Are you sure it's a real invitation?"

"Sure I'm sure! And I want to tell them that I'll be there! Wouldn't you like to go on a trip to Morial? I could wait for your train at the station in Winnipeg and we'd go the rest of the way together. We'd have two whole days for a good chat, it'd be fun, we never see each other ..."

"If you think that'll make me want to go ... No, right here is fine for me ..."

"I'm sure you're as bored in Regina as I am in Saint-Boniface."

"I don't like moving, Bebette, you know that. I never have. It was hard enough to go to Saint-Boniface when your Rosaire died and then Méo left."

"I can't imagine you not coming! Your brother-in-law and your own brother! Even you couldn't be that hard-hearted!"

"Don't change the subject ... If I get an invitation, I'll see ... Meanwhile ..."

"I knew it, you're jealous!"

"I just don't want to go if I'm not invited. Can you see the look on them if we show up when they didn't expect us? What'll they say? Where'll they put us? What'll they do with us? Maybe we'll be in their way more than anything."

"Régina! We aren't children, we can take care of ourselves. They're inviting us! They're at the other end of the world, they could just not tell us Rhéauna's getting married, we wouldn't know, that's all! They don't *have* to tell us. But if they bother to invite us it's because they want us, don't they?"

"Not me, they don't. I didn't get anything."

"All right, okay, drop it. We're going in circles. If it goes on like this we'll be repeating the same thing till you get your mail tomorrow morning. If you get an invitation tomorrow, you'll call me back?"

"If I don't you'll never know if I got one or not."

"Quit talking nonsense ... I'll call you, same time tomorrow."

"Who says that I'll tell you the truth? That I'll say any old thing to get rid of you?"

"Don't make me waste my money, Régina-Cœli Desrosiers! It's expensive, a long-distance call, you know that as well as me."

"Don't throw your money out the window! And quit picking on me! If I don't want to go to Morial it's my business!"

Régina hangs up.

She is holding her invitation. Bebette described it well. The turtledoves are there, the ribbons, the wreaths, the gold letters. And the little handwritten note at the bottom, most likely by Rhéauna: "Do you think you could play a little piece on the piano? You play so well. It would make me so happy."

She'd looked at it for a long time before opening it. She'd guessed right away what it was.

An invitation to go to Morial when she's been unable to leave her own house for weeks, how ironic! Still happy that she has a telephone and can order in the small amount of food that she manages to consume ...

It had started out weirdly. For years, from April to September, at the end of every afternoon she would play a few piano pieces for her neighbours. She would open the windows and the front door, sit at the piano, take out a music book, and for half an hour play her favourite pieces. The spectators would gather on the sidewalk and listen religiously. These past few years some have brought chairs that they set on the lawn of her minuscule garden. As none of them can afford a concert ticket, they take advantage of it. It costs nothing and it's so beautiful! When she has finished they applaud. The applause is discreet, brief, and sincere. Sometimes Régina-Cœli Desrosiers goes out on her balcony, makes a little bow, blushing, or waves her hand. The garden and the sidewalk are vacated, the small crowd disperses, Régina closes the door, happy to have played. For herself and for them.

But the first time she gave what she calls her *late afternoon concert*, some weeks earlier – it was a wonderful April day, so warm that it seemed like late May – she realized as she was about to go out and make her bow she was incapable of crossing her own doorstep. She'd got up from the piano, headed for the balcony as usual, and froze. She couldn't take a single step. Everything outside, the people smiling, applauding, the cars passing – suddenly seemed hostile. She was convinced that she would put herself in danger if she went out onto the balcony. That something terrible would happen. Assuming it was a fleeting uneasiness, she thought: "Go out, go out, they just want to thank you, it would be crazy if they hold something against you, they didn't before, why would they today? Her two feet, too heavy, stayed nailed to the floor and, panicked, she had abruptly shut the door. Without saying goodbye, without her little wave, modelled – she'd seen it at the movies – on that of Queen Mary of England.

She told herself that she would wave the next day, apologize to them for being rude, for closing the door in their faces, then ate her supper without thinking about it anymore. A tiny bit of concern was gnawing at her, though, a malaise that she couldn't explain and that was making her heart beat a little faster. There must be a reason for what had just happened, these things don't occur overnight, they're planned, maybe long before. And what if it were the beginning of a serious illness?

And genuine panic, the kind that makes you go weak in the knees, that gives you the sense that you're slipping, sinking, that produces an unpleasant sense of lightness in your stomach and makes you clutch just about anything to keep from falling, had flung itself at her when she opened the door after supper to go out and rock on the balcony and found herself in the same situation as a few hours earlier. Feet of lead. The hostility of everything that was outside her house. The conviction that some danger was lying in wait. The uncontrollable fear of seeing someone or something open the garden gate, run up the two or three steps to the veranda, and violently lunge at her … That was it! A little girl's nightmare! A monster in the closet! An uncontrollable, total, childhood terror! She tried to lift one foot to take a step. Nothing. The whole world was mad at her. For some reason she didn't know. And if she took one step forward, if she crossed the threshold of her house, she would pay dearly. Like when she was a child and the worst monsters in the universe hid in the closet or under the bed.

It has gone on for weeks. She has no problem walking around in the house, going about her everyday affairs, she plays the piano, fixes meals, takes long hot baths, and manages sometimes to concentrate on reading a novel, but as soon as she glances in the direction of the front door...

Up till now she has refused to ask for help. She hasn't called her doctor because she is afraid she'll be told she's crazy – which is most likely true – and end up in an asylum with some dangerous lunatics – another ridiculous fear of a little girl with too much imagination.

Her food is delivered to her door, she no longer speaks to anyone, she shuts herself more and more into a kind of padded cocoon, which consists of spending hours motionless in her rocking chair, mind blank and a false tranquility in her heart.

The arrival of the invitation to Rhéauna's wedding has done nothing, then, to reassure her. Nor has the phone call from her sister. How, in fact, can you plan such a journey when you can't even leave your own house? She could have confided in Bebette, cried out for help, asked her to come and pick her up, force her out of this slump she's sinking into deeper and deeper. She couldn't do it. Pride?

No. Something else.

A ton of bricks lands all at once on her shoulders. She gets out of her chair, pours a glass of water, gulps it down. Then bends double over the sink and starts to vomit her breakfast.

She has just realized that contrary to what she had been thinking until then, she's just fine the way she is.

With the certainty that she is safe from everything. And everyone.

# Gabriel, Josaphat

Elbows on the oilcloth, heads bowed, the two men have been bent over their cups of cold coffee for a while now. The visit to the apartment finished – barely two minutes, it's so small – Josaphat offered Gabriel a coffee. He accepted. They drank it in the kitchen because they'd have been cramped in the living room jammed to the ceiling with useless things gleaned here and there, an impressive collection of everything that the inhabitants of a big city used to getting tired of objects threw away before they have taken full advantage of them and replaced with others that they'll soon lose interest in. So thinks Josaphat during his forays into the lanes in his neighbourhood on those mornings when he doesn't feel like playing his fiddle in the department stores, which he devotes to exploring the backs of houses and sheds that are easy to open.

Showing Gabriel what was piled up in the room – furniture, stacks of newspapers, kitchen utensils, armloads of clothes, both women's and men's, in every size and every colour – Josaphat assumed a pitiful expression.

"Don't go thinking I've turned into a ragman, Gabriel. It's just that I can't understand people throwing things away before they're finished! There's stuff in there that's still in good shape, stuff I might need some day."

"If you can find your way around in all this muddle! Let's say that one of these days you need something, mon oncle, and you know that you've got it, will you be brave enough to root around in here? Right to the bottom, underneath everything by the window, or behind the sofa? Do you remember where you've thrown all these things you've picked up? I'm sure you don't."

"Maybe not. But I know I've got them."

Gabriel had surrendered before a logic that was incomprehensible to him. And he's beginning to regret his uncle's invitation.

It's the first time Josaphat has invited him to his place. Their usual meeting place is the Taverne Normand, at the corner of Fabre and Mont-Royal, not far from L.N. Messier. With his little concert finished – usually on Saturday afternoon, Gabriel's day off – Josaphat goes into the Taverne Normand, says hello to Gabriel if he's there, and joins him at his table. They don't talk any more than they've done this morning but it's a public place, the sound of conversations is sometimes deafening, and they use that as an excuse to drink in silence.

Gabriel thinks to himself that something has to happen, that he ought to try to start a conversation.

"How long've you lived here?"

What a stupid question!

"A couple years ... But it's damp in winter. You see, my boy, there's nothing below my apartment, it's the passage that leads to the back of the house. There used to be a stable with horses and all that till quite recently ... Still smells when it's damp. Plus my floor's not well insulated, you can't heat the apartment, so all winter I freeze."

"How come you stay?"

"It's cheap."

Gabriel fiddles with the handle of his mug before he comes out with the question he's dying to ask. And that question isn't stupid.

"D'you earn your living with your violin, mon oncle?"

Josaphat leans back in his chair, sips, makes a face because the coffee is cold.

"I earn it. Some parts of the year are better than others. Winter's tough. Except around Christmas, of course. Then all of a sudden everybody wants to hear a fiddle ... But I'm lucky I found my little job year-round at Messier ... At least I don't spend my days outside.

There's other places too where I play ... Weddings, family parties."

"Why don't you go to the department stores in the west of the city? Maybe they'd pay better."

"The Anglos aren't interested in fiddles. They like bagpipes better."

"Why d'you say that? Did you ever go and look?"

"No. That's true. You're right. I guess I'm lazy."

"I didn't say you were lazy!"

Josaphat doesn't answer right away.

"I know it. Let's just call it a good old prejudice. They've got prejudices about us, why shouldn't we have some too? But see, in those big stores west of here, I'd feel like I was begging. Another poor French Canadian holding out his hand to the rich Anglos. On Mont-Royal, I feel like I'm playing for my people. They don't give me money out of pity, they give it because they think what I play is beautiful."

"Anglos might find it beautiful too."

"Maybe that's why I don't want to play for them, Gabriel ... I just told you, I wanna play for my people ..."

Without trying any harder, Gabriel gets up, takes the cups to the sink.

"D'you ever miss the countryside?"

Josaphat closes his eyes. Gabriel, whose back is turned, doesn't notice.

"Yes. Every day."

Gabriel comes back, holding the coffee pot.

"I think it's still hot."

"No thanks, I've had enough for this morning."

"Why don't you go back there? To the countryside?"

His eyes mist over, then Josaphat turns his head towards the window. Gabriel realizes that if his uncle could escape through the open window and fly away to Duhamel, he'd do it.

"Because there's things that keep me here."

Gabriel leans over the table in the hope that his uncle will go on speaking, but the confession stops there. His confidences won't go any further.

To hide his embarrassment, the young man adds a little milk to his coffee, a lot of sugar, stirs it all up, clinking his spoon against the china.

"Have you made any friends at least? I mean here, in the city?"

Josaphat replies without looking back into the room.

"Yes ... There's some women next door ..."

Gabriel startles, smiles, stretches his arm across the table to pat his uncle's hand.

"You old rascal! Women! So that's what's keeping you in the city! How about that! Now that's a good one."

Josaphat seems to come back to earth all at once. He shrugs, blushing.

"Not that kind of woman, that's not what I'm talking about ... They're neighbours ... Folks I used to know in Duhamel, then I met up with them here ... They live right next door."

"Did I know them too when I was little? I'd like to meet them, see if I recognize them ..."

"No. You can't see them."

"What do you mean I can't see them?"

Josaphat gets up, as if he wants to avoid the subject or feels that he's said too much, and heads for the apartment door.

"Sorry, Gabriel, the crapper's outside, at the back of the yard, and I gotta go ..."

"But what does it mean that I can't see those women?"

Josaphat opens the door, takes a look in the corridor.

"It just means they aren't there. Today. They've gone away. Maybe to Duhamel, they didn't tell me."

"If I come back will you introduce me to them?"

Josaphat turns towards his nephew before going out.

"There's plenty of things you don't know about me, Gabriel. Plenty of things. And it's best if you don't try and work them out. It'd make us even unhappier, all of us ... Don't lock the door when you leave ... And come back whenever you want, now you know where to find me. I'd be glad if you'd come and visit now and then ... And about your wedding, I'll have to talk to your mother about it before I give you my answer."

# Maria

At the corner of Dorchester and Montcalm, Maria spots three of her children sitting on the balcony of their apartment. Rhéauna has Théo on her lap and seems to be telling him a story. The little boy is drinking in her words and looking at her as if she were the incarnation of what she's describing: it's not her that he sees, it's the crusader imprisoned by the Saracen in the Holy Land, or Snow White's wicked stepmother, or the Queen of Hearts giving a tongue-lashing to Alice. "Off with her head!" He laughs because she has made a sound with her voice that he thinks is funny.

Maria's Alice – whose head she would often like to cut off – is sitting on the top step of the staircase, smoking a cigarette as she too listens to the story. Like her brother, she smiles when Rhéauna puts on a comical voice. It must bring back memories. Of Saskatchewan, as much as here.

Maria understands right away what Alice is doing in this charming tableau: she has lost her job. She'll have shown them one of the numerous bitchy sides of her nature and they'll have sacked her. Probably not for the last time; Alice has serious problems with authority.

That's all she needs. Not only does she have no money for Rhéauna's wedding but on top of it, one of her children has just lost her job.

But she mustn't show her despair. She must at all costs avoid worrying Rhéauna, who knows nothing about the loan that she tried to obtain: she'll find a way to unearth that money somewhere, she already has a pretty good idea – a final sacrifice she'll make for her big girl whom she adores in her way – she knows she just has to make a single phone call and the person at the other end will accept right away, no questions asked. One more humiliation in a day that's already been well supplied with them. When all's said and done, Victoire, Gabriel's mother, will have been right.

She pushes open the little wrought-iron fence that surrounds the poorly kept up little garden. Alice mashes her cigarette with her shoe.

"Don't scream and yell at me, Moman, it wasn't my fault!"

"I'm not screaming."

"No, but you were going to, I know it ..."

"No, I wasn't ... If you're here it's because they already yelled at you at the factory ... And once a day is enough ..."

"Twice ... Don't forget you yelled when I left this morning."

"That's true. One more reason not to start doing it again. We can explain ourselves without yelling and screaming like banshees. We'll try anyway ... Did you eat your banana at least?"

"Yes. It was really good. Thanks."

"I don't like it when you put on that little expression, Alice. If you want to make fun of me, wait at least till I'm not here. Don't do it to my face."

"What do you want me to tell you? It was a banana. It tasted like a banana."

Rhéauna has sat Théo on the floor. He resists because the story isn't finished.

"It's nearly time for you to go back to school, Théo."

Maria takes her daughter's place in the rocking chair.

"Did he eat something at least?"

"No more than usual."

"I'll never understand it. He eats like a little pig in the morning, so you tell me anyway, he devours everything on his plate in the evening, even the most boring vegetables, so why doesn't he eat a thing at noon?"

Alice gets up, brushes the cigarette ashes off her skirt.

"Don't you know?"

The other two women look at her, surprised.

"And you do?"

Théo gives her a pleading look; with a frown, Alice makes him understand that she won't tell on him and pushes open the front door. He is wondering what it will cost him, what she's going to ask him in return or impose on him. "Hardly. I just thought you knew. And I wish you'd told me. I'm sorry..."

To Théo's great relief she disappears into the bedroom she shares with Béa.

Rhéauna is already in the kitchen.

"Do you want me to make you a little something? A sandwich? We've still got some of Madame Desbaillets's cretons. They're real good."

"No, just make me some strong tea."

"You have to eat something."

"If you've got some soda biscuits, with a little butter..."

"Moman... You need something more serious than that. We've got a big afternoon ahead of us..."

Dupuis Frères. The wedding gown. Maria had nearly forgotten.

"You're right. Make me whatever you want. No cretons though. They've been giving me trouble for a while now. Madame Desbaillets uses too much fat, I've told her a hundred times."

While they are eating – Théo, whose mother has insisted he go back to his place at the table instead of leaving for school, clears his plate to avoid being scolded even if the food disgusts him – Maria regards her three children. She would like to get up from the table, go to each one in turn, gather them into her arms, embrace them. To reassure them. Rhéauna, because she is about to throw herself headlong into a new life about which, an intelligent woman, she already senses the difficulties; Alice, because on account of her damn personality, she is doomed to go from job to job until she meets a boy who's enough of an idiot to ask her to marry him and will suffer the consequences; and Théo... Théo, the frailest of her four children, who always needs reassurance. As he has since birth. And she senses, from the way he has looked at Rhéauna ever since he has known that she is about to leave the house, that the prospect of losing his second mother, the one who has actually looked after him the most during these past years, terrifies him. She could tell them it will be fine, everything will turn out well, that Rhéauna will be happy with her Gabriel, that Alice will find an interesting job with a good salary, that she herself will devote more time to Théo in the future, become an exemplary mother. But she's never been motherly with them, never cuddled them, never acted – this is the first time – on those impulses that encourage mothers to throw themselves on their children, caress them, kiss them, bite their cheeks, while vowing eternal love. The effort that would take – get up, bend over each of them, place her lips on a neck or the top of a head, say something sweet or comforting – is that beyond her reach? Is she really incapable of doing that?

She is on the point of doing it, she has just set her hands on either side of her plate, she is about to give herself a push to stand up when a thought goes through her mind and nails her to her chair.

It's not the children who need reassurance. It's her.

She has no money to pay for her daughter's wedding. In a few hours she and Rhéauna will be in a fitting room in front of some very expensive gowns. The invitations have gone out, the replies will come in soon. She is going to lose her eldest daughter who took her place with her brother and her sisters so long ago now. How will she manage? How will she get out of it?

Help me, somebody. I need someone to hold out a hand. To reassure me. Reassure me.

She should do it right now, make that phone call, even if she doesn't feel brave enough. That, at least, would reassure her. An exorbitant price to pay for a moment of peace of mind.

She sits there over her cup of strong tea and her ham sandwich. Rhéauna looks at her, frowning.

Théo gets out of his chair and runs to the bathroom to vomit.

Alice laughs idiotically.

## Tititte, Teena

"Why bother coming to a restaurant if you just order a ham sandwich! Honestly!"

"I like ham sandwiches, Teena!"

"Sure, but you can make one at home. When I go out to eat I want a Swiss steak or a chicken à la king, not something we can make at home whenever we want…"

"I don't know why but I don't trust them here. It wouldn't say it looks dirty but I wouldn't say it looks clean either… I told myself I won't have anything fancy, just a ham sandwich, you can't mess that up."

"Me, my *tourtière du Lac-Saint-Jean* is terrific."

"It's so greasy your lips are all shiny." Teena wipes her mouth with her table napkin, leaving lipstick on it along with the juice from the meat.

Despite her sister's reaction, she liked this restaurant as soon as they arrived. It smelled good, the waitresses seemed pleasant, they don't bow and scrape like they do in the chic restaurants she hates so much because she feels out of place there. True, the food is fairly greasy, but it's delicious, and most of all Teena doesn't feel as if someone has an eye on every move she makes. She's not being judged. If she makes a gaffe, no one is going to put their hand over their mouth to hide a contemptuous smile. After all, she isn't here for people to watch her eat, she's here to stuff her face.

She fans herself with her hand.

"You're right, though, it is kind of heavy for noon ..."

"It's kind of heavy for any time if you want my opinion ... Seems to me you could've picked something lighter ... There was a nice sole meunière ..."

"You know as well as I do I hate fish! I don't go to a restaurant to punish myself, I go to a restaurant to give myself a treat."

"After this you'll complain about indigestion ..."

"Even your ham sandwich would give me indigestion so I might as well spoil myself ..."

She takes one last forkful of tourtière, chews slowly with her eyes closed.

"This is really good. They're lucky up in Lac-Saint-Jean, they can eat this every day ..."

Tititte puts her hand over her heart.

"Stop that! Just thinking you could eat that every day gives me palpitations!"

The waitress comes to pick up their plates, asks if they want dessert. From the look her sister gives her, Teena understands that she'd best decline and contents herself with ordering a cup of tea. Looking at the menu earlier, she'd noticed that the dessert of the day was a cream puff topped with whipped cream.

The restaurant Comme au Lac is across from Dupuis Frères department store. Through the restaurant window, Teena watches the crowd parading down rue Sainte-Catherine and wonders where they all come from, especially the men who are constantly going in and out of the department store. Don't they work? Don't they have anything else to do?

She shrugs and starts tapping the tabletop with her fingernails.

"Stop that, Teena, you know it gets on my nerves!"

Teena joins her hands as if in prayer.

"Hey! You're a heck of a grump today. Everything gets on your nerves!"

Tititte wipes her lips, then pulls her veil over her face. Teena heaves a sigh.

"You're the only woman who still wears a veil in the middle of the afternoon! Anyhow, nobody ever wears one anymore … And don't tell me that the veil's another of the grande dame's final touches, I'll slap your face!"

Tititte takes a pair of gloves from her purse. Black leather, very soft, with seams so fine you can hardly see them.

"We can't look like a bunch of penniless beggars this afternoon! What we have to do is important!"

"If we look too chic they'll raise the price of the gown!"

Very cautiously, Tititte pulls on each finger of her gloves, as if they were extremely delicate individual girdles.

"There's times you make me feel discouraged, Teena."

"And you discourage me all the time!"

Tititte pays. With a two-dollar bill that she holds aloft like a weapon.

They still have fifteen minutes to kill before their appointment. Teena takes Tititte's arm as they are leaving Comme au Lac.

"I hope you aren't ashamed of me even if I haven't got gloves and a veil?"

"If I were ashamed I wouldn't show myself in public with you."

"D'you think people realize we're sisters?"

"I sure hope not!"

"You don't think we look alike?"

"No, I don't think we look alike! Maybe they think you're my maid!"

"Don't be silly!"

They smile. After forty years of teasing, each of them still finds the other one funny.

"You'd've liked to have a maid, wouldn't you?"

"What I really would've liked was a sister that followed my advice better."

"If I followed your advice better I'd wear a hat with a veil, over-heated gloves, and dinner would've been a tomato sandwich. Thanks but no thanks!"

They look in some store windows, make unflattering remarks about what's on display, complain about the price of everything.

Tititte squeezes her sister's arm lightly.

"I wanted to talk to you about something."

"Okay, here we go again ... I had the impression I'd end up paying for my free meal ..."

"No, no, don't worry, it's got nothing to do with you."

"That's a relief. For once."

"I wanted to ask you something."

"Go ahead. As long as it doesn't involve a hat with a little veil and kid gloves ..."

Tititte hesitates briefly before she speaks.

"Don't you think he's a bit of a drip?"

"What *he*?"

"You know ... The fiancé."

"Gabriel? You think he's a drip?"

"Don't you?"

"Nope. Not at all."

"I don't know if *drip* is the right word ... You know, for Nana, I'd've imagined somebody more ... I don't know. Somebody that had more going for him. I've got nothing against him, he seems like a nice guy and all that, but ... Seems to me that Nana deserves more. He's deaf in one ear and he barely earns a living."

"Who says he barely earns a living?"

"Have you seen what he looks like? He sure as heck doesn't look like somebody who's a big money-maker!"

"I make a good living but you're always criticizing how I look."

"As far as that's concerned ... Maybe his taste is as bad as yours ... But ... I think he hasn't got much personality, he hardly says a word when we run into him."

"If he's half-deaf ..."

"Exactly. If he's half-deaf what kind of life will it be for her, will you tell me that?"

"The main thing is, they get along together and they love each other, right? And it's none of our business! So mind your own business, Tititte Desrosiers!"

"I want her to be happy."

"We all want her to be happy, Tititte! She must know what she's doing, she's bright! If she waits around for your ideas about Prince Charming she'll be an old maid at our age. Like us ... She might just as well marry a good guy who'll take care of her than wait too long and end up like all old maids, wearing St. Catherine's hat five years from now."

Tititte stops in the middle of the sidewalk and looks at her sister as if she's never laid eyes on her till now.

' "I didn't think I'd ever say this, Teena, but know what? For once you're right! I'm getting involved in something that's none of my business. It's her life, after all, she must know what she's doing ..."

Teena straightens her bust – which is imposing and even impressive.

"If you listened to me more often you'd realize I'm not that silly."

Tititte shrugs as she turns around because it's nearly time for their appointment.

"Now just because I pay you a compliment it doesn't mean I'll agree with everything you say, Ernestine Desrosiers! If I listened to you more often I certainly wouldn't be where I am now!"

She takes the initiative, holding down her hat because a wind, an early warning of rain, has just come up.

"Don't tell me it's going to rain! I put on my patent-leather boots. If they get wet they've had it!"

When they arrive at the first Dupuis Frères window, she stops and grabs Teena by the arm again.

"I don't care, I still think he's a drip."

Seeing that her sister is not replying, she glances in her direction and realizes that Teena, red as a beet, has just inserted her forefinger between the collar of her blouse and her skin.

"Good grief, Teena, don't tell me you're having a hot flash in the middle of rue Sainte-Catherine!"

Her sister gives her a murderous look.

"D'you think we choose when these things happen, or where? Wait till it's your turn, kiddo."

A few months earlier, the doctor had told Teena that she was a little young for menopause, but that it wasn't all that rare. She had to sit tight, accept every episode without getting upset, that it was neither serious nor dangerous, that all women go through it, it was natural, it was their destiny. She had felt like telling him that women had a few too many destinies for her liking, that men didn't know how lucky they are, that nature didn't remind them every month with unbearable pain, and they were never overwhelmed in the prime of life by those goddamn hot flashes that make them want to break everything, then throw themselves into an ice-water bath to keep from suffocating. She had restrained herself. After all, it wasn't his fault, poor man, he was only the messenger responsible for delivering the bad news.

She is panting, sweating, her body is blazing hot, if she didn't hold back she'd tear off her clothes and run stark naked along rue Sainte-Catherine to cool off. But she knows it would be pointless, that nothing can soothe her, that she has to wait for it to pass.

Tititte dares not approach her, she knows that Teena can't tolerate any physical contact during these attacks.

"Good grief, Teena, you look like you're going to explode!"

Teena undoes the collar of her blouse.

"I'm going to explode too! Some fine day it really will happen, it makes no sense to feel like this."

"Shall I grab a taxi? You can't pick out a wedding gown in that state!"

"Are you out of your mind? D'you think I'd miss that? No, don't worry, it'll pass ... Good thing it didn't hit me in the middle of the fitting! I don't even know if Nana realizes she'll go through it one day too. Maybe her mother hasn't warned her yet, poor child. My Lord I'm hot!"

"Do you want me to get you a glass of water?"

"I don't need a glass of water, I need a fifty-pound block of ice! I'd sit on it and wait for it to melt. Go on ahead, go up to the fifth floor, tell Maria and Nana that I'm running late but I'll get there ... Meanwhile I'll go to the ladies' room and freshen up."

"I'll go with you ... I can't just leave you like that ..."

"You can't do anything to help me, you'd just get in the way. Let me have my attack alone, I'm used to it… Goddamn hot flashes! Goddamn hot flashes! C'mon, go or you'll end up late!"

Tititte starts, pushes her sister to the window.

"Hurry up, Teena, hide, there they are! Go to the door on Berri, I'll go and join them, they're right in front of the entrance on Saint-André. Here, take my bottle of Lait Des Dames Romaines, it'll cool you off."

"It smells too strong, it makes me sick…"

"Hey! It costs practically a buck a bottle!"

"I don't care if it costs practically a buck a bottle, it still smells too strong! I'll splash some cold water on my face."

Tititte waits until she has turned the corner before going back to join Maria and Nana who recognized her by her hat and are now waving at her.

"Isn't Teena with you?"

She kisses their cheeks through her veil.

"She'll be coming soon. She's on her way."

Maria frowns.

"Gosh, you look funny. Is something the matter?"

Tititte gestures in Nana's direction with her head to tell her sister that she'll speak to her later.

"No, no. Everything's fine. She'll be here soon."

They step inside the store just as the rain starts to fall.

## Josaphat

Empty beer bottles are strewn across the table. Josaphat has slept for a few minutes, forehead resting on the oilcloth. He dreamed of greenery, of the scent of pine trees, of a radiant sun mirrored in a lake. Of a small house that looked over a small valley. Of a tremendous happiness followed by a tremendous woe. He moaned, uttered some incoherent words. When he woke up, with his tongue coated and a pain behind his right eye heralding one of those terrible headaches that strike him when he drinks too much, the four women who live next door were standing on the other side of the table. Had they watched him sleep for a long time, had they just arrived? Were they really there?

He didn't speak to them right away. He stood up, opened the door of the icebox. He was out of beer. He came back and sat down after filling a glass with water. That tasted bad.

Florence pulled out a chair, sat down.

"You promised us you'd never drink again during the day, Josaphat."

Josaphat raised his hand in a sign of protest.

"That was before they announced the wedding. It was before I met my future daughter-in-law. It was before I realized I can't take it anymore. All of it. The secrets. The goddamn secrets that have been suffocating me for so long. My two children who call me *mon oncle*. My future grandchildren who'll call me *mon oncle*. The love of my life who is moping around in the basement of a house on the ruelle des Fortifications."

She has placed her hand on his right hand. The one that holds the bow, that interprets the musical line, the one that draws out the notes and makes them spin into space, forming melodious ribbons of indescribable beauty.

"How are you going to be able to play later on?"

"I'm not going to play later on. I don't even know if I'll play tomorrow. Or the day after. I'm fed up. Totally fed up. For a long time now. But goddamn it, I can't take it anymore!"

He downed his glass of water in one gulp. For the first time he dared to lock eyes with Florence.

"I know you aren't there, y'know. That it's just in my head. Always has been. Everything. The moon, the horses. The importance of what I do every month. Every single thing. I'm fed up with that too. It saved my life, it helped me put up with everything since I was a child, true. But now, when I take out my fiddle when the moon is full, when I go out on my balcony, holding the bow, I feel ridiculous. I'm not a child, I can't believe in those things. I'm nearly fifty and I still believe that it's me that makes the full moon come up every month! She's gonna come up without me, that goddamn full moon, for millions of years she's been coming up without me, who do I think I am? The saviour of the world? The new Messiah?"

Rose, Violette, and Mauve, at a discreet signal from their mother, have retired to the living room while he was talking.

Florence got up, took her chair, walked around the table, and sat down next to him. She brings her face close to Josaphat's.

"You're the one that chooses, Josaphat. To believe or not. We can't do anything about it. But we're there. And we'll stay there. In case you change your mind. But let me say it again: It's true that you make the moon come up every month, it's true that you spare the horses from hideous suffering and you prevent the sky from being covered with blood ..."

"But if all that's just in my head, it's not you talking to me, it's me talking to myself! It's me that wants to convince myself that it's all true! Because I'm crazy!"

"But you need it, Josaphat!"

"Exactly! I don't need it anymore!"

"You might think differently tomorrow."

"Then I'll go and get you, that's all. But meanwhile, here and now, I'm fed up with everything! If I had a case of beer I'd drown myself in it! Happily, for that matter! I want to forget, do you understand? I want to forget everything that's happened since Duhamel, go back to when Gabriel was little and we all lived in peace, the three of us, in the backwoods of the Laurentians!"

"You know perfectly well that you can't go back to the past."

"Yes I can! Beer takes me back to where I want to be!"

"Beer knocks you out and gives you headaches."

Josaphat gets up, slaps the tabletop.

"Beer helps me live, goddamn it! It used to be the fiddle, now it's beer!"

He sweeps the table with a broad, furious swipe; empty bottles land on the floor, some of them break. He collapses rather than sits on his chair. He covers his face with his hands, sobbing.

"Sorry. I'm sorry. I don't know which way to turn! Before, I just believed in it, I didn't think about it, you were there and that was enough for me … When I left Duhamel and you stayed there, I was desperate. Then when you found me years later, I thought you would save me from the questions I was starting to ask myself … I'd like that, not to ask myself any more questions! It was so much better when I didn't ask myself any questions!"

He looks at her, looks at her face, her good, kind face, for a truth that he knows he will not find.

"It's hard to accept that you're crazy, you know!"

Florence gets up and for the first time since they've known one another, she goes behind him, hugs him, and plants a kiss on the top of his head.

"You aren't crazy, Josaphat."

"I didn't want some great destiny, you know. I didn't want to be the man that others don't see, who can do things that others can't. Play the fiddle without studying. True, you gave me an amazing gift with the fiddle. I'll be surprised till the end of my days with those sounds that it produces. I'd've been happy with that. But the price you put on it was too high. The responsibility you imposed on me was much too great. When I go out on the balcony now, when I lay my bow on my instrument in the light of the full moon ... It didn't used to happen, never, but now, I wonder every time what would happen if I didn't play. In fact I'm pretty well sure there'd be nothing, it's all in my head. And more and more I feel like doing nothing at all, not playing, just to see ... Then the beer helps me forget all that."

"It's not true that nothing would happen, Josaphat, and you know it."

"So you say. Anyway, I think it's you that says so, I'm not even sure about that either. But I don't believe you anymore. I'm too tired. Too fed up. Everything's going too badly."

He extricates himself from her embrace, gets up, walks away from her.

"Take your girls to knit inside your house, you aren't welcome here anymore."

He closes his eyes.

Florence takes a few steps back.

"If you change your mind ..."

"Yeah, yeah, I know."

After a few seconds, he hears the rustling of a skirt, some words spoken in an undertone in the living room. As soon as the apartment door is shut, he opens his eyes.

"I loved you all so much. So much."

## Alice, Béa

She walked all over the cookie factory, sticking her nose into most of the boxes, each one giving off aromas more exciting than the rest. She opened the lid, leaned over, took a big sniff. Let out excited little cries over the maple-leaf cookies and the fig squares, her favourites, but finally chose a large royal cake, all sticky because it was hot inside and the cookies were starting to suffer.

"It must be terrible in the middle of the summer, they must all melt! D'you sell cookie soup in the summer, Madame Guillemette?"

She thinks she's made a joke, laughs. Then turns serious again as she looks at the royal cake that is already staining her fingers.

"That would be good with a glass of milk."

Béa takes a worried look out the window.

"This isn't a restaurant, we don't eat cookies here, we sell them! Even if I had any milk I wouldn't give it to you. Anyway, who gave you permission to take one? If Madame Guillemette shows up... D'you want me to lose my job? Just because you haven't got one at least you can respect other people that do!"

Alice sets the pastry on the counter, takes a hanky out of her little purse, wipes her hands, then uses it to pick up the cake and plunks the whole thing in her mouth.

"Gi... me o... fo''éo..."

Her sister sighs, exasperated.

"How many times has Nana told you to swallow what's in your mouth before you speak? I didn't understand a word!"

Alice chews faster, swallows, chokes a bit, clears her throat.

"That's who I wanted to talk about... And Moman. During dinner at noon they just about guessed that you give Théo cookies practically every morning. He'd gobbled them all and he wasn't hungry. Moman made him eat anyway and he got sick."

"The little brat! He always told me he waited till after dinner to eat those damn cookie pieces!"

"And you believed him! How naive can you get? As if a nine-year-old could resist cookies!"

"First of all, they aren't cookies. Not all the time anyway... They're pieces of broken cookies."

"They're still cookies, pea brain! And they still cut his appetite!"

"First of all, how do you happen to know that? I didn't say a word to anybody!"

"Actually, he told me. A boy of nine can no more keep a secret than he can resist cookies. You're lucky he didn't let it out in front of Moman or Nana."

"Wait till I see him tonight..."

Alice is bending over another rack of cookies.

"Hands off, Alice!"

"I'm not touching, I'm looking..."

"I know you. First thing I know you'll have your fat, dirty hand in the cookie tin."

"My hands aren't fat and they aren't dirty either, Béa Rathier!"

"Maybe they aren't fat, but did you wash them when you left the shop? And after dinner?"

Alice wipes her hands with her handkerchief a second time. Béa shrugs.

"I knew it, you still smell of tobacco!"

"Enjoy it, this is the last time!"

She brings her hands to her sister's nose, laughing. Béa pushes them away.

"I washed them before dinner; I've got manners!"

Béa heads for the factory door, opens it.

"You got what you wanted, you managed to steal a cookie from me, now take your dirty tricks somewhere else!"

"Béa. I'm not nine years old like our brother, you can't boss me around like that. And I came to see you because I thought about something ..."

"I hope you won't be surprised if I tell you that has me worried."

Alice goes behind the counter, puts her hands on the metal cash register.

"D'you think your boss could use another salesgirl?"

Béa jumps as if she's just been stung by a wasp.

"Are you out of your mind? You wouldn't want to work here."

"Why not? It'd be fun. We'd be together all day."

"We'd kill each other by the first weekend! And that personality of yours would send the customers running!"

"I can be nice when I want."

"But that's not often. Anyway it's pointless to talk about it, there's never enough people here to keep two girls busy, come on ..."

"But two good lookers like us could attract men ... Hardly anybody comes in here except women with babies or little old ladies. Anyway, men've got more money to spend."

"Who do you think you are anyway? Men won't break the doors down to buy our cookies because you work here! You aren't ugly but honestly, that's going too far! Nobody'd take you for Gloria Swanson!"

"Gloria Swanson isn't even pretty. And they say she's a midget! Anyway, it sure as heck isn't Madame Guillemette that attracts men here."

"Madame Guillemette can do whatever she wants with her cookie factory and you aren't about to change that!"

"It wouldn't cost anything to ask."

Béa brought her face close to her sister's.

"And you never thought of asking if I wanted to work with you?"

"Why wouldn't you?"

"First of all, because you're unbearable, and second of all because I don't want to watch you swiping cookies from the boxes the minute Madame Guillemette's back is turned!"

"'Cause you want to keep them for yourself!"

"What d'you mean? You're hen-headed! As if I spend the whole day eating cookies!"

"Greedy guts like you? I wouldn't be surprised at all."

"See? See what I mean? D'you think I want to listen to remarks like that all day long? I'm fine here, Alice, don't come and spoil my pleasure! Leave me my job and go find another one for yourself."

Alice runs her hand through her hair the way she does when she's nervous.

"Okay, okay. Don't get on your high horse. Excuse me for having a good idea."

"It wasn't anything like a good idea!"

"It was an *excellent* idea! But you're scared I'd be a better saleswoman than you, is that it? You're jealous of me before I even start working here ... It's always the same thing ..."

And there it is, the eternal conflict is showing the tip of its nose.

Alice has been accusing Béa of jealousy for years. And she's not totally wrong, Béa has always envied her slimness, her naturally curly hair, the way the boys look at her on the street, and she often uses that to infuriate her sister, and the arguments that her unkind remarks set off are hopeless and endless.

As usual, Béa bursts into tears and Alice regrets what she just said.

"Okay, Béa. Keep your goddamn job! Anyhow it must be deadly dull, selling cookies by the pound."

"First of all I suppose there's nothing dull about shaking tobacco leaves under a burst of steam."

"That's true. You're right. It was dull. And it was hard. I'll look somewhere else. I won't be underfoot. I'll only stop by and swipe a cookie now and then."

At that point, Madame Guillemette arrives, arms full of packages.

"Alice, why are you here at this time of day? Were they out of tobacco to shake? Did everybody decide to stop smoking?"

She sets her purchases on the counter.

"People complain that cookies cost too much. Let me tell you, it isn't just cookies! I was scandalized, *scandalized*, my friends, when I saw the price of vegetables!"

Realizing that Madame Guillemette is going to complain about the price of everything for most of the rest of the afternoon – Béa is always saying that she's a penny-pincher – Alice takes off, relieved actually that she doesn't have to put up with her whining and moaning every day.

Where will she go now? She hates doing nothing and she's anxious at the prospect of the hours she'll have to spend wandering the neighbourhood while she waits for supper.

## Rhéauna, Maria, Teena, Tititte

Teena hasn't dared express an opinion ever since they've arrived at the Salon de la Mariée on the fifth floor of Dupuis Frères. Rhéauna has already tried on three gowns that her aunt thought were hideous and now she's just emerged from the fitting room in a kind of shapeless outfit that, in her opinion, is the furthest thing from a wedding dress. Maria seems to think everything is beautiful from the outset, as if she wants to get rid of a thankless task as fast as possible; even Tititte has words of praise for outfits that obviously she ought to realize are hideous. What's going on? All of a sudden they have no taste? And so she decides to jump in, come what may.

"Seems to me a bride ought to look like a princess ... Don't you think so? I don't see anything in there that resembles a princess ..."

Maria looks daggers at her.

"So what does a princess look like, in your opinion?"

"Nothing like that, that's for sure."

Teena fans herself with a large-size magazine she's taken off the counter without permission. It's too heavy and she has to wave it in both hands to create a little air that doesn't even cool her. A blast of hot flashes strikes her head again and she doesn't want people to see them. She knows that she should've gone home when she came out of the ladies' room, but curiosity won out.

"First of all, a princess wears a floor-length gown. But that one shows her feet. I don't think a bride should show her feet."

"Where'd you get that one?"

"I don't know where I got it, but I think it!"

"You think like a little old lady! This is the twentieth century! Dresses are getting shorter every day!"

"I know dresses are getting shorter! I wear them myself. It's more convenient, 'specially in winter. I understand all that. But seems to me that's no reason for wedding gowns not to fall to the floor! In June there's no snow, no mud either, no danger that she'd get it dirty... Unless it rains... But don't let's think about that..."

Gesturing discreetly, Tititte tells her sister to be quiet, then she turns towards Rhéauna who doesn't seem sure that she likes the dress she has on, though a few minutes earlier she came out of the fitting room with a big smile, saying that she might have found the right one.

"Nana wants to look like a modern bride, Teena, not a leftover from the last century like us. Maria's right, you have to keep up with the times."

Teena shrugs.

"You talk about keeping up with the times when you still wear hats with veils!"

"I'm not a little girl like her, I don't have to follow the fashion!"

Rhéauna turns to the three women.

"Will you quit talking about me as if I wasn't here! If I'd known that you'd give me such a hard time I'd've come by myself. Sure, I want you to make remarks, give me advice, that's what you're here for, but it's me who decides what I'll wear for my wedding, not you! It's me who's going to wear the dress!"

Tititte places a hand she intends to be soothing on Rhéauna's arm. This only makes Rhéauna more upset.

"I want to look lovely, do you understand? If other people aren't happy, tough. I have to feel good, comfortable, and most of all I want Gabriel to think he's dreaming when he sees me! In this dress I think I look beautiful and I know he'll think I'm beautiful too.

That's the main thing. And the veil that comes with it is really long, I can try it on if you want. That at least will fall to the ground if that'll make you happy, ma tante Teena! And quit fanning yourself like that, it gets on my nerves!"

Teena flings the fashion magazine on the counter as if it were burning her hands.

"I wonder what the real reason is why I insisted on coming here ... I'd've been better off staying home."

Tititte goes up to her and speaks in a low voice.

"Nobody's keeping you, Teena. In the state you're in, people would understand ..."

"There's just you that knows what state I'm in ..."

"I could explain."

"Never mind. I'm just afraid of what you could say ... I know you, you always exaggerate."

The saleswoman, long and lean and sallow but very well turned out – the four women hated her at first sight because of the superior manner she assumes – takes Rhéauna's hand and makes her spin around. She's afraid the sale will get away from her if the squabbling between the four women goes on, and she wants to change the subject, draw their attention to something other than the length of the gown.

"You will notice what's unusual about this gown, ladies. With the sash at the waist and the seam at the knee, it's a three-tiered dress! As if the bride had three dresses one on top of the other ... Well, maybe not three but two anyway ..."

Teena heaves an exasperated sigh.

"Exactly. There should be a third one. To the floor."

The saleswoman acts as if she's heard nothing.

"In any case, it's a thing of beauty. Very, very, very original ... With such a long veil it's magical, a real princess."

Teena shrugs. As for Tititte, she'd like to tell the nasty saleswoman that they can see for themselves, they don't need her descriptions to appreciate how beautiful the gown is; she holds back so as not to escalate matters. Already Teena nearly ruined everything with remarks that were mean and inappropriate.

The saleswoman lifts a section of the white lace that covers the wedding gown.

"Besides, under the layer of lovely fine Belgian lace it's as delicate as a spider's web and you can see that the dress is peau de soie."

Tititte startles.

"What's that? Poo-*de-soie*? Silk doesn't come from poo, it comes from worms! You say silk worms, not poop worms. That's a good one."

The saleswoman looks down on them, as if she were wondering where this woman, though chic, comes from if she doesn't know peau de soie.

"It's not *poo*, Madame, it's *peau, p-e-a-u*! Look it up in your dictionary. If you have one."

Tititte stands with arms akimbo and rushes to her, red with fury. She'd like to grab that cow by the throat like bandits in American comedies and give her a good shaking.

"Listen here! You aren't gonna teach me how to spell *poo* right now, I know how to write it. And I'll have you know that I work in the most elegant store in this whole city! Not some pitiful place like this! I'm the main saleslady in the glove department at Ogilvy's and I'd like to remind you, it's the most fashionable one in this city and maybe all of Canada, and peau de soie is peau de soie!"

The saleswoman forgets her concern about losing a sale and angrily gets up on tiptoe.

"Maybe you work at Ogilvy's and think you're the centre of the universe, I can't help it if you don't know *poult-de-soie*!"

"I know it, but I know it under its real name! Peau de soie! Anyway, it sounds nicer. Who's going to buy a gown made out of poo?"

She realizes how ridiculous she's been, backs up a few steps, brings her hand to her heart. What if the saleswoman was right? After all, Ogilvy's is an English store and maybe they pronounce the name of the fabric incorrectly. All the same, *poo-de-soie* or *poult-de-soie*, it's very ugly for such lovely fabric! Panicking, she looks towards her sisters in search of encouragement. How humiliating if the saleswoman were right! She coughs into her fist.

"Anyways, we aren't here to talk about things like that, we're here to buy a wedding gown for my niece."

Rhéauna places the veil she'd been slipping onto her head on the counter next to the magazine.

"Okay, that's it for today. I'll be back tomorrow. By myself. It's stupid to squabble over something so silly. You upset me too much, I can't see a thing!"

Her mother and her two aunts, in the face of such fierceness in a girl who's usually so calm, surround her immediately, soon joined by the panic-stricken saleswoman. They protest, apologize, Teena even says that she thinks the gown is ravishing, finally, that Rhéauna should take it, that she'll be the most beautiful bride, that she mustn't listen to what she just said, she's just an old fool – though she's not all that old…

Rhéauna calms down a little, looks at the gown in the big mirror again.

"It really is gorgeous. And I like it more than the others I tried on. How long would it take for the alterations?"

The saleswoman is professional again. All smiles, she trots out from behind the counter and looks at an order pad.

"I've just got one more for the moment. It would just take a few days… You told me that you work here, Mademoiselle Rathier? You're entitled, then, to an interesting staff discount… You'll see, you won't regret it, you'll be so beautiful on the most beautiful day of your life."

Maria rests her elbows on the counter, brings her face to the saleswoman's, speaks to her very softly.

"If I give a down payment of ten percent today, would that be okay? I'll bring the rest when we come to pick it up."

The saleswoman looks at her, frowning.

"It's because Mademoiselle Rathier works here, I'll trust you… We don't usually but…"

Maria feels the moment coming when she won't be able to hold back. She imagines her hand being raised, making a round trip to the saleswoman's face, and then, rummaging in her chignon, taking out the hairpins, pulling the hair, tearing out a few… No. Patience. It will all be over in a few minutes.

While Rhéauna is making her way to the fitting room, Maria turns to her sister Teena.

"Will you tell me what's got into you? And why were you fanning yourself like that, it's not that hot in here! It can't be the change of life, you're way too young!"

# Rose

When she saw the mailman approach the house, walking next to his bicycle, Rose raced down the steps to meet him. Monsieur Poisson comes to her place only rarely for the simple reason that she hardly ever receives any mail. The last time it was her aunt Bebette, a few years earlier, informing her of the death of her uncle Méo. She was still wiping her hands on her apron – she'd been doing the dishes – when she caught up with Monsieur Poisson who had stopped to catch his breath. He hadn't wanted to leave his bike on the road, even if there was practically no risk of it being stolen, and descending the bumpy road through the expanse of green that ran from the dirt road to the shore of the little lake where Rose and Simon's house was located had worn him out. Tree roots, stones, clumps of early wild ferns had forced him to hoist his bicycle onto his shoulder and several times he'd cursed the goddamn envelope from the city.

He was getting old and word had been going around that it was his last summer, he would be replaced in the fall by a youngster who probably knew nothing about the complicated labyrinth of roads around Duhamel and was liable to get lost in the woods. It had taken Monsieur Poisson years to get used to the postal route of the region and the local population had no desire to constantly have to go looking for their mailman lost in some hidden corner of the forest just as they'd had to do during the first year Monsieur Poisson had the job.

In winter there was no mail delivery in Duhamel. It had to be fetched from the postmistress, the dreaded Emma Poisson; in spring and summer, however, a small, a very small budget had been voted by the town council to allow Jos Poisson, her husband, to criss-cross the main roads and the secondary routes on his bicycle, a leather bag over his shoulder, to deliver to the locals the mail long awaited or feared.

"Good grief, Monsieur Poisson, did somebody die? It's been years you haven't been up here!"

Monsieur Poisson has set his bag on the ground, wiped his forehead, blown his nose, taken time to recover a little before replying to Simon's woman whom he'd always taken a shine to and who still sets off troubling heartbeats in him. If his wife found out ...

"No, I don't think so. Anyway, there's no black line around the envelope ... I'd say it's more likely an invitation. With such a pretty envelope it can't be bad news ... And you can see that it's not a letter either ..."

Rose nearly tore the envelope from his hands and ripped it open in front of him.

"Sorry, I can't wait, I'm too scared ..."

After noting what was in the invitation, she jumped for joy and planted two loud smacks on his rough beard, which smelled a little of pipe tobacco and a lot of grime.

"Would you care for a little pick-me-up, Monsieur Poisson? Simon brewed some *bagosse* just last week."

"I won't say no to that. I gotta go back up that road with my bike and I don't know how I'll do it ..."


He laid his bicycle in the dust of the road and followed Rose into her kitchen, which was fragrant with apple pie and sisters' sighs with cinnamon.

"Would you be shocked if I asked you for a sister's sigh? I'm feeling a bit peckish ..."

"I sure wouldn't be shocked, on the contrary, it's a compliment! You've brought me such good news: just think, I've got a little niece, or maybe she's a little cousin, anyway I can't keep track of who's related to who but she's getting married, in Morial, and me and Simon are invited!"

"Are you gonna go? That's a long ways away, Morial!"

"Are you crazy? I haven't got a thing to wear! Simon neither. There's just little Ernest, he's got his First Communion outfit. But I'm so glad she's getting married!"

Simon has arrived while the mailman was finishing his pastry. The two men greeted each other coolly. Simon's not the most popular person in Duhamel and Monsieur Poisson's not the last one to malign him. Rose told him the good news. He didn't show as much excitement as she did but he said, maybe to make her happy, that it was good news.

Simon nonetheless offered to put Monsieur Poisson's bicycle back on the road. He accepted, of course. We may not get along, but we know our manners.

While her husband was out, Rose reread the invitation several times.

She saw again the serious little girl who'd been so nice to Ernest the year when she'd come for a week with her mother, her aunts, and her little brother and who had gone into raptures over the beauty of the Laurentians. She'd been brought up on the western prairies and had never seen mountains before. She'd spent days walking all over, holding a book, sometimes accompanied by her little brother. She would come home with armfuls of wildflowers, pink with pleasure and always ready to lend a hand. She'd laughed as she talked about the slight anxiety she'd experienced at the proximity of the mountains because she was used to a flat and empty horizon. Or the aroma of fir and spruce, so strong, so fragrant, that she adored and couldn't get used to. And here she was about to be married. Rose hoped Nana's man would be as fantastic as hers.

She was smiling when Simon came back.

Now he is sitting across from her, holding a glass of homebrew.
"Isn't it a bit early for that, Simon?"

He smiles, runs his hand through his hair, which he wears shoulder-length. He knows that his wife likes this gesture, finds it exciting, and takes advantage of every opportunity that comes along to make it, flexing the muscles in his arm. He knows the rewards he can garner from it.

"You gave the mailman some."

"Out of politeness. And the poor old guy was exhausted."

"Not too exhausted to gawk at you."

"Cut that out! In your opinion, men are always gawking at me."

"And they are! Good thing we live far from the village! There's not so much danger!"

He laughs, slaps his knee.

She leans over, tucks away a strand of hair.

"Silly!"

He takes her by the hand, forces her to her feet, takes her outside.

It's the time of day when the late-afternoon sun passes just over the lake. They sit together on the top front step. Simon takes Rose in his arms. The water's surface burns their eyes. Waves of light dance on the lake, streaking it with golden slashes that run aground, murmuring, on the edge of the beach.

"I was thinking about that on the way back from driving the mailman to the road ... What would you say to taking a drive to Morial?"

Rose startles, moves away from her husband.

"You can't mean it! Morial! I was telling Monsieur Poisson just now that we probably wouldn't be able to go to the wedding because I don't have a stitch to wear ..."

"They didn't invite us for our clothes, Rose, it's because they want us to be there ..."

"Maybe it doesn't matter to you, Simon, but it does to me! I don't want to show up there looking like the ragpicker's daughter! And you've never been to Morial. For me it's been centuries! We'd be lost!"

"Exactly! It's the perfect time! The wedding doesn't interest me all that much, it's the trip! Let's go there and get lost, Rose darling, Rhéauna'd never seen the mountains when she came here, Ernest's never seen the big city… There's lots for the youngsters to learn."

"You're just saying that because you want to go there."

"For sure! But it's also true that little Ernest could learn a bunch of things… Listen, somebody could come and take us to the train to Papineauville… Or I could leave the horse and cart with one of my brothers along the way… The train, Rose, we'd take the train from Papineauville to Morial! Like rich folks!"

"But Morial, Simon, do you realize what you're talking about?"

"I could take you wherever you want…"

"With what money?"

"Money – you can always find money."

"You won't be going out poaching again?"

"Never mind where I'm going to get the money, Rose, just think about what you'll do with it… We've got nearly a month till the wedding, loads of time to get dolled up."

"No stealing from stores, mind you…"

"I promise that when I go into a store it'll be to buy something for you."

Rose goes down the stairs, heads for the lakeshore.

"Still too early for swimming, I guess?"

"Me, I went in swimming when I got up this morning."

"Oh you – everybody knows you'd break the ice in the middle of January to tan your hide!"

She is about to give in. Morial. The big city. The sounds. The crowds, everywhere, all the time. The lights, the evenings, the theatres, the movies.

"And little Ernest? His school?"

"Weddings are always on Saturday. He'll miss Friday and maybe Monday."

"But it'll be nearly exam time…"

"Rose, stop looking for reasons to duck out of it… It's either yes or no… You want to or you don't."

"You know it's not because I don't want to! For years now I've been dreaming about it!"

"Then say yes and stop thinking about it!"

"If I say yes, Simon, I'll have to think about it! A trip like that, you have to get ready for it! You'd be just as happy waltzing in your moccasins, your hunting pants, and your checkered shirt, but this isn't a village wedding we're going to, we're going to a wedding in a big city! It'll be huge, it'll be stylish, there'll be tons of people I haven't seen for centuries, people I won't recognize who won't recognize me either!"

"Does that mean it's yes?"

She throws her arms around him, kisses him on the mouth.

"That means I'll think about it."

She takes his hand now and brings him back into the house.

"You taste of booze. If you'll give me a little glassful maybe that'll tempt me to say thank you in my own way, if you get the picture ..."

"What if little Ernest shows up?"

"He won't be back from school for half an hour ... And we'll tell him we were taking a nap."

"He's getting to be too old to believe that ... Even though I haven't talked to him about those things yet ..."

"Me neither ... But we'd better do it fast."

"Yeah, but if we talk about those things we'll have to hide when we want to take naps ..."

They laugh their way into the house.

## Rhéauna, Josaphat

To the great relief of Tititte, the rain has stopped by the time the four women leave the department store. The sidewalks have had time to dry but the street, on the other hand, is disgustingly filthy. The mud runs into waterholes, car wheels squirt dirty water that mixes with road apples and litter dropped by heedless passersby.

Laughing, Teena points to Tititte's boots.

"Poor Tititte, I'm afraid your old boots've had it. You'll have to wear shoes like the rest of us. Come and see me at the store, we've just taken delivery of some nice ones ... At the same time you could get rid of those little veils ... It's your turn to play the modern woman."

Tititte stares wide-eyed at rue Sainte-Catherine, wondering if she'll ever be able to cross it. Rhéauna senses her discomfort and lays a hand on her arm.

"Ma tante Teena's right. Get those boots good and dirty once and for all, then throw them in the garbage!"

Tititte straightens up, holds her purse tightly against herself.

"Those new things are for youngsters like you, Nana. Us ..."

"You aren't old, ma tante ... Far from it."

"In the world we live in, my dear, past forty-five ..."

"That's just it, if you wore shoes instead of boots like in the olden days, it might make you look younger ..."

"If you think shoes are going to make me young ..."

All the same, she bends down at the edge of the sidewalk, selects a particularly disgusting puddle, and steps into it with her right foot.

"There we go. Modern times have just entered my life."

She turns towards her sister.

"Teena, we'll go to your store. I need some shoes."

At the corner of Saint-André and Sainte-Catherine, the four women meet a scruffy gentleman who is staggering a little as he watches them approach. Rhéauna stops in front of him, smiles.

"Didn't you bring your fiddle today, mon oncle Josaphat?"

The man raises his arms in a gesture of helplessness.

"My fiddle didn't want to leave his case today. He can be temperamental if he wants … But it's no coincidence for us to meet, Nana. Gabriel told me you'd be coming here to buy your wedding dress this afternoon, and I wanted to talk to you …"

The three others approach. Rhéauna makes the introductions.

"This is Gabriel's uncle Josaphat … He's the artist in the family … I told you about him, Moman. He's the one who plays the fiddle …"

Teena interrupts her.

"Yes, I know him. He plays every day at Messier's, next door to where I work. And does he ever play good!"

She addresses Josaphat, placing her hands on her heart.

"I talked to you this morning when you went past Giroux et Deslauriers where I work …"

"Yes, I remember …"

"I didn't know you were related to Gabriel."

Josaphat turns red, clears his throat.

"He's my sister Victoire's boy. I think of him as my own son …"

Now it's Rhéauna's turn to feel uncomfortable. She thinks she knows what Josaphat will have to tell her and she absolutely does not want to have that conversation in the middle of rue Sainte-Catherine. And in front of witnesses. She speaks to him very softly.

"Come over after supper. Usually the dishes are done around six-thirty. And Gabriel won't be there before eight. If you arrive around seven we'll have loads of time to talk."

She takes his arm, walks a few steps to get him away from the other three women.

"You smell of booze, mon oncle Josaphat. I don't want us to talk when you're in this state. I want you to know that if you show up like that tonight I won't even open the door ... But if you're sober we'll sit out on the front balcony and chat while we drink lemonade. Lemonade, mon oncle Josaphat, nothing stronger."

He hunches his shoulders without replying and walks away without answering, not even turning around to say goodbye to the four women.

Tititte, insulted, heaves an exasperated sigh.

"That man! He's got no manners. Already pie-eyed at four in the afternoon!"

Rhéauna takes her arm, pushes her into the mud on rue Saint-André.

"That man is more miserable than the four of us together. For years he's been hiding a terrible secret ..."

Teena grabs her other arm.

"A secret? I *love* secrets!"

Rhéauna looks down, takes a long step to avoid a dirty puddle.

"Let me tell you, ma tante Teena, you wouldn't like this one."

Her aunt turns her head and looks towards Maria, who is following them.

"You haven't said much since we left chez Dupuis, Maria. Are you hiding a big secret too?"

With a sad smile, Maria says:

"If I told you all my secrets, Teena, you wouldn't want to call me your sister."

Teena comes out with a bell-like laugh that shows her teeth with their gold fillings and makes some heads turn.

"As far as that's concerned, if you knew mine ..."

Tititte climbs onto the south sidewalk of rue Sainte-Catherine, looks at her feet, dejected.

"Is this some kind of contest? Are we playing who's got the biggest secrets? Because if I join in ..."

The three sisters laugh. Only Rhéauna is still serious. She doesn't feel brave enough to confront Josaphat and surprises herself hoping that he'll go on drinking and won't show up after supper.

She's relieved, though, that her aunt Teena didn't recognize him after all these years. Twelve years ago she'd bought his house in Duhamel to bring up little Ernest there ... And if he had recognized her, he didn't show it.

# Aunt Alice, Uncle Ernest

She could have not given him the invitation. Put it in the garbage. Or burned it in the stove. Maintain later on, if Ernest ever found out that Rhéauna had been married and asked her questions, that they'd never received it, that it must have got lost in the mail.

But as soon as he came home from work, and without really knowing why, she held out the envelope to him. A conditioned reflex. He is rereading the short text printed in gold letters, frowning, a bitter fold at the corner of his mouth. He hadn't uttered a single word since he'd taken the small rectangular card from the envelope. She had hoped that he'd tear it into little pieces, drop them into an ashtray, set fire to it – to everything it represented – and that it would never be brought up between them again. As if the thing had never existed. The past is past, we don't go back to it. He did not tear it up. He even forgot to light himself a cigar. She fears the worst.

And the worst happened.

He rests his head against the back of his easy chair, closes his eyes. She realizes that he is moved – Ernest, moved! – maybe on the verge of tears, this man she's never seen cry. She should have made the invitation disappear. She regrets her weakness, her honesty, her spinelessness; she sees again the ridiculous gesture of submission, the arm extended, the eyes lowered, with the invitation hanging between her thumb and forefinger. She had just wakened from her nap when he came back from work, everything was hazy, she'd barely recovered from her last late-afternoon "glass of water," remembered that the mail had arrived ... No, it's not that. It's obedience, obedience again. It's her role, a woman gives her husband his mail no matter what it contains or what the possible consequences may be. She knows that if she hadn't seen Monsieur and *Madame* Ernest Desrosiers, she wouldn't have allowed herself to open the invitation, and all at once she's mad at herself for the cowardice she's been dragging around for all these years. A single movement of revolt, of disobedience, could have spared her the calamity that she is certain will come crashing down on her at any moment.

Adding insult to injury, when he starts to speak it's in French, as happens every time it's about his whole damn family. When he talks about his sisters, about Sainte-Maria-de-Saskatchewan, his childhood, his mother tongue comes back to him, all broken into pieces because he no longer uses it, and he seems to savour the words that emerge from his mouth. He gives the impression that he's listening to what he says and finds it beautiful. Even since he kicked Maria out of his house and Teena and Tititte cut ties with him. He also knows that his wife doesn't understand everything, that she'll have to fill in the blanks because her French vocabulary is inadequate, she'll have to guess a large part of the true meaning of what he says. But he can't help himself; he is talking about his niece, about her wedding, and that has to happen in French. While Alice listens to him, motionless, his obedient little wife listening to him express himself in a language she doesn't understand, that she has always refused to learn, eyes closed, on the verge of exploding. She pictures herself getting up, crossing the living room, running to the kitchen, rummaging around under the sink, taking out the bottle, pouring herself a big glass of consolation and oblivion. But she won't do it.

She understands through the bits she can grasp that he considers this invitation as a respite, an appeal for reconciliation, that he is convinced that Maria is holding out her hand to him by inviting them to her daughter's wedding. Holding her hand out to *him*, not to *them*. It's about him and him only. He blows his nose, wipes his eyes, talks about buying a new suit, about taking her to Ogilvy's where she can select the most beautiful dress. They will get all dressed up, they'll go to the church, embrace everyone ...

Why isn't she getting up and isn't she going to slap him? He has said so many horrible things about his sisters in recent years, called them every name in the book, accused them – at last, she knew it, knew how mean those women were and he'd never seen it – of the most destructive intentions, and now all at once he's ready to forget everything, forgive everything, throw in the sponge!

She's shaking. With anger as much as from her need to drink.

*Forgive and forget?*

*Forgive, maybe. Forget, never!*

## Maria

"How come you're asking me on the phone?"

"You know I could never ask it to your face."

"Your goddamn pride?"

"My goddamn pride. I told you a thousand times, I don't want to owe you anything."

"That's not the same thing ..."

"It is too the same thing. It's a loan, it's money I'll owe you. And who knows when I'll be able to pay you back?"

"If you'd come to see me right away instead of running to a batch of highway robbers ..."

"I don't want to talk about that. Ever. You can tell me yes or you can tell me no, but I don't want to hear another word about it. You'll be getting your two bucks a week for years, but we won't talk about it when I come to give them to you. We'll disguise it as a restaurant meal if you want."

"You know I don't want your two bucks ... I don't need them."

"Go on like that and I'll hang up on you."

"You're the one borrowing money from me and on top of it all, you're going to hang up on me?"

"Well, that's the way it goes. Take it or leave it."

He laughs. It's not a mocking laugh, it's the amused laugh of someone appreciating a witty remark or – as in the present case – a comical situation.

"Listen here, Maria, we're going to do two things. And I'm the one that sets the conditions."

"I don't want any conditions, you know that. It's humiliating enough as it is."

"For once I'll be the one that has the upper hand, and you're going to listen to me. First of all about those two dollars: instead of giving them to me you're going to set them aside. You'll hide them in a shoebox or at the back of a closet. If you want, I'll take care of it, I'll open a bank account, say, that'll be more convenient. That way, you'll have to save money for the next marriage! It won't be long before your other two daughters meet boys…"

"That money is yours, you'll keep it…"

He raises his voice for the first time.

"Maria, shut up and listen!"

Maria moves the phone away from her ear. She is on the verge of hanging up when he cries out even louder: "Don't be pigheaded for once, and for once listen to common sense!"

She knows perfectly well that he's right. That he is her last hope. That she won't know where to go if she refuses his conditions, of which the first one, in fact, is very generous. But why do there have to be two? If the first one is generous, what's hiding behind the second one? Another marriage proposal? She couldn't bear that. She's been refusing to marry him for more than ten years, he should have got it by now. She nearly gave in a few years earlier, after a good meal in a fancy restaurant, but she pulled herself together in time and held on to her independence, which had cost her so dearly but that she's so proud of… Why does he keep coming back to it? She is satisfied with their arrangement: they don't live in the same house, their relations take place mainly when the children are absent, Monsieur Rambert has agreed not to overly spoil Théo who continues to suspect nothing and thinks that he's a Rathier like his three sisters.

"Are you there?"

"Of course I'm here."

"Now listen to me…"

She closes her eyes. If he dares to mention marriage, she'll hang up and refuse to see him again.

"There's something I've been asking you for a long time ..."

Right, here it is. Her last chance to come up with the money for Rhéauna's wedding has just gone up in smoke. Now what does she do?

"Maria, are you listening to me?"

"Of course I'm listening to you, Monsieur Rambert ..."

"That's exactly what I want to talk about. About your *Monsieur Rambert*. You've never agreed to call me anything else. My second condition is that as of today, you're going to call me *Fulgence*. That's all I'm asking for. I'm not even asking you to say *tu*."

She leans her head against the telephone mouthpiece.

That's all. Just that. It's a relief and at the same time an anxiety. Because she's going to be obliged to give in in the face of such generosity.

"That, I'll do. But the other ..."

"The other, I'll handle. You're going to collect money without realizing it and then when Béa or Alice get married ..."

"I may have more money then. I may not need your ..."

"It will be yours, Maria."

"No. It will always be yours ... Your money ... Fulgence."

She imagines his smile, that of a well-dressed old gentleman, that glimmer of happiness deep in his grey eyes. And it cost so little.

"Come and join me after work, we'll talk about all that ..."

She hangs up.

She's angry at herself. She should have refused. Everything. The money and Fulgence. No concessions. Ever.

In the midst of all this, Rhéauna comes into the kitchen, where the telephone is.

"Don't forget, Moman, I'll have two visitors tonight. Gabriel's coming around eight and then his uncle Josaphat wants to talk to me."

"What d'you think he wants?"

"I don't know. I think he loves Gabriel very much and he wants to talk about him to me. He'll be here around seven, and then when Gabriel arrives, he'll leave."

"It's strange though, isn't it, an uncle coming to visit a girl that isn't even his niece yet."

"Moman, don't start being suspicious."

"No, you're right. I see danger everywhere when you kids are involved ... But fix it so Madame Desbaillets doesn't see you, you know what she's like ..."

Rhéauna leaves the kitchen, laughing, then comes back, retracing her steps.

"Thank you again for the gown, Moman. It's really gorgeous. I'll pay for part of it ... You can't pay for the whole thing."

"Out of the question!"

"I know you have to make sacrifices ..."

"Not that many ... I'd put aside some money."

"I'm not sure I believe you."

"That's your problem."

"Promise me you'll come and see me if you ever have any problems."

"Sure, of course. But I won't have any."

Maria listens to her walk away down the corridor.

Problems. She already has problems. That she doesn't know how she'll get out of.

Because this is all for her. For the happiness of this child.

## *Régina-Cœli*

She has rested her head against the frame of the door to her apartment. She just has to take a step, only one little step, just has to lift one foot, point it forward, the threshold would be crossed in a fraction of a second and nothing will change, no danger will loom up at the corner of the street, she knows that perfectly well, no disaster will befall her and she'll be liberated from the weight, cold and heavy, that for too long has imprisoned her heart. From the fear too that persists in making her heart pound at the mere thought of leaving her apartment. Why? How did it all happen? What could have set off such a ridiculous phobia? And out of the blue, when she hadn't seen anything coming?

She misses her walks through the neighbourhood, the errands she did in the morning before there were too many people on the streets, the streetcar ride downtown. Movies. ZaSu Pitts and Gloria Swanson and, most of all, Rudolph Valentino. She feels as if depriving herself of Valentino's films makes her even more unhappy than not being able to leave her house. That animal agility with which he moves, the gaze where she reads something other than desire, a morbid melancholy – maybe a touch of neurasthenia? – that makes him so seductive, the exotic costumes that he handles as if he'd always worn them. Is all that in the past because she will never leave her house again?

Something else that she misses is buying potatoes, choosing

them one by one and arguing with the grocer, who has a tendency, she's seen him do it, to press his thumb on the scale to cheat his customers, even the most faithful, even her whom he always addresses by her full name, Régina-Cœli Desrosiers, because he claims that it's the most beautiful name he's ever heard. When he says Régina-Cœli Desrosiers with his lovely French-from-France accent, she feels almost the same as when she looks into the eyes of Rudolph Valentino. She feels important, or in any case, special. And she misses that. A lot.

And she misses summer evenings spent watching the sky over Regina where, unlike the big modern cities, you can still see the stars and lose yourself there while dreaming of a better life. You can't dream of a better life when you're shut away inside your house, unable to leave it.

She'd been sitting on her sofa a few minutes earlier and as she'd done every day now for weeks, she was analyzing everything, trying to make out *why*, to find reasons for her sickness, didn't find any, as usual, which infuriates her. At herself. At her weakness. It would take just a small amount of will, she's convinced of it. She has plenty, though, she has will to spare ... She hasn't spent her life all alone, giving children with no talent piano lessons they'd forget as soon as they were out the door, without showing a bit of will or courage. Courage she's had all her life as a respectable young lady who had never been visited by love, because it takes courage to survive solitude day after day. But now the mere thought of opening the door of her house ... Why? Why such fear?

She turns around, crosses the corridor, comes back to the living room. She looks at the old beige sofa with its bashed-in cushions on which she has spent the past weeks. She stayed there for hours every day, hands flat on her knees, her head sometimes resting against the back, sometimes bent forward, terrified simply at the thought of going outside, often crying with rage or roaring with laughter at her own stupidity. And without coming up with the reason for her condition. Is that all the future has in store for her? An old maid in her sixties – she's pushing seventy but refuses to admit it – who mopes around in her living room because she's afraid (for no reason, absolutely no reason!) of the world outside?

No. It's too unfair. She looks at her watch. Soon it will be time for her little daily concert. Is she going to end up fearing that too? Will the time come when even her neighbours' applause will start to terrorize her because it comes from outside? Is her sickness soon to be transformed into madness? Will she end up completely hidden, a willing recluse who lets herself die of fear without a struggle and who refuses any contact with reality?

She runs to the piano, lifts the lid, plinks at any key at all. A lunatic's scales. Furious cacophony. Rage expressed through sounds that emerge from a musical instrument but are not music. That is what she's going to offer them today. A concert of modern music. Enough to make their ears ring for hours. To drive them away. Persuade them not to come back. Because the old maid who used to play such beautiful, comforting pieces for them has lost her mind, maybe is dangerous. Chopin waltzes played backwards or read diagonally or any old way, played any old way. A child seated for the first time at a piano that they take for a big toy and treat like a game of blocks, pounding it hard to demolish it.

And without realizing it too much, amid demented arpeggios, without having really wanted to, she gets up, crosses the corridor again, stops on the threshold of her house, breathless. It's now or never. Either she accepts her condition and lets herself slip into the madness that lies in wait for her, or here and now she takes the step that can bring her back to a normal existence.

It's so beautiful. The trees don't have leaves yet but the buds are glistening in the late afternoon sun. It smells of spring, of freedom, why confine herself to the terror and rage of winter?

She'll get there. No.

She straightens up, closes her eyes, holds her nose, and as she'd done the one and only time in her life when she jumped into a lake, so long ago, at the end of her childhood, she's not even sure where, she puts her feet together, takes a run, and jumps. The tiniest little jump that will enable her to cross a single little step.

When she opens her eyes she is on her balcony, next to her rocking chair. People are already walking up the street to come and listen to her. The concert, in the end, will be no different from the one the day before.

And for the first time in a long time she will go out onto the balcony and bow, blushing. From joy. She is going to feel again the joy of bowing to people she'll have made happy for a brief half-hour. And then take a long walk in the neighbourhood.

As she makes her way to her piano she finds the invitation that she'd left on an armchair. She picks it up, rereads it, and before she begins her little recital, she makes her way to the telephone.

# Maria, Her Family

Usually the evening meal is the liveliest of the day. Théo talks about what happened at school, Alice dishes the latest dirt from the tobacco factory, Béa describes the customers who've been in the cookie store and what they bought. Maria puts in her two cents' worth and reports, choosing her words carefully, part of what happened at the Paradise the night before. Nana tries to put it all in order, untangle the revelations flying around the table, meaningless though they may be, to find a way to see to it that the wave of words unfurling in the kitchen manages to take the way and the form of a nearly normal conversation. Most of the time that's impossible because no one listens to anyone else, each one wanting to monopolize the conversation, and because the anecdotes recounted, instead of being an exchange between members of a family, arrive only very rarely at the person they were intended for and come back, having been ignored, to the person who had expressed them.

That night, however, a peculiar silence reigns over the Rathiers' table. Théo is still playing with his plate, barely touching his food, while now and then looking desperately in Nana's direction, though she pretends not to notice. She is waiting to be alone with him to explain that she's not leaving him all by himself, that they'll see each other often after her marriage, that eventually he'll forget that she ever lived with them because she is not nearly as important as he thinks ... Alice, tired of describing her altercation with her boss and her sensational resignation – and who is still mad at Béa for not encouraging her to come and work with her at the cookie factory – closes herself inside a sulky silence astonishing in this young girl who is constantly moving and talking too loudly. Béa, who knows that in any case no one is ever interested in her stories about the cookie store, is eating more than usual – a *pâté chinois* thrown together by Rhéauna on her return from Dupuis Frères – without lifting her nose from her plate. She is concentrating on the flavours of meat and vegetables that she won't taste again for a while. She suspects that the task of making the French Canadian shepherd's pie will be her responsibility from now on and she is terrified at the thought of not being up to it. Rhéauna is an excellent cook, Béa is only an excellent eater.

Maria also has an eye on Rhéauna. What does she know about what's going on around her marriage? What has she guessed? Not much, most likely, or she would refuse the sacrifices her mother is making to organize a suitable wedding for her. More than suitable. A rich person's wedding paid for by a woman who can't afford it.

The shepherd's pie is delicious; Rhéauna has used plenty of canned corn – kernels as well as cream-style – to please her, but she's afraid that she won't be able to digest it because of her terrible case of nerves at the prospect of the compromise she is preparing to make.

"You look wistful, Moman..."

Maria looks up. She must avoid at all costs making Rhéauna worry.

"It's a big production, you know, a wedding..."

"If you haven't got the money, if that's what you're worried about, I told you I could help out – a little."

Poor little girl. If she only knew.

She forces a smile that from Rhéauna's expression she doubts is working.

"No, no, no, it's not the money. It's... It's organizing everything, the arrangements, it all has to be ready on time, it all has to go well, you and Gabriel have to be happy with everything, but that's normal, don't worry, it's normal for a mother to worry, you'll see when you've got your own children, that things often get complicated and it can be overwhelming…"

"If you'd let me help out too…"

"I don't want help, Nana, I can work things out on my own. I've lived through things a lot worse than this."

She gets up, walks around the table, gives Théo an affectionate slap upside the head.

"You often have a fit so Nana will make a *pâté chinois*, Théo, so enjoy this one instead of playing with it."

Alice ends her silence and everyone guesses that what will emerge from her mouth will be unpleasant for someone at the table.

"'Specially because starting in June you'll be stuck with Béa's cooking. That she'll likely make with cookie crumbs instead of potatoes!"

## *Rhéauna, Josaphat*

It has been raining for long minutes. He wipes his eyes and nose with his shirt sleeve which is now soaking wet. Rhéauna offers to get him a handkerchief because he doesn't have one on him, he refuses while pleading with her to stay on the balcony with him because he couldn't stand to be alone in such a moment of distress. Sometimes he sits perfectly stiff in his chair, staring at her without a word, sometimes he bends over towards the railing – he even rested his forehead on it just now, as if he were going to vomit. He still smells a little of alcohol and a lot of stale cigarettes. He has changed his clothes but these are as shabby as the rags he'd had on outside Dupuis Frères a few hours earlier. And he's shivering. You'd think that he's cold whereas it's a beautiful, mild evening in May. When he's not sobbing, his lips quiver and he stays silent in the face of the enormity of what he has just found out. He's the one who is surprised, when he'd been afraid of shocking Rhéauna with his account, maybe even to the point of driving her away from his son, whom she loves and is about to marry. He can't let this wedding take place, he thinks, unless she knows the truth.

But now the revelations have come not from him but from her. He didn't expect that, of course, and all the lovely sentences, the grand explanations, the various excuses he'd prepared since the afternoon turn out to be unnecessary. He is the one who is shocked.

By Rhéauna's amazing understanding and her tremendous tolerance of something that anyone else would find monstrous.

She informed him first of all that she'd spent a week in his former house in Duhamel a few years ago, and then, choosing her words carefully, said that she had read the fantastic tales he'd written to explain, to justify the existence of Gabriel, which Simon, who'd found them by chance when he was rummaging in the attic, had given her because he'd noticed that she liked to read and he didn't know that the notebook contained shameful secrets. She quickly added that she'd thought the tales were magnificent. That much later, after she'd met Gabriel, she'd been particularly taken aback by the incredible coincidence when in the end she had guessed their meaning. Shocked too, yes, beyond the slightest doubt, because the unbelievable love story of him and Victoire was not only unconventional but reprehensible and wrong in the eyes of society. She was holding his hand while she was speaking, she wanted him to know that she wasn't judging him even if she'd been unable to grasp everything. Not Josaphat's love for Victoire and Victoire's for Josaphat, she could understand love, she was convinced that she was living one herself, no, it was their life as outcasts, their ostracism by the population of their village, the tattletales, the insults, what they'd had to put up with and how they had managed to survive it that she didn't understand. She couldn't make him feel all of that simply by squeezing his hand, of that she was aware. If she put into it all the warmth of which she was capable, though, maybe in the end he would stop crying and find the courage to answer her.

Finally, his first words were to accept her offer to get him a handkerchief. She brought two and he used them both, very noisily. Then he took a deep breath before looking up towards the starlit sky where some shreds of clouds were racing.

"I left my fiddle at our place. I think I need it really bad right now."

Rhéauna is still standing, leaning against the guardrail. All at once Josaphat seems very small in his chair. She would like to bend down, put her arms around him, and rock him. She'd also like to hit him. Because he could have ruined everything between Gabriel and her with his tremendous need to confess his terrible secret. If she could have a good look at his face she suspects that she would realize that he has aged ten years since he arrived. He blows his nose one last time, isn't sure what to do with the soiled handkerchief, finally stuffs it in his pocket on top of the other one.

"He doesn't know nothing, you know. We never said nothing, not me or Victoire or Télesphore..."

"How come you wanted to tell me?"

"It was me that wanted, not the other two. The other two don't know I'm here... The other two, they'd never think to confess to anybody at all... We've kept it buried for so long! Me, I didn't want you to marry Gabriel unless you knew everything. Him, he isn't strong enough to accept it or even to understand. I'd've been scared of his reaction."

"You weren't scared of mine?"

"No. I haven't seen that much of you but, it's funny, I knew you'd be able to accept it... There's something about you, Nana, something that makes people want to talk... Even about all that."

"It could have destroyed my life."

"No. You're too strong. The proof is you knew it but it didn't destroy nothing."

"But if I hadn't known, mon oncle, if I'd had a bad reaction! Have you thought about that?"

She crouched down in front of him. His smell, that of unwashed old man, rises to her nose and she struggles not to make a face. Now she hasn't the slightest desire to take him in her arms and rock him. All she feels at the moment, when scarcely a few minutes earlier her generosity had carried her away, is a black fury that sends a shiver down her spine and that she has trouble overcoming.

"I'm not mad at you, mon oncle Josaphat, but there's one thing I want to tell you. It wasn't so that I'd know everything you came to tell me tonight... You came here tonight for yourself, to make yourself feel better, to unburden your conscience, to get rid of a secret so heavy that you couldn't stand it anymore. If you didn't know why you came here, well, now you know. You risked jeopardizing our marriage to relieve yourself, that's your business. And I've felt sorry for you ever since I met you because I knew what you've put up with in your life. When a person suffers I guess they can do something dangerous without thinking of the consequences. I hope you hadn't thought about the consequences. I'm telling you again that I'm not mad at you, but let me tell you, what you've just done is something a person doesn't do. You just don't do it! It's selfish! You've been selfish and you're incredibly lucky you haven't destroyed anything! What I want now is for you to leave. I've had a really tough day and now I have to rest."

He has a hard time getting to his feet. As if the fiddler full of energy whom she used to know doesn't exist anymore. It's a broken man who is trying to hold himself up in front of her.

"Gabriel asked me to play the fiddle at your wedding. I suppose that's out of the question now ..."

She lays a hand on his arm, lifts it as if she were regretting a moment of weakness.

"You can come if you want. I can't deny you that. You're an important guest for Gabriel. And he must not suspect, never, that we've talked tonight."

Heading north on rue Montcalm, Josaphat becomes fully aware of what he's just done and he starts sobbing again.

## Madame Desbaillets

If she didn't hear what was being said on the Desrosiers' balcony that night it was not for lack of trying. Her balcony looks down on her neighbours' and not infrequently she will bring her chair to the railing on the right and prick up her ears, especially since it's been mild and Rhéauna has been entertaining her sweetheart, a tall, lanky individual, the one lover Maria Desrosiers speaks highly of, but who strikes Madame Desbaillets as lacking in personality.

She wonders what Rhéauna can see in him. She is too smart, too beautiful, too witty to be interested in an ordinary nice guy who works in a print shop. And what she's heard from this much-touted Gabriel – he speaks loudly because apparently he's partly deaf – hasn't impressed her at all. He seems kind, appears to adore Rhéauna, that's all well and good, but will he be able to offer her a life worthy of her, spoil her as she deserves? Madame Desbaillets doubts it and is sad when she sees them groping one another's hands and kissing, twice a week, under the little electric lantern that barely lights up the balcony.

But what she has just witnessed – absolutely by chance for once, she'd gone out on the balcony for some fresh air after finishing the dishes and because her husband was getting on her nerves – intrigued her tremendously. Who was that strange man, dishevelled and dressed in rags, whom Rhéauna had caused to cry? Gabriel's father? You don't bring tears to the father of your future husband less than a month before the wedding! Who is he then? And what made him burst out sobbing after the long monologue by the girl who seemed more than serious, mysterious, you'd have almost called it a confession, filled with secrets murmured in an undertone?

She'll have to ask Rhéauna, subtly, because she is hard to trip up, unlike her mother, or else one of her two sisters. Surely they know who that man is ...

Maria leaves the apartment and immediately looks in her direction. Madame Desbaillets makes as if she has just settled into her chair, smooths the skirt of her dress, sips her coffee, acts as if she were looking towards her neighbours' balcony by chance, mimes a startled surprise, waves to Maria.

Damn her, she's caught her spying again.

Maria is talking to her daughter who in turn is looking in her direction.

She sees them smile. They're talking about her. She has to say something to hide her embarrassment. She sits up, sips some more coffee.

"Lovely day, isn't it? I just came out ... I wanted a little fresh air before I picked up my knitting again."

She regrets at once what she's just said. She should have kept quiet, not come out with a pointless explanation.

Maria smiles, shrugs.

"It's your balcony, Madame Desbaillets, do whatever you want on it, it's none of our business."

Rhéauna goes inside without saying hello – she who's usually so polite.

Maria takes out a cigarette, lights it.

"Have you thought about what I asked you, Madame Desbaillets?"

A few days earlier, Maria Desrosiers had knocked at her door, not to invite her to her daughter's wedding, which would have been totally normal, even though they'd been more or less squabbling for years, but to ask her a favour. She needed someone to look after the buffet and the drinks table that she'll have set up in the yard on the day of the wedding, and she wondered if Madame Desbaillets would be so kind as to look after it.

Insulted, Madame Desbaillets didn't know what to say at first. Tell her where to get off? Tell her to do it herself or to hire one of her fellow waitresses at the Paradise? It was their job, serving people, not hers. Then she had heard herself saying that she'd think it over and shut her door to keep from jumping down her neighbour's throat. The nerve of her, to ask for such a thing! She was a neighbour, she should've been a guest, not a servant!

They hadn't spoken again since that incident. And once more Madame Desbaillets doesn't know what to say. She ought to tell her to piss off once and for all, that's what she ought to do. But if she agrees, in any case if she offers to talk it over with Maria Desrosiers at her place, it might give her a chance to worm some information out of Alice or Béa about the mysterious visitor.

And to add insult to injury, Maria says:

"I could pay you, you know."

## Béa, Alice, Théo

Béa and Alice are sitting at the end of their little brother's bed. Each is holding one of his hands. He had a serious crying jag just as their mother was leaving for work, and they didn't want to disturb Rhéauna, who was waiting for her Gabriel on the balcony, so they did what they could to console him. He refused to say why he was crying but his sisters suspect that it had to do with the wedding plans. They cuddled him, kissed him, tickled him. He's calmer now. He wants them to read him a story or to tell him one to put him to sleep. They tell him he's too old to be read to before falling asleep, that it's something for babies, he persists, whimpers, they sense that another crying fit is about to burst, and glance around the room in search of a book.

In the end, Béa finds the solution.

Rather than try to turn Théo's attention away from Rhéauna's wedding, she launches into a description of the fabulous day it will be, the unbelievable party that's going to take place right here, in their house. She paints a picture in words of the ceremony in the church, the most gorgeous one he'll ever have seen – the organ that makes the walls tremble, the beauty of the voices that will sing hymns from up in the choir screen. She talks to him about the members of their family come from as far away as western Canada, who will fill the house with shouting and laughing, decorations all over the house, because there will be music, heavenly music, maybe even square dances or reels. She describes the masses of food, the food in particular, actually – fancy sandwiches in every colour, cut into triangles that he'll be able to eat till he's sick if he wants, celery sticks with cream cheese, masses of stuffed olives, mustard pickles, the soft drinks that he loves and that for once they won't keep track of, chicken à la king, the main course, with its yummy white sauce and its peas and carrots, the four- or five-layer cake all slathered with white icing that he'll be able to gorge himself on for days and days, he'll be so fat! Because she knows what a glutton he is, almost as much as herself. He opens his eyes, listens to everything she says without blinking. All at once he's looking forward to the wedding. He forgets all the consequences and all the complications that will happen after Rhéauna leaves. He sees himself wallowing in the pyramids of sandwiches and dishes of pimento-stuffed olives, dipping a piece of a tushie bun in the chicken à la king sauce, washing it all down with soft drinks that sting his throat and make him burp. And he imagines himself over a humungous slice of white cake with white icing adorned with little balls of silver sugar that creak under your teeth. He sketches a smile, takes his hands away from those of his sisters, turns on his side, pulls the blanket up to his chin.

Béa heaves a sigh of relief while Alice gives her a sign of appreciation.

"You going to sleep now?"

He opens his eyes, looks at her.

"Yes. But you made me hungry. I want a piece of pie and a glass of milk."

## Rhéauna, Gabriel

They are sitting on the top step of the short flight that goes to the balcony. Gabriel has asked permission to smoke a cigarette. He has put his arm around Rhéauna's waist and she has leaned her head on his shoulder. They're talking about the future. Gabriel is more concerned than Rhéauna, who is doing all she can to reassure him.

"Think about the new job you might be getting, Gabriel. And if you don't get that one we'll manage with what you're earning now, what I make at Dupuis Frères, even if it's not much. We'll get along, you'll see. Don't worry about that ..."

"There'll be children, Nana. Gotta think about that."

"Maybe not right away, though ..."

"You told me you wanted one right away, that you wanted lots of children ..."

"If we have to wait, we'll wait."

"You can't just order them ..."

"We'll just be careful, Gabriel."

She blushed. She hopes that he won't notice anything. Fiancés aren't supposed to talk about those things before the wedding. She has just wandered into a prohibited zone and what surprises her is that despite turning red – she suspects that Gabriel is as ignorant as she is in that area – she's not ashamed of having brought up the subject. The ground is slippery but she feels up to it. Gabriel's embrace has loosened, however, she senses that all the same, she has to change the subject.

"Besides, I'm sure you'll get that job ... You deserve to anyway. We're going to be happy in our new house, you'll see ..."

They have rented a tiny apartment on Papineau, just north of Mont-Royal. It was Gabriel who discovered it while strolling the streets where he knew he'd be able to find an inexpensive place to live. At first he was a little ashamed to show it to Rhéauna: not only is it small, it's not much to look at. Two rooms in a row, to the left of the front door. They'll be the living room and bedroom; then, a corridor leading to the tiny kitchen. Behind the tiny kitchen, a tiny bathroom. No hot water. The most basic heating system – sheet-metal pipes fuelled by a coal furnace, run to the ceiling. Gabriel will have to dismantle them every year to clean out the soot. He asked if it could be heated in the winter, he was told that it was more than bearable, except in January.

"If I get that job, if I make more money, believe you me, we won't be there very long. We'll spend one winter, then if we aren't happy we'll go somewhere else."

"Don't you worry. You'll see, I'll fix it up and it's going to look good. Maybe it's the people that stay there that don't know what to do with it ... I've already got some ideas that won't cost very much."

He lights another cigarette, takes a long drag while he looks at the sky decorated with a small crescent moon and brilliant stars.

"Just think, in a month we'll be in La Malbaie."

She smiles, happy at the diversion.

"A whole week doing nothing, Gabriel ..."

"I don't intend to do nothing, you know!"

He blushes at the innuendo he's just spoken. Rhéauna slaps him on the arm. He tries to make up for it.

"I mean, we're gonna spend a night at the Château Frontenac in Québec City, we'll visit the old city before we leave for La Malbaie. And once we get there maybe we'll see some whales ..."

"That'll cost a lot. The train, the hotels, the whales ... Where did you get all that money? I hope you didn't borrow it ..."

Now he's the one who taps her arm.

"Don't worry about that. It's my turn to tell you not to worry. I've been working since I was twelve years old, I've had time to put aside a little money ..."

"That money could go towards something else ..."

"No, Nana. It's going to go to making wonderful memories for us. And we'll take pictures. Lots of pictures. And if it doesn't work out, later on, we'll take out our albums of wedding pictures and we'll tell ourselves that we paid no attention to what we were spending for one whole week... Now get yourself ready for loads of surprises ..."

"You're crazy, Gabriel, but you're right."

He kisses her. She's not sure that she likes the taste of tobacco that Gabriel's mouth always gives off. She'll have to talk to him about it.

Gabriel's hand ventures where it shouldn't. Rhéauna pushes it away gently.

"That's also going to wait for the Château Frontenac, Gabriel ..."

Her wonderful laugh rises into the sky above rue Montcalm.

Gabriel drops his cigarette butt to the ground, steps on it.

"A month is a long time ..."

She gets up, looks at her watch.

"We'll have a whole lifetime to catch up, Gabriel. Meanwhile, go to bed, you have to work tomorrow."

## *Josaphat*

Somewhere in the house a light comes on. Someone pulls the curtain on the front door. The sound of a bolt. A voice.

"D'you know what time it is, Josaphat?"

The man staggers, leans his shoulder against the door frame.

"I'm drunk and I wanna play the fiddle."

The door is now wide open. Florence goes out on the balcony.

"I thought you didn't want to play any more ..."

Josaphat raises the arm that is holding his instrument.

"I'm drunk, I wanna play the fiddle, and I'd like you to accompany me."

"In the middle of the night?"

"It's not that late."

"But it's too late to be playing music."

"We won't play loud. I'm drunk, I wanna play the fiddle, and I want you to accompany me and we'll play really, really quietly. You're just gonna brush the piano keys, I'm just gonna brush the strings of my fiddle. I wanna play something sad and long, something that doesn't ever end, not till the sun comes up anyway. Something too beautiful for us to share it with the rest of the world. Something just for us. Just for us."

"Why don't you play by yourself at home? You said you didn't need us any more, you didn't believe in us any more ..."

He falls to his knees, arms stretched out on either side of him, the fiddle in one hand, the bow in the other.

"I was wrong to say what I said this afternoon. It's not true that I don't need you. You're all I still have in my life. And if you didn't exist, if I really am crazy, tough luck. I'd rather be crazy with you than sane all alone in my corner! I'm drunk, I wanna play the fiddle. I want you to accompany me, I wanna play something so sweet and consoling, and I wanna do it with you 'cause you're all I've got."

She gestures to him to come in.

The old upright piano takes up nearly an entire wall in the small room. Florence sits down, lifts the cover.

"Do you want us to play something that already exists or something we're going to invent?"

Josaphat places his instrument on his left shoulder, raises his bow.

"I'm too sad to play something that already exists. Let's invent."

Rose, Violette, and Mauve have entered the room. Like their mother, they're in nightgowns and still daubed with sleep. They settle onto the big sofa, hands crossed on their knees. Josaphat takes a deep bow that makes them smile. Their mother turns in their direction.

"Josaphat is drunk, he wants to play the fiddle, he wants me to accompany him on something sweet that will console him, something that doesn't exist yet, that we're going to invent. Josaphat is back."

# THAT EVENING ...

... Régina-Cœli went to bed early, exhausted and on edge. Not only had she been able to go out on her balcony to bow to her neighbours who were applauding her victory, but she had also been able for the first time to work up the courage to speak to them. After thanking them for their kindness and their generosity, she informed them that she was going to be obliged to leave town for at least one week in May: she was taking a trip to Montréal, at the other end of the country, so there wouldn't be a concert during that time; but when she comes home she was going to play for them every day, including Saturday and Sunday, until September. She spent the rest of the evening congratulating herself for being so fearless and went to bed early, hoping that she would dream about Rhéauna's wedding or at least about her own journey to the metropolis of Canada, which she's been dreaming of for so long.

... Bebette took out all the railway schedules that her husband had collected throughout his life. She's organized an itinerary that would take herself and her sister, after meeting in the station in Winnipeg, from Winnipeg to Toronto, from Toronto to Ottawa, and from Ottawa to Montréal. Unlike Rhéauna nine years earlier, who'd had to change trains at every city because her grandparents didn't want her to spend the night there, these travellers will have to make just one transfer, in Ottawa, where they'll spend one night. They would have time to visit their niece, Louise, the famous Ti-Lou, but neither she nor her sister is the type to hang around with hookers – what would they say to those women, how to behave with them? – and will have to content themselves with a hotel that's not so chic as the Château Laurier. She imagines everything they'll see in the big city and all the people they're going to visit, and she can't get a wink of sleep.

… Ti-Lou took an inventory of her wardrobe and decided that she possesses nothing worthy of a wedding. In any case she has been thinking for a while now about having a couturière make a new outfit from the most ravishing and costly fabrics. And the most extravagant hat. She doesn't like the new cloche hats that in her opinion give women a boyish look, and even if it means surprising everyone she's considered buying a big, floppy, broad-brimmed hat trimmed with peacock feathers that she'd spotted in the boutique of her favourite milliner in Ottawa. She has already reserved, for a week, a room at the Ritz-Carlton on Sherbrooke – the swankiest hotel on the chicest street in the whole city, according to her clients who spend time in the metropolis – and promises herself to look for an apartment, maybe in the area around boulevard Saint-Joseph, stronghold of professionals in the eastern part of the city. She wants to settle in the east end, among francophones. Though he doesn't notice for a moment, she is somewhat absent during her frolics with her last client of the evening.

… Télesphore found his copy of *The Contemplations* which Victoire had hidden in the breadbox, under a stale crust. "La vieille chanson du jeune temps" floats through the apartment. Once again Télesphore takes himself for Victor Hugo, adopting a stentorian voice that keeps everybody awake in the sub-basement of the house on the ruelle des Fortifications: "I wasn't thinking about Rose; / Rose of the woods who was with me; / We were talking about something, / But I can't remember what." Victoire shrugs as she pushes open the door to Édouard's room.

"Really! If you don't know what you were talking about, shut up! Write a poem about somebody that can't remember what they've said! You gotta have a lot of time to waste."

As he does whenever his father recites poems late at night, Édouard has left his bedside lamp on and now he's listening.

"You like that, eh, when he's like that?"

"They're things you don't hear anywhere but here, Moman ..."

"A good thing too! If every woman was stuck with a sourpuss like mine ..."

"He doesn't hurt anybody, he recites poems ..."

"He could recite them at a normal time of day. As long as he doesn't launch into 'La fête chez Thérèse!' That one goes on for ten minutes and it's so boring you could die without asking for help. I can describe a party, sure, and call it poetry! 'La fête chez Thérèse!' Why not 'Victoire's Ill-Starred Party' while you're at it!"

"It's poetry, Moman ..."

"I know that! Don't worry, I don't think I'm Victor Hugo. One of those in the house is enough."

"Sometimes I tell myself I'm lucky. Nobody else in my school knows who Victor Hugo is. Let them laugh, I couldn't care less!"

"You sure are your father's son! As if that could do you any good! Anyhow, if you're still interested in poetry when you grow up, don't drink alcohol, little boy ..."

She pulls his sheet up to his chin.

"Shut your light off. You'll hear poetry just as well in the dark. Even better, maybe."

"Night, Moman."

"Night, sweetheart. Don't dream about being Victor Hugo, that would give you bad ideas for your future ..."

When she leaves the room, Télesphore strikes up Lamartine's "Le lac." She wishes she could run away from the house, howling. Though Albertine doesn't answer when she knocks on the door of the room she shares with her little sister, Madeleine, Victoire gives herself permission to open it. Every night Madeleine waits for her mother to tuck her in before she goes to sleep. She is fast asleep now for once, a thumb planted firmly in her mouth. Albertine is reading a fashion magazine; she doesn't hear her mother knock on the door because she'd plugged her ears with cotton batting. She takes it out it when she sees her come in.

"So do I kill him right away or wait for you to?"

Victoire sits on the edge of her daughter's bed.

"You told me once you couldn't hear a thing when you've got cotton in your ears."

"I don't hear a thing but it isn't normal to have to use it so I can sleep because my father recites poems all night long! At least it's not the full moon though! He'd send us off adrift in the 'Bateau ivre.' A pie-eyed father and a drunken boat!"

"He won't go on reading all night. I'll figure out a way to get him into bed."

"Sure, you always say that ... And he always wins. True, he's nicer when he's loaded but he's so tiresome! When the girls ask me what my father does I'm too ashamed to say he's a janitor ... But for sure I won't say he's a poet, they'd laugh at me!"

"So tell them he's a translator, that's his real job."

"Yeah, but he hasn't worked for so long he can't even remember how to do it! Anyways I didn't inherit that from him, poetry I mean, and it's the last thing I'd want. Before you see me with a book of poems in my hands ..."

Victoire's heart sinks. If she only knew. If she only knew that her real father is more of a poet and more dissipated than the one who recites Lamartine and Victor Hugo in the living room ... But she'll never know that. Just as she'll never know why she gets along so well with her uncle Josaphat.

"I'm going to stay with you a little longer if you'll let me, Bartine. I'll just lie down beside you ..."

"Yeah sure, and you'll still be there tomorrow morning ..."

"Do you mind?"

"I don't mind, but I think it's sad."

In the living room, Télesphore puts *The Contemplations* back under the stale crust of bread. He needs something more serious, darker, to express the weight on his heart, the spleen that is tearing him to pieces. He goes looking for *Les Fleurs du mal* that Victoire knows is on the Index and that she's hidden somewhere less obvious than the breadbox. He will turn the house upside down if he has to, but he is determined to find it.

… Aunt Alice has no memory of what happened in the course of the evening. At one point she sensed that someone – she laughs: someone, why someone, it could only be Ernest – undressed her unceremoniously, tore her clothes off, twisting her arms to pull off the sleeves of her dress, cursing because she was too limp. She laughed. He yelled at her. She whimpered. He yelled even louder. She can't get back to sleep. Yet she'd fallen with her nose in her plate during supper. But now, no. Nothing. Just a bad taste in her mouth. She looks at the ceiling. She heaves a long sigh, in any event they certainly won't see her at that wedding. Why bow and scrape to people who despise her and always have? Not the bride, no, it's true that Rhéauna has always been nice to her … But the mother! And the mother's sisters! She smiles unpleasantly. After all it could be fun to go to the wedding, bring along a bottle … of water and drink under everyone's eyes. To show them that she doesn't drink. That's it. That's what she ought to do. Stretched out beside her, Ernest dares not move in case Alice is asleep. He may admit tomorrow morning that he had called her sister Maria early that evening to tell her that they'd both be there, that all was forgotten, all was forgiven. What he will not admit, though, is that Maria hung up on him after she'd told him that he was welcome but that he had nothing to forget and nothing to forgive her for because she hadn't done anything to him.

… As soon as night had fallen, Simon crept out of the house. He went to the shed to count the money he'd been putting aside for a while now for a surprise for his wife. While he had no idea yet of what to buy her, the opportunity that had arisen now was like a dream come true. He hides part of his income from poaching, so he won't have to depopulate the woods around the house to pay for their train trip, which Rose had feared. He opens his tool chest, empties it. There, at the very bottom, a metal box of Turret tobacco. A wad of bills, rolled up carefully, nice and tight. He counts them. It's not huge but it'll do. For new clothes. Train tickets. Restaurants. As for a place to stay, they'll find a dump with some relatives or other. Maybe with Teena, little Ernest's mother ... She owes them that. As for Rose, she dreams of window-shopping along the city streets, going into department stores and chic boutiques, just to see, to snoop really, not to make herself jealous, no – what would she do with jewels and fancy outfits in Duhamel? – just to smell the expensive perfumes, for once, and spy on the well-dressed women. She'll take little Ernest to Eaton's, to the chalet on the mountain, to île Sainte-Hélène. She and Simon will taste food that they couldn't imagine even existed and sip cocktails invented for grandes dames. She thinks about her own wardrobe. Simon says not to worry, but what old shapeless, nearly colourless thing will she be obliged to mend? Where will she find gloves? And a new hat? Most likely they will be the poorest guests at the wedding. Provided that she doesn't make anyone feel ashamed. After all Maria could have simply not invited them, she knows how impoverished they are. As soon as he found out that they were going on a trip to Montréal, little Ernest, before he showed the slightest enthusiasm over this unexpected adventure, asked his mother if they would have to see the lady who comes to visit them every summer and who now and then sends money for them and presents for him. She ran her fingers through his hair.

"Yes. But not very much. Just once."


... Alice intends to go and see Madame Guillemette in secret the next day to ask her for work. Selling cookies is easy compared with what she's been obliged to do to earn her living for so long. If the pay isn't so attractive, at least she wouldn't be confined to one end of a table in a noisy factory; no more tobacco-shaking, infernal noise, appalling heat, the advances of her boss. A clean shop not far from the house, nice polite customers, tons of cookies she can dip into whenever she wants ... As for her sister Béa, she'll just have to get used to her being there. Béa, on the other hand, intends to warn Madame Guillemette the next morning about Alice's little schemes. She knows that her sister is capable of visiting the owner of the Biscuiterie Ontario to ask for work. And nothing in the world excites her less than the prospect of having to work with her sister who'll spend the whole day laughing at her, making dumb jokes about her weight, chain-smoking until the luscious aroma of cookies is obliterated. She'll tell Madame Guillemette that Alice is liable to drive customers away with her pigheadedness and her foul temper. No, no. Anything but that. Théo spends part of the night with his nose in gigantic plates of triangular coloured sandwiches or monumental slices of white cake covered with white icing and silver sugar beads. But in the middle of his feast something sneaks around him and spoils his pleasure. He doesn't know what it is, he doesn't even want to think about it, he wants to concentrate on the chopped ham that tastes of cloves and the sweet fragrance of vanilla that emanates from the cake. A shadow falls onto his plate. He looks up. It's her! It's Rhéauna! She's wearing a long white veil! And she has come to bid him farewell! He cries out in his sleep so loudly that he wakes up the whole house. Rhéauna tries to console him. Screaming, he pushes her away.

... Tititte and Teena are playing a card game for two at Teena's place. They are talking, of course, about the upcoming event in June. Teena still considers that the dress Rhéauna has chosen isn't a wedding gown and Tititte tells her once again to be quiet because she doesn't know a thing about fashion. Endless discussion ensues. Cards are slapped onto the table with unusual briskness, fists are pounded on the oilcloth. Never would they admit it but they don't mind this shouting match all that much, one of the most exciting and most passionate, hence the most successful, in a long time. Reconciliation over pound cake and a cup of tea will be all the more touching. They spend their lives squabbling, then reconciling, every time they see one another, it's their way of expressing affection. Always has been. The phone rings in the middle of the evening. It's tante Bebette calling from Saint-Boniface to ask Teena if she can put them up, her and her sister Régina-Cœli, while they are in town. Teena, who didn't even know that the aunts had been invited to the wedding or that tante Bebette actually has her phone number, was speechless for long seconds before replying that she has a studio couch in the living room … Once she'd hung up she came back to her place at the table.

"What'll I do with them? It's way too small in here for three, it's ridiculous." Titite pinches her nose before replying: "Maybe I could take one of them …"


… Madame Desbaillets, lying on her side in bed, with one hand under the pillow, listens to her husband snore while hatching plans that will no doubt make Maria Desrosiers furious: she will promise to help her on the wedding day and then won't show up. Imagining the chaos that will set off at the reception she smiles with pleasure, then asks herself why she wants to be so mean with her neighbour, why the two of them hate one another so much, thinks of no valid reason, and for the first time feels an embryonic guilt that makes her even wider awake. Especially because she's quite fond of Rhéauna and playing such a trick on her wedding day would be terribly cruel.


… Monsieur Rambert went to the Paradise for a beer just before closing. The singer hired for the month of May, drunk, gave hell to the drinkers who weren't listening to her. They answered back. There was nearly a fight. She wanted to come down off the small stage to go and beat them, they wanted to go up to deal with her. Summer was coming, tempers were running high. Monsieur Rambert took Maria by the hand. "Let your boss handle his problems, we're leaving." She refused and asked him to wait until it was all over. "It's my job to take care of these things. I know it bothers you but that's the way it is." Once the singer was shut up in her dressing room, the drinkers kicked out, the tables and chairs tidied up, Maria's boss told her that she could go. Monsieur Rambert offered to take her home, she accepted. It's chilly. A little wind from the north had driven away the afternoon clouds and subdued the humidity that had descended on the city over the past few days. Monsieur Rambert takes off his jacket, drapes it over Maria's shoulders. She takes his arm. Boulevard Saint-Laurent and rue Sainte-Catherine are swarming with people. The nightclubs are closing, a wave of drinkers including a few women is taking over the sidewalks, filling them with singing, shouting, laughing, yelling. It's almost like in August with a full moon. Monsieur Rambert points to a couple who seem to be about to come to blows.

"Looks like they let the loonies out tonight."

Maria shrugs.

"It's always the same at this time of night ..."

They quicken their pace. They're not talking to each other. Words would be pointless. Maria knows she can't offer any thanks on the matter of the goddamn loan and Monsieur Rambert doesn't expect any. Arrived at her place, they kiss. No danger they'll be seen, it's too late. Even Madame Desbaillets must be asleep. Before going onto her balcony, Maria turns towards Monsieur Rambert.

"I'm real worried about their future, Fulgence."

She doesn't see him smile.

"That's normal. But you'll see, they'll work things out."

... Rhéauna can't get to sleep. She's worried about their future.

... Gabriel can't get to sleep. He's worried about their future.

... They made music a good part of the night. They played sonatas and rigadoons, waltzes and reels, impromptus and folk ballads, they wept as they performed the first movement of Schubert's Piano Trio opus 100 without knowing what it was, without ever having learned it, and by two players even though it was a trio, they had tons of fun during the "Rigodon don-daine," Florence and her daughters even stamped their feet at one point, as if they were at a family party, and Josaphat crooned out of tune in the middle of the "Méditation" from *Thaïs*. At times the music caressed them in ethereal whirls, at times it inflamed their nerves and made them vibrate as much as their instruments. Rose, Violette, and Mauve danced a minuet – it was slow, pretty, dainty – and Josaphat nearly broke his bow during a pyrotechnical piece by Paganini. No one in the neighbourhood complained. Maybe because they didn't hear anything. Or there was no music to hear. At the end of an over-whelming, totally calm improvisation in which piano and violin moaned nearly always in unison, like after a long attack of sobbing when the body is exhausted and eyes are burning, Florence closed her instrument. "It's late, Josaphat. That's enough for today. You can come back whenever you want." He did not protest. He put his fiddle back in its case. The four women thought that he was going to leave without a word when he turned towards them. "I'm in such terrible pain. If you only knew."

# PART TWO

# THE GRAND
# MELEE

On the eve of the wedding, Ti-Lou arrived on the train from Ottawa. After powdering her nose and refreshing her lipstick, she climbed down from the first-class car head high and torso straight. She had decided to travel light and the porter wasn't panting too hard under the weight of the two huge, half-empty trunks that she intended to fill to the brim with luxurious clothes and accessories of all kinds during her stay in the city. At the exit to Windsor Station, heads turned as she passed by, she was used to it, but the fact that genuine city dwellers were appreciating her bearing, the small of her back, and her décolletage was flattering and she allowed herself to do something that she'd always refused in Ottawa: she responded with a knowing smile to certain discreet signs, to several tipped hats. The women she met were not mistaken about her profession and she suffered some shrugs and a good many accusing looks that were intended to be insulting but that only amused her. She hailed a taxi and shouted rather loudly to the chauffeur before getting into the car: "The Ritz-Carlton, please!" She was treating herself to the chicest hotel in town and wanted it known. Rue Peel streamed by at full speed, the car drove past the Hôtel Windsor – her second choice if there'd been nothing available at the Ritz – she studied the ladies walking in Dominion Square. She didn't like the way they were dressed – too modern, too short, too revealing, lacking mystery – and she wondered if some day she'd feel able to dress like them. She shrugged. We'll see about that when the time comes. Meanwhile it was a beautiful day, it smelled like a real city that is hot, and all at once everything seemed possible, the wildest things and the most eccentric movements. When the taxi crossed rue Sainte-Catherine, she gazed hungrily at both sides of the street.

Bebette and Régina-Cœli had spotted Ti-Lou on the platform of the Ottawa train station just before she boarded the train. Bebette wanted to say hello but Régina had held her back by the sleeve. "Leave her be. Don't pay any attention to her." "But she's our niece, Régina, our sister's daughter!" "She stopped being our sister's daughter when she chose that profession, Bebette!" "Good Lord, when did you start being so high-minded, Régina-Cœli Desrosiers!" "I'm not high-minded but I don't feel like chattering with a slut between Ottawa and Montréal, that's all!" "Nobody's asking you to spend hours with her, I just would've liked to say hello …" "I know you, Bebette, you're never happy just saying hello to somebody. You have to know everything about them!" "If you don't want to talk to her what'll you do tomorrow at the wedding?" "I'll say hello if I have to but that's all. Meanwhile quit gawking at her, she'll notice …" When they'd seen her board the first-class car, Régina had let out a disapproving sigh. "Oh we know, those women only travel first class. It must be a man that buys the ticket!" Bebette tapped her arm. "She's likely got more money than you and me put together! I'm sure she could pay for a first-class ticket." "Yeah, with dirty money." "Régina! What's wrong with you this morning? You're so crabby! We've just spent two days together and you haven't been mean like that." Régina-Cœli had opened the door to their car and pushed her sister up the three metal steps. "I hadn't thought about the guests who'll be there tomorrow. There'll be all kinds of people, Bebette, not just the relatives we want to see …" "Well I want to see everybody! Even the ones I don't know!" "That's just like you, you always want to jump on everybody and talk to them …" "That's called being sociable, Régina." "Yeah … It's also called liking to snoop …" This minor altercation didn't prevent them from going on gabbing during the long hours it took the train to travel from Ottawa to Montréal.

At the tiny station in Papineauville, Rose, Simon, and little Ernest boarded the same car as Régina-Cœli and Bebette. Since they had never met, Rose always being absent from the house of

Méo Desrosiers, her adoptive father, when his two sisters visited Sainte-Maria-de-Saskatchewan, they didn't say hello. They were far from imagining that they would meet up at the same wedding the next morning. All the same, Rose and Simon had giggled at the two old ladies because they were shouting, with a hint of English accent that was kind of funny, and they were always contradicting one another without realizing it, as usual. Sisters, most likely. Old maids. Though on second thought the more corpulent was the type who'd have brought up a large family and run it with an iron hand. Now and then she'd let out a thundering *saperlipopette* that made heads turn and that reminded Rose of something, though she couldn't remember what. As for little Ernest who'd never been out of Duhamel, he had gawked at everything he'd seen since they'd left early that morning. From the window of the train Papineauville had seemed huge to him, and Rose had told him that Montréal would be a hundred times more impressive. "It's so big, Ernest, you can't go all the way across it on foot. It would take days. Get ready for lots of surprises, kiddo! Houses five or six storeys high, streetcars, electricity everywhere, even in the toilets! And toilets in just about every house!" That might be what struck little Ernest most: toilets inside houses and all of them with electric lighting. Not to freeze your bum when you have to pee during the night in the middle of winter! No metal bucket next to the bed! "Is it heated even in the toilets?" Rose runs her hand through his hair as she does when he says something that touches her. "I think they've even got heating in their beds, Ernest!" He believed her. When Simon signalled to his wife to take back what she'd said, she responded with a big grin. "It's his dream week, Simon, let him dream ..."

That same afternoon Rhéauna and Maria went to Dupuis Frères to fetch the wedding gown and the accessories that Rhéauna had picked out on her own a few days after the excruciating scene in the fitting room. They stopped on the ground floor for the perfume and jewellery, and the second floor for the shoes. Maria paid with crisp new bills just withdrawn from the bank, an impressive wad that Fulgence had brought her the night before when she was on her way out of the Paradise. They left the department store, arms full of boxes and bags. The apartment on rue Montcalm wasn't far, so they walked. Rhéauna looked at herself in all the store windows she came to, telling herself, at this time tomorrow you'll be married! She couldn't believe it and clung to her packages, tangible proof that it really was the day before her wedding and that it wasn't all a dream that would burst like a soap bubble when she woke up. She was more worried than excited: given the choice, she'd have preferred a private wedding with just her close loved ones and Gabriel's. It was Maria who'd had the idea of a big wedding; a big family reunion; guests – on their side anyway – who would come from the four corners of the country, as far away as Regina; who'd suggested food in industrial quantities; music all day long; dancing; plenty to drink. "You just get married once, Nana, and if the honeymoon doesn't last and you're stuck with an asshole for life, at least you'll be able to say it was a fantastic party!" Seeing how important it was to her mother, Rhéauna hadn't protested too much and finally let herself be won over by Maria's enthusiasm. They spent part of the afternoon at the hairdresser's, a lady named Olivine Dubuc who had just opened a salon very close to their place, to whom all the women in the neighbourhood were rushing because she offered a free movie ticket to her new clients. The women weren't thrilled with their hairdos when they left the salon but they consoled themselves by saying that Rhéauna's veil and her mother's cloche hat would cover up Madame Dubuc's professional deficiencies.

Ti-Lou entered the Ritz-Carlton like a queen entering her castle. She immediately spotted the manager, the bellboys, the concierge, nodded to each of them, and made her way to the reception desk, asking the porter to set her suitcase beside her. If the hotel staff were aware of her profession, none of them let it show. She was clearly a woman of means, she had reserved one of the most expensive suites for a long week, no matter the source of her money. There were, however, limits not to go beyond: when Ti-Lou asked for the bar, the manager replied, choosing his words carefully, that they couldn't serve alcohol at the bar to an unaccompanied lady, and that if she wasn't expecting someone she must order her drinks in her suite. She got around that without losing her smile, made her way to the bar, chose the most discreet table – partially hidden by a column of fake marble – and in a strong voice ordered a dry martini with two olives and a strip of lemon rind. To the manager who had followed her to her table she slipped an outsized tip and murmured to him like a woman of the world: "An establishment like yours needs women like me to adorn the bar. To encourage the men to drink. I'm on vacation here and I'm not letting stupid regulations spoil it. I'm not here to work, I'm here to celebrate the wedding of my second cousin and the bill that I'll pay after a week will mitigate all the rules I'll have overstepped during my stay here." Two men raised their glasses to her health. The manager saw them, understood at once the advantage that Ti-Lou's presence in his hotel could represent, and withdrew without another word. Ti-Lou raised her glass in the direction of the two men who immediately came up to her table.

Rose, Simon, and Ernest got lost as soon as they left Windsor Station. They headed north up Peel after they'd asked for rue Dorchester where they had rented a room after Teena told them that she couldn't accommodate them because she was going to put up the two aunts from the Canadian Prairies. One more expense. Where did all that money come from? They walked right by it, at the corner of Dorchester, because they were looking up and heading for rue Sainte-Catherine when they noticed the Hôtel Windsor, which was the most beautiful building they'd ever seen. Rose had put her suitcase on the sidewalk. "I wonder who can afford to stay in this place ... Not us, that's for sure ..." Simon pretended to climb the steps in front of the hotel, under the bewildered gaze of his wife – and that of the doorman in red-and-gold livery that made him look like a retired British soldier – who burst out laughing. "Silly fool! I believed you for a minute!" Ernest, who'd stayed on the sidewalk, went into ecstasies over the grandeur of Dominion Square across the street which in his opinion could have contained the entire village of Duhamel. Rose took him by the hand. "And it's far from being the biggest park in Morial, Ernest ... When I take you to parc La Fontaine you won't believe your eyes. Anyways, they say it's quite a sight ..." They retraced their steps, found rue Dorchester, turned east. They asked a passerby if rue Amherst was far from there and after she'd told them that yes, it would be a good half-hour's walk, they bravely picked up their suitcases in the powerful early June sun. Rose looked around her. "Doesn't seem to be any big stores on this street ... I'll have to find a hairdresser before tonight ..." Whenever she has her hair done – which isn't often – Simon and Ernest laugh and elbow each other, pretending they don't recognize her and it makes her furious. Simon leans over to Ernest. "Maybe we should go easy on her tonight ... She's worked up enough as it is ..."

Settling Régina and Bebette at Teena's wasn't simple. While the reunions were tearful and punctuated with cries of joy – Régina-Cœli kept being amazed at having travelled so far from home and shared her reactions way too often without realizing it, her voice higher-pitched than ever, her movements capricious like those of an overexcited little girl – the silence that settled into the room when the two aunts saw the davenport that they'd have to share was eloquent. "*Saperlipopette!* Are you sure there's room for two on that, Teena?" Who, exercising patience and holding back the urge to kick them out – already! – gave a succinct demonstration: she opened the sofa, fetched two pillows, and placed them side by side. "See that, you can put two pillows, which means that two can sleep there." Régina sat on the upholstered chair beside the davenport. "I've never slept that close to anybody." Then, realizing the implication of what she'd just said, she blushed to the roots of her hair. Bebette turned towards her niece. "I'm too fat to sleep with somebody on that. Even if Régina's skinny. And I twitch and shake in my sleep." "It's for just a few nights, ma tante." "That's just it, we're worn out and we need a good night's sleep!" Teena sat on the bed, took a pillow and held it against herself. "Tititte offered to take one of you if ..." Bebette shrugged and swept aside the suggestion. "We don't want to separate! We didn't come all this way to end up separated!" And so, yes, Teena made the sacrifice of offering her own bedroom to her aunts. Her bed, wider, could accommodate both of them and they would be closer to the bathroom. Strangely enough, what shocked her most was that the aunts didn't thank her, as if it was perfectly normal that she would make a sacrifice for them.

Victoire spent the day fiddling with the least worn out of her children's and her husband's clothes. She added a flounce to the hem of Albertine's red dress; she lengthened a yellow tunic for Madeleine, who's grown too quickly and will soon find all her clothes too tight; she cut two wide ribbons to make sashes for them. For Télesphore and Édouard, she simply pounded their suits with a wooden spoon and pressed them with a very hot iron, taking care to make the crease in the trousers perfectly straight. As for herself, she took out the dark violet, nearly black dress that she kept for funerals, brushed it, steamed it, added a lace collar taken off a dress of Albertine's, redid the hem which drooped on one side, and took off the belt that emphasized her stoutness around the middle. Alterations complete, she tried it on, studied herself at length in the mirror, finally told herself that with her black spring coat, it wouldn't be too disastrous. With garments scattered all over the living room, she made herself a cup of tea and thought about her big son who is going to cut his ties with the ruelle des Fortifications, perhaps definitively, having already taken his leave by renting an apartment. He promised to come back to see them as often as possible, but she knows that a married man, in the beginning in any case, concentrates on his new life and she's going to see even less of him. The eldest of her four children had found freedom, broken away once and for all from this family where bad luck had made its nest. The others would follow, each in turn. And good for them. When no one was left in the empty house but Télesphore and her, when she'll have no responsibilities but that of janitor, maybe the vulture will finally have the courage to take responsibility for its actions to the bitter end, who knows?

During the final try-on of the wedding gown, in Maria's living room, Théo couldn't stay away from his sister. He showered her with compliments, insisted they let him climb up on a chair because he wanted to kiss her once again, barely touching her with the edge of his lips so he wouldn't soil anything, he talked loudly, he gesticulated, so much so that several times his mother had to threaten to send him to his own room. He didn't calm down but he restrained himself. To keep from howling with sadness and fear. Alice and

Béa seemed to swoon, saying they'd never seen such a gorgeous wedding gown, that Rhéauna looked not just like a princess but like a genuine queen. Rhéauna replied, laughing, that they were going too far, and besides, they'd only ever seen a bride in fashion magazines so they couldn't make comparisons. Alice told her that if she didn't want compliments she could say so. Rhéauna apologized, blaming her reaction on nerves. When she was all dressed except for the bouquet of peach-coloured roses that they'd left in the icebox to keep fresh, what she saw in the big mirror in her mother's room thrilled her: a beautiful woman in a magnificent gown under a veil that swathed her like a cloud of lace. Herself. In beauty. For the time being she was calm, contrary to what she'd told her sisters, no doubts perturbed her, no serious worry except, of course, about how the next day would unfold. She was going to walk up the central aisle of the church confidently, she would say a good sonorous "I do," she would kiss her new husband with all her heart ... As for the rest, their precarious financial situation, the new life as a couple with someone she might not know quite as well as she'd have liked, there would be time to think about that when she came back from her wedding trip. Maria, not choosing the best time, took her hand and pulled her towards the bed. "There's a conversation we've never had, Rhéauna ... There are things I ought to talk to you about tomorrow night, when you get to Québec City ..." Rhéauna burst out laughing, "Moman! Do you think I'm still fifteen years old? Other girls may be ignorant when they get married but not me! I've found out things!" Maria was so relieved that she burst into tears.

As she does every evening, Tititte had two plates to wash, a knife, a fork, a glass. Her task done – she rinsed the glass several times because it didn't shine enough for her liking – she cleaned the splatter of bacon fat off the stove, wiped the table, put everything away in the small kitchen cupboard. Then she settled on the balcony in her rocking chair to watch the night fall. Streaks of pure gold crossed the sky after the sun set, darkness was a long time coming, as if the evening were too beautiful for it to turn dark. There was the scent of the lily-of-the-valley drying in the flower bed. An aroma of First Communion on the eve of a wedding. Strollers walked past the house, a very small number of them greeted her. After so many years she was still an outsider in her own neighbourhood. Arms crossed on her chest, a cup of tea sitting on the small table next to her rocking chair, she thought a little about the next day and a lot about what her own life would have been like if her marriage had been a success. She saw again her disastrous wedding trip to London with a man who had all the merits aside from being interested in what a woman could offer him; her horror before what the future could offer her with a frigid husband; her hasty return to Montréal; the awkward explanations to her family and her friends that, when all was said and done, were only lies. She rarely lets herself think about it but she tried to imagine what her existence would have been if she'd had children ... She would be old enough to have grandchildren, she would go to the Church of Saint-Pierre-Apôtre accompanied by how many, seven individuals, eight? More? Children who would have become professionals, grandchildren who would be her delight, a husband considerate and loving after so many years ... She didn't cry, though it would have done her good. All that she felt was regret. Then she saw herself behind her counter at Ogilvy's, the leather, suede, or woollen gloves arranged tidily in their racks, the customers who don't even bother thinking that in front of them is a human being whom they treat as if she were a robot. For them Tititte is only there to present her merchandise and collect the cash they hold out to her when they deign to buy something. At that, she cried. And it didn't make her feel any better.

Madame Desbaillets had got the surprise of her life a few days earlier when she realized that managing Rhéauna's wedding was so fascinating. Maria Desrosiers had asked her not only to see to the details of the party – passing plates, drinks, in such a way that everyone wouldn't congregate in front of the tables of victuals and the bar, and that the flow of guests be natural and smooth – but she had also assigned her the total administration of the reception: receive the suppliers while everyone was in the church; have the tables set up in the yard by the young neighbours requisitioned for the occasion, whom she'd have to pay from the small budget she'd been allotted; trim them with ribbons and bows purchased from that same budget; set the wedding cake in the very middle of the space in such a way that the reception would move around it; greet the guests as they arrived. Maria Desrosiers had told her that she would be the "governess" of the wedding and she'd been flattered. Before such a sign of confidence and even friendship – it didn't cross her mind that once again she was letting herself be manipulated and that her neighbour could be taking advantage of her – all her resentment against Maria, the rancour she'd been dragging around ever since they'd swapped apartments six years earlier; the squabbles that were extinguished on their own and then were reborn, who knows why, like a bushfire – they had flown away all at once and she had pitched in with an enthusiasm she hadn't felt for a long time. Finally she had something useful and important to do and she was thrilled by it. She went down to Madame Desrosiers' after supper, reassured her: nothing to worry about, all is well, everything would be ready when they came back from the church, she'd be happy and it would be a glorious wedding. Maria thanked her, praised her in advance, told her she'd always known, in spite of the minor problems between them, that she could count on her. Madame Desbaillets sang as she climbed upstairs.

When supper was over and before she passed out, Uncle Ernest laid his hand on that of his wife. "Now listen here, Alice. Not one drop of *water* when you get up tomorrow morning, no flask hidden in your purse to cool off or wet your whistle. You're going to stay far away from the bar during the reception and you're going to eat and drink what I give you. Understand? And don't claim you're sick when you wake up; if I have to drag you to that wedding I'll do it. You can be discreet if you're bored but you're going to be polite and even nice when somebody speaks to you. Meanwhile, go and lie down, you need to sleep off your *water*." Ernest had decided to wear his full RCMP outfit, the puffy khaki breeches, the red serge tunic, the leather belt, the broad-brimmed hat that always – or so he hopes – makes people forget the size of his nose. He sincerely believes that he will bring some decorum to the religious ceremony and to the reception at Maria's. A bit of class. Something serious and official. Alice lies down in their bed which is too narrow now that Ernest has become rather corpulent. She looks at the clothes they will wear the next day, now hanging on the closet doors: her new dress which she chose deliberately in a colour she hates, an Irish green that's too young for her and that is unbecoming to her complexion. She's going to wear that dress, she'll no doubt get laughed at (who, for that matter, dresses in Irish green for a wedding except the Irish themselves, when the background of her own ancestors was Scottish?) and she decides to spend the day hidden in a corner without talking to anyone, especially not to her husband's sisters. Let them laugh, it's all the same to her. They don't come up to her ankles. In spite of her slightly shaky hands, she falls asleep, smiling.

Gabriel's fellow workers from *Le Devoir* – pressmen, typographers, proofreaders – had organized a stag for him. It was held at the premises of the Syndicat catholique so it was agreeable and rather innocuous. They offered up some call-and-response songs, some love songs too, the beer – permission granted thanks to Gabriel's boss – though it wasn't flowing, still caused some tempers to flare: double meanings began to circulate after a few minutes; sexually explicit jokes that turned the men telling them as red as the man they'd been addressed to, made the rounds, someone even questioned Gabriel's virginity. A subject on which he was discreet. He merely asked his friends how many of them had known women before getting married. Which shut them up on the spot. There were no farces in bad taste, no one poured molasses onto Gabriel, no one plastered him with shaving cream or feathers, they didn't get him drunk and walk him around the neighbourhood with his pants down as was often done at this kind of party that were mostly marred by forced bad taste. It ended early, before midnight, because the groom would be taking communion the next day. His boss drove Gabriel home in his car. He was a little the worse for wear but not too much, and before sinking into sleep he wondered what state his father would show up in the next morning, and whether his uncle Josaphat would show up. With or without his fiddle.

As for Monsieur Rambert, he's fallen asleep with a smile on his face. The Sunday before the wedding Maria and Rhéauna asked him officially – it was unexpected and he nearly burst into tears – to serve as the father of the bride and lead her to the altar, an honour he didn't feel worthy of but in the end, he accepted, moved by the urging of the two women. His suit, perfectly clean, was hanging on a chair, his well-polished shoes next to it, his new necktie, displayed on his white shirt like a badge of honour. He was going to lead his mistress's daughter to the altar before the eyes of Théo, his illegitimate son who suspected nothing and whom he adored.

Josaphat hadn't drunk a drop in case he worked up the courage to appear at the wedding.

Télesphore hadn't drunk a drop in case Josaphat worked up the courage to appear at the wedding.

No fiddle that night. No poetry either.

Rhéauna wakes up feeling anxious. It takes her a few seconds to realize why. That's it! It's today! She has just spent her last night in her girl's single bed. At this time tomorrow morning she will be in Québec City, at the Château Frontenac, and she'll be a woman. Whatever that means aside from ... Don't think about that, there will be enough vexing things going on between now and their entrance into their hotel room ... Opening her eyes she spies Théo standing at the foot of her bed. "Just what d'you think you're doing there?" He goes up to her, puts his arms around her neck. "We'll never see you anymore, will we?" Rose emits deathly screams as she gets out of bed. "That's all we needed! We've never had bedbugs in Duhamel, we had to come here to get them." Her back and legs are covered with nasty red bites. "Besides looking ugly, I'll be scratching my back all day like a cat with fleas!" Simon hides his laughter behind his fist. "How come I haven't got any? Are you sure they're bedbug bites?" "You and your Native blood, we know you never get bitten! Even famished blackflies get sick to their stomach at the sight of you in the spring!" Little Ernest bursts out laughing. "You're funny when you talk like that, Moman!" "If you were in my place, buster, you wouldn't think it was funny! Wouldn't it be something if I passed on the bugs to other guests?" "You're going to take a long bath, Rose, a long hot bath and the bugs will be on their way ... I hope." "Yeah, sure. Unless they decide to follow us to Duhamel ..." "Don't talk about bad luck! And don't talk so loud! What if all of a sudden they heard you?" "Who, the bedbugs?" "You never know ... don't take any chances, don't give them a taste for travel!" He gets a slap upside the head. Ti-Lou wakes up in the arms of a Greek shipowner – or so he claimed when he approached her at the bar, though his accent sounded more Italian. He wants to start over again, she pushes him away reminding him that she has to be at the church in less than two hours. He doesn't push it, dresses without washing or shaving and leaves her an enormous "gift" on the bedside table. No matter if the money comes from building boats or making olive oil, Ti-Lou resolves to rent a limousine to get to the church and to enjoy a royal feast in one of the most spectacular restaurants in Montréal. Unwrapped the day before and hanging prominently, her sumptuous new dress puts a big smile on her face. Bebette and Régina declare that they'd slept well while Teena aches all over because the mattress in the davenport was so hard. It takes her a good five minutes to extricate herself from the bed and she walks into the kitchen bent nearly double. Bebette holds out a cup of coffee. "Good Lord, Teena, you look like you spent the whole night partying!" Régina butters two slices of toast and puts them in front of her niece. "Is it on account of the davenport?" "What d'you think? It's as stiff as an iron bar." "Good thing we didn't have to sleep on it!" and they go on gabbing as if nothing had happened. Teena would like to strangle them. Télesphore, who claims he can stop drinking whenever he wants, gets up fresh as a daisy. He's almost humming as he gives himself a close shave, spends more time than usual washing and grooming himself, puts on the clothes that Victoire has left out on the back of a chair. He studies himself in the big mirror hanging behind their bedroom door. He thinks that he cuts a fine figure and wonders if it occurred to his wife to brush his hat, which has ended up more than once in the gutter on ruelle des Fortifications these past weeks. Victoire inspects her three children in the girls' room. It's not as catastrophic as she had expected. Albertine looks cranky, as usual, but her dress is pretty and Victoire has managed to tame her oily hair by putting it into two braids that she hopes will last all day. Madeleine and Édouard look like two poor but clean children, which they are. Victoire hopes they'll go unnoticed. She's not yet dressed herself, as her husband points out. She walks past him without even a glance. "My dress is so old I'm scared it'll die on my back, so I'll put it on as late as possible." Télesphore, thinking it's a joke, laughs. Maria, who'd taken the day before off work, spent an agitated night. She reproached herself several times, claiming she was selfish and heartless, but she couldn't help thinking once again about what was going to become of the house and its inhabitants when Rhéauna was no longer there. No one has done anything yet about the transfer of power, no one has wondered who'll do what, when, and why, because they're used to everything being done without their realizing. Nothing is going to happen now as it used to, she realizes that, and she is horrified when she thinks of the weeks to come. Ask Alice to stay home and replace Rhéauna? She wouldn't wish it on her worst enemy. That's what they'll have to do. For the first time. When she gets out of bed she realizes that not once has she thought about her daughter's happiness. Going into the kitchen, hair straight and wrinkles on the pillowcase still printed on her face, she's surprised to see Madame Desbaillets, curly as a sheep and sparkling in an unflattering flame-red dress. "You're here already?" "The delivery man from the Pâtisserie Parisienne is on his way with the lunch and the cake ..." "He'll be here early ..." "It'll take time, organizing everything." "Speaking of that, Madame Desbaillets, I don't know what I'd do without you ..." Pink with pleasure, Madame Desbaillets plunges her face into her coffee. "We should drop the *Madame*. I'm Monique ..." Maria puts two slices of bread on the stove burner. "No. I prefer Madame Desbaillets ..." Josaphat wakes up in a sweat. His hands are shaking. He gets up, looks at himself in the mirror he's hung on the back of the door to his room. Eyes red, bleary. His beard dirty. A skeleton. Less than a skeleton. A ghost. What to do? Go back to bed? Forget it all, open a beer while he's fixing his coffee, and spend the day cursing? Or take his courage in both hands, put his clothes on, pick up his fiddle ... But the effort that would take would be colossal ... Gabriel invited him, though, Rhéauna hasn't objected ... Try to play the fiddle on an empty stomach? That hasn't happened to him in years! And what to wear? How to dress for his son's wedding? Gabriel is paralyzed in his bed. He doesn't want to get up, dress, go to the church, put a rope around his neck. He's scared. Of everything. Of getting married, of having children, of spending the rest of his life as a responsible man. All at once even changing jobs terrifies him. He's just fine as he is, he has a good job, some friends, an orderly life, a girl he adores and who adores him … Only his desire for Rhéauna, to see her body at last, explore it, possess it, gives him the courage to jump out of bed. He's mad at himself for not being more excited by the day now beginning, no doubt the most important one in his life – maybe that's it, in the end, the ceremony, the reception, the congratulations, the speeches, the toasts, the bad jokes, the bustle around the buffet, the strong drinks too early in the day, and too fast, that's putting him off: he would gladly take Rhéauna by the hand, they would go together to the Provincial Transport terminus, board the first bus for Québec City, and he would fulfill as fast as he could his curiosity about physical love that's been driving him crazy for months, ever since he's known that he will soon be getting married. That profoundly selfish thought makes him turn red with shame. He has to think about her, too, about Rhéauna whom he loves so much. He has to follow the rules of his society, of his religion, do like everyone else, stop thinking about his desires and concentrate on the meaning of marriage, the importance of living with someone, of loving his wife, respecting her, making children, bringing them up … That's all well and good but what really awaits him and Rhéauna when they come back from their wedding trip? The poverty he's always known? But worse? Living from hand to mouth for the rest of his life? Constantly on his toes, in pursuit of money that doesn't exist and of an illusory happiness, promised but never delivered? Aside, of course, from the time spent in bed with his wife? And if he didn't get dressed? If he didn't turn up at the church? Of course he knows that's impossible, but it's what he would do, he thinks, if he had the courage. A coward's courage. Uncle Ernest still cuts a fine figure in his Mountie's uniform, or so he thinks, though it's a little snug around the waist and the seams are starting to rip, and the buttonholes. He thinks he's imposing when he studies his reflection in the bedroom mirror. Eyes forward, shoulders square, the false ease in his bearing that was ingrained in him so long ago, it's become second nature – to appear sure of yourself, especially when you aren't, because you represent justice … He'll make quite an impression! Beside him, sitting at the foot of the bed, his wife is trembling. It started with her hands, at breakfast time, unable to hold the cup of tea, then, as she was getting ready – donning slip, silk stockings, her new dress, trying to hide the redness of her cheeks, those ugly purplish blood vessels too that streak her face – the trembling spread to her whole body. Ernest had to put on her shoes, lace them. She won't be able to make it through the event. She pleaded with him to leave her at home but he refused to bend. Her place is at his side at the wedding of their niece, and that's that. He takes off his broad khaki hat and sits down beside her. "I'm going to do something, Alice. I'm going to let you have a drink before we leave the house. One drink. Not two. One. And you can take along a flask if you want … Don't overdo it, though. If I see you heading for the bathroom more than two or three times in the day I'll take it away from you … And I don't want to see you taking it out in the church! Even though you aren't Catholic! Understand?" Alice's entire body is tensed, she jumps up, runs to the kitchen. And for the first time in their shared existence she drinks a glass of gin without hiding. Rhéauna is standing right in the middle of the living room, waiting for comments. They were all dumbfounded when she entered the room. Théo is the first to speak and with his limited child's vocabulary, he talks about a princess out of a book, even if fairy tales aren't his favourites. The magic word having been uttered, the three women start to talk all at the same time. Compliments fly out, hands are clapped, Béa has brought her hand to her throat and is laughing like a loony, she's so excited. "I knew you were beautiful, Nana, but that gown … I don't know … You ought to never take it off, I think!" Alice, who's never in a good mood in the morning, tries out a little waltz. "I can't wait to see you two dancing, Nana! It'll be so romantic!" Maria puts her arms around her daughter. "I knew it would be a beautiful wedding and that you'd be a gorgeous bride. I knew it. Make the most of it, I've done it all for you …" Rhéauna walks back and forth in the living room. She turns around to check the lightness of her veil that hangs behind her, to check what her bouquet looks like against the pearly lustre of her gown. She can only see the upper part of her body in the mirror hung horizontally above the false fireplace. The veil conceals the unsuccessful hairdo, the collar emphasizes the beauty of her neck, the discreet makeup on her lips and cheeks hides her nervous pallor. Her eyes are feverish, which makes them lively. Yes, she will be a beautiful bride. She smiles as she wonders whether Gabriel will be a handsome bridegroom. With what she knows of his taste ... Madame Desbaillets emerges into the living room, out of breath. "I just saw the Pâtisserie Parisienne truck turn the corner ... Stay in the living room, the rest of the house will be taken over and ..." She stops mid-sentence. "Oh my Lord, Nana, you look absolutely gorgeous! A real princess!" Théo pulls at her sleeve. "I said it first." Initially, the taxi driver refused to take five passengers, claiming that his car was too small. Télesphore looked him up and down for long seconds without a word, then he took a dollar bill out of his pocket. "Is a buck enough to enlarge your car?" The driver, who'd been expecting it, grabbed the banknote, gesturing to the five passengers to get inside. Victoire wonders where her husband found it. A dollar! A fortune! Télesphore got in beside the driver while Victoire, Albertine, Édouard, and Madeleine piled onto the back seat. The driver turned to Victoire. "They told me it was for a wedding but they didn't tell me what parish ..." Télesphore pulled off his kid-leather gloves. He's hot, all of a sudden, and nervous. Still there's a big difference between reciting poems at the top of your lungs in a tavern full of drunks who aren't listening and leading your son to the altar under the eyes of two whole families. On an empty stomach. "We're going to the Church of Saint-Pierre-Apôtre. Somewhere in the east, on Dorchester near Wolfe or Montcalm, I'm not sure which ..." "Will you need a taxi to get to the reception afterwards?" "Nope, it's at the bride's house and it's not even a five-minute walk ... I think the whole wedding party'll go on foot." While she and her two aunts are waiting for their taxi, Teena experiences the worst hot flash in recent days. All decked out in their best finery – Teena wonders, in fact, what Tititte will have to say about her new outfit – the three of them are standing on the front balcony. Bebette keeps craning her neck to see if the car is coming. She's already let out three ringing *saperlipopette*s and is tapping impatiently with her fingertips on the guardrail. Régina tries to calm her. "We're ahead of time, Bebette, we won't miss anything!" "Oh sure, we're early as long as we aren't late! If Montréal taxi drivers are as slow as the ones in Saint-Boniface …" "If Montréal taxi drivers are as slow as the ones in Saint-Boniface I know for a fact we'll get there before everybody else!" "I'm anxious to see who'll be there, Régina, I'm entitled to that!" "That's no reason to have a fit!" "I'm not having a fit, I'm just nervous!" "Calm down, then!" And it's then that Teena turns red and brings her hand to her throat as she takes a seat in the rocking chair. Her two aunts are already on her. "Good Lord, Teena, what's the matter?" Bebette quickly realizes what's happening and undoes the collar of her niece's dress. "Poor you, what bad timing!" Teena tugs at her collar, undoes the mother-of-pearl buttons. "I'm hot, I'm so hot, I can't believe how hot I am!" Régina fans her with her gloves, which she's just pulled off. "You're soaking wet! Your face is all shiny!" Teena unbuttons her dress to the waist. "I have to loosen my belt or I'll feel as if the sweat's collecting above my waist till I drown in it!" Bebette holds out her arm to help her up. "You can't go there like that, you look terrible! Go and change!" "Are you crazy? It'll pass, don't worry. I'll just go and freshen up … Look, there's a taxi coming … Take it and I'll call for another one in fifteen minutes." "Are you sure?" "Sure I'm sure, go on …" "You absolutely don't want me to stay with you?" "Ma tante! You just said you were dying to see who all's there, so go … I'm telling you, I won't be long …" The taxi honks its horn. Bebette and Régina-Cœli go reluctantly down the few steps. Teena runs into the house. "Shoot! That's all I needed!" The square in front of the Church of Saint-Pierre-Apôtre hadn't seen such excitement in years. Relatives who haven't seen each other in a dog's age embrace, the hugs are endless, the handshakes too, the slaps on the shoulders; there's laughter, they try to remember the last time they saw one another. Especially on the Desrosiers side, which is a lot more expressive than Gabriel's family, which tends to be discreet, even fearful. The two groups don't mingle yet. That may happen later, during the reception at Maria's, when the official speeches have been delivered and drinks have started to bring down defences. Each one stays on their side of the church, Victoire and her entourage on the north side of the main door, Maria and hers on the south. Which doesn't stop anyone from babbling while they glance impatiently at the same door, which an altar boy has just opened but no one has dared yet to step inside. Someone, a remote uncle on Gabriel's side, can be heard, a heavy man surrounded by his wife and their seven children: "We have to wait for the bride and her witness. We aren't allowed to go in the church before that ... We have to follow them ..." His wife elbows him hard. "Where'd you pick that up, idiot? We can go inside whenever we want! Me, it's the bride's arrival I want to see. Last wedding we went to, the bride was so fat she could hardly get through the door!" Her husband shrugs. "Are you sure that wasn't our wedding?" His children burst out laughing. Not his wife. When Tititte sees her aunts Régina and Bebette arrive she rushes at them and asks where Teena is instead of welcoming them and saying how glad she is to see them again. Régina straightens her hat which got caught on the top of the door of the taxi. "Of all things, she had a really bad hot flash just before we left! She had to stay behind and change ..." Tititte is exasperated. "Don't tell me she'll have to wear that damn orange dress ..." Maria, who has come to welcome her aunts and has heard everything, frowns. "It's not orange, Tititte, it's gold ..." "Whatever, that's what she said, that's what she wanted us to think, but I'm telling you that dress is not gold, it's orange! Teena looks like a fat hen in it!" After she has embraced her aunts, Maria moves away. "If she looked like a fat hen in that dress like you claim, the dress would be lemon, Tititte, not orange!" Tititte shrugs and finally asks her aunts how they are, whether they had a good trip, and if they'd slept well at Teena's. Maria tugs at her sleeve. "Teena has hot flashes already?" Tititte gestures impatiently. "For a while now." "And you didn't tell me ..." "You had enough to be upset about, you didn't need that ..." Régina lays her hand on Maria's arm. "This isn't the best place to talk about it, Maria ..." Who turns her back and walks away. "If we never talk about it how can we help each other!" Rose, Simon, and little Ernest, after saying hello to a few people and realizing that their clothes – even Rose's new dress – aren't right for a wedding, take refuge near the statue of the Sacré-Coeur that overlooks the steps of the church. Simon and Ernest are leaning against the fence that surrounds the statue. Rose has studied the outfit of every one of the guests. "When more people get here we can show ourselves again. Not before. Maybe they won't notice us so much in the crowd..." Simon embraces her, kisses her. "How many times have I told you, it's not for our clothes they invited us?" "Maybe, but that's no reason to shame them!" Maria is the first who dares to cross the boundary between the two families. She heads straight for Victoire, takes her in her arms, kisses her. "I'm so glad to see you." "Me too." "This is the big day, isn't it, the day it's happening ... The day we lose our two big children!" A woebegone look passes between them. Maria is the first to pull herself together and attempts to make a sad smile. "I wanted to tell you, don't worry, Victoire, all will be well, I've worked things out..." "That's good! I was really worried about you!" "I figured it out better than I thought I would aside from that ... You'll see, it's going to be quite some wedding! Not a high mass, but I don't think that matters too much..." "And the lovely Nana, is she on her way?" "Yes, I left her at home with Monsieur Rambert who's going to act as father ... She has to arrive last, you understand ... Gabriel mustn't see her before she goes into the church ... Apparently that would bring bad luck ... And she didn't want us to stay with her ... My children and me, we came on foot, it's right next door ... Not even a five-minute walk..." She's explaining too much, realizes it, and keeps quiet after she's said: "Hey, it's hard on the nerves, all this!" The same altar boy emerges from the church. "Monsieur le curé says you can start going in ... The church mustn't be empty when the bride and groom arrive." The aunt on Gabriel's side turns to her husband. "What'd I tell you, Oscar?" He pushes her towards the church door. "Yeah, yeah, we know you always know everything, Berthe. But you won't see the arrival of the bride, that I can tell you ..." "I want to see her arrive. I think I'll wait outside. Go in, the rest of you." "Okay, you'll try and find us afterwards ..." Just then a babel of voices rise up in the street right in front of the church. A horn blows, all heads turn. A magnificent, pure white

Packard has just parked next to the sidewalk. Thinking the bride has arrived – but where's the groom? – everyone rushes towards the car. Télesphore frowns. "If Gabriel arrives after Rhéauna I'll kill him with my own hands!" Victoire cranes her neck, stands up on tiptoe. "I don't see him. You shoulda gone and got him too ..." "He didn't want me to. I guess he must've been worried about what shape I'd be in ..." The Packard's door opens and the lady who steps out is so beautiful and so elegant that a murmur of admiration can be heard passing between the two families. Everything about her outfit: her dress, lace and silk; her extravagant hat trimmed with long peacock feathers; her jewels which sparkle in the sun; her high-heeled shoes – a novelty; and even her eyeshadow, absolutely everything is lilac. Her bearing is regal but nothing in her face betrays condescension. She is a creature such as no one in this crowd has ever seen, and the silence that settles on the church steps is only broken by the cry of joy of Maria, who throws herself into the lady's arms. Those on Gabriel's side who don't know who she is wonder if Nana has a rich aunt; those on the Desrosiers side who have recognized her step back a few paces, though they can't take their eyes off her. La tante Bebette pulls a handkerchief from her purse, dabs her eyes. "She isn't ordinary beautiful." Régina-Cœli's sigh is disdainful. "Those women, they got nothing to do but primp at the mirror and get all dolled up." Her sister gives her a look as if she's just said something idiotic. "You think so? You think she didn't earn that dress?" Régina looks away. "If that's what you need to do to get a dress like that I'd rather look like how I look!" This time it's the *curé* himself who comes out of the church. "Please! If you want it to start ... The bride and groom are on their way." And just then Gabriel arrives, pale and out of breath. He embraces his mother, says hello to Télesphore. "I came partway on foot, I was too wound up ..." His mother straightens his tie. "If I'd been there to help you, you'd be all neat and tidy ..." "I'm fine, Moman, Nana's not marrying me for my clothes." "Maybe not but the guests want to see what the man she's marrying looks like, y'know ..." Gabriel leans over to his brother Édouard ... "Did you bring everything I gave you?" Édouard sticks out his chest. "I sure did! Everything's in my pocket. Look ..."

While he is showing Gabriel the contents of his pocket, Victoire approaches them. "What's this paper, Édouard? Aren't you just supposed to give the rings to the bride and groom?" Gabriel gestures to her to be quiet. "It's a present. For Nana. That she'll get just before we exchange rings …" Victoire frowns. Everyone wants to go into the church right after the beautiful woman who goes through the main door of Saint-Pierre-Apôtre as if she were going to officiate at some mysterious ceremony. A human gridlock forms in the doorway, despite its width, unpleasant words are exchanged, backs are pushed. As soon as they're through the portal everyone pounces on the best seats, Gabriel's family on the left, Rhéauna's on the right. Maria guides Ti-Lou towards the second pew, just behind Rhéauna's immediate family. The entire Desrosiers clan is insulted. Aunt Alice opens her purse, her husband stops her from rummaging in it. In the crush that forms near the door no one notices a frail and badly dressed man who has taken refuge in the last pew on Gabriel's side, holding a violin case against himself. He watches everyone pass, avoids the eyes of those who recognize him. Passing close to him, Victoire brings her hand to her mouth. She seems to be on the point of saying something, changes her mind. Édouard, though, doesn't hold back. "Mon oncle Josaphat! Come and sit up front with the rest of us!" Josaphat shakes his head and tells Édouard to follow his mother. Teena arrives, out of breath. In her gold dress, already soaking wet at the collar and under the arms. She looks for her sister Tititte, finds her sitting with the two aunts from the West. Spotting her arrival, Tititte rolls her eyes. Teena would like to slap her but she holds back. "I put some rags in my armpits but it still shows, it's not my fault!" Télesphore and Gabriel, who are pacing outside in front of the church, await in silence the signal to go inside, while Josaphat is miserable in the back row, his fiddle beside him. An hour earlier he was the first to arrive at the door. He wanted to sneak discreetly inside and hide in a corner while he waited for people to arrive and the ceremony to begin. He didn't want to meet the guests, mingle with them, sail from group to chattering group, asking his relatives what's new. He just wanted to witness the ceremony, see his son marry the woman he loves. After that he would find a place to hide in Maria's house until someone came to ask him to play a piece for the newlyweds. If they don't forget that he's there, of course, amid the feasting and festivities that will shake up the house all day long. When the beadle came to unlock the front door, Josaphat followed him inside. He stood there, frozen, in the middle of the portico. The only church he had attended was the little chapel in Duhamel, a square and ugly edifice topped with a ridiculous belfry where now and then a tiny bell tinkled with a tinny sound. The beauty, the majesty of Saint-Pierre-Apôtre, the light that streamed into it and its huge Gothic stained-glass windows had him rooted to the spot. The nave, exceptionally long and staggeringly high, was crowned with a ceiling separated into huge caissons in the shape of triangles and diamonds painted sea-green and peach. The high altar was a masterpiece of carved wood with gilded mouldings that shone in the morning sun, and the five stained-glass windows that girded it on three sides cast daubs of shimmering colours dancing with motes of dust into the church. It smelled of stale incense and beeswax. His mother in her great naïveté would have said that it smelled of the good Lord. He had forgotten to hide and so he sat in the last row, on the left, the bridegroom's side. Not to pray, no, he hasn't done that since childhood, but to admire it all, that wealth of colour, nearly happy now, and lets himself be permeated with the peace emanating from it. When the beadle comes to tell the two men that the time has come to go into the church, Gabriel leans against the door frame, closing his eyes, Télesphore grabs him by the shoulders. "What's the matter, Gabriel, you're as white as a sheet!" Gabriel straightens up, runs his hands over his face. "It's nothing, really nothing. I didn't sleep well and I didn't eat this morning because I'm taking communion." "You had the right to drink a little water." "I drank some, but it's not nourishing … Let's go, I'll be okay." They pass through the doorway, Télesphore ramrod straight, Gabriel slightly hunched, stepping hesitantly. All eyes turn towards them. Télesphore is about to turn his head to the right, to the left, very "lord of the manor," when he spies Josaphat who hasn't had time to react and is still riveted to his pew. Télesphore stops dead. Gabriel takes a couple of steps before he realizes that

Télesphore is throwing himself onto Josaphat and grabbing him by the collar. "What do you think you're doing? You've got no business here!" Gabriel comes back, pulls him by the arm. "I'm the one that asked him to come..." Télesphore frees himself, points towards Josaphat's nose. "Get outta here now or I won't be responsible for what I'll do. In front of everybody!" Josaphat gets up, ready to give in. Gabriel, who seems to have gotten his strength back, grabs the arm of the man he believes to be his father and bends over his ear. "You're going to stop that right now, Poppa! Right now! I don't know what it is between you two, I know it's been going on for years, but you're not gonna deal with it here, at my wedding." Télesphore straightens up, turns towards Gabriel. "What's between us two, kid..." Then, behind Gabriel's shoulder, he sees the guests looking at him. In particular he sees Victoire standing in the aisle, one hand raised in front of her as if to protect herself. He realizes that what he was getting ready to say and the violence he'd have put into it would have killed her on the spot. Restrain yourself. Restrain yourself once again. He's hot, his heart is pounding, he feels a dizzy spell coming. It's not Gabriel who's going to collapse, it's him. He has to support himself on the shoulder of Josaphat, his eternal rival, so he won't fall. A few seconds pass in deathly silence. He takes some breaths, moves away from Josaphat, and says out loud: "Sorry, everybody. I had a weak spell. Emotion. Nothing serious. It's gone now." Before moving away he turns towards Josaphat. "And is that what I think it is, that damn fiddle of yours?" Josaphat holds his gaze. "Yes. Gabriel asked me to play at his wedding." "Not here at the church, though?" "Nope. Later on. At the reception." Télesphore looks at Gabriel and sighs before going back to Josaphat. "Okay. Fine. But afterwards I don't wanna see hide nor hair of you. Never. I want you out of my life and Victoire's and Gabriel's. You don't belong here." He joins Gabriel and together they walk down the central aisle. Albertine has tugged on her mother's sleeve, forcing her to sit down. Ti-Lou leans towards Maria, sitting just in front of her. "Am I right or did something gruesome nearly happen here?" The two men make their way to the high altar where the priest, frowning, is waiting for them. In front of the church, the few guests who have stayed on the front steps follow the approach of the limousine that has just turned onto rue de la Visitation. Excited as a flea, an aunt on Gabriel's side practically runs down the steps to the sidewalk. "It's her! It's her, she's here!" The car stops opposite the main door and Fulgence Rambert, red with emotion, gets out. He opens the door, holds out his arm. A cascade of lace, of silk, of tulle appears, unfolds, a gloved hand holding a bouquet of peach-coloured roses rests on the hand of the elegant gentleman accompanying her. Some applause is heard. La tante Berthe brings her hand to her heart. "That's the most beautiful thing I've ever seen!" Rhéauna and Monsieur Rambert hastily climb the steps, obviously eager to be inside the church. When he sees the bride, bathed in light, outlined against the door, the *curé* gestures to the parish organist, Madame Gariépy who, though totally lacking in talent, has officiated at the organ of Saint-Pierre-Apôtre for eons. Immediately she strikes up the wedding march from *Lohengrin*. The congregation rises as one, turns towards the entrance. Ti-Lou can't stop herself from humming along with the music: *Here comes the bride, all dressed in light...* Maria takes a handkerchief from her purse, dabs her eyes. Rhéauna and Monsieur Rambert walk up the aisle, this time without haste. The bride, whose face can't be seen behind the veil, nods briefly to the people she knows, especially those who've come a long distance, Rose, Simon, little Ernest, then Bebette and Régina-Cœli, and finally, Ti-Lou, so resplendent all in lilac. She raises her bouquet, as if offering it, towards her mother and then towards Victoire who is holding her purse tightly against her, trembling, cheeks bathed in tears. Arriving at Gabriel's side, she lays her hand on his arm. You might think that she wants to reassure him. He brings her hand to his lips. "Are you ever beautiful!" She runs a finger over his forehead, lifts a rebellious strand of hair. "Are you ever handsome!" Télesphore and Monsieur Rambert have left to take their places in the two chairs assigned to them. The *curé* leaves the high altar, which is weighed down by flowers the same colour as Rhéauna's bouquet, and coughs into his fist to get the attention of the bridal couple. "We are gathered together this morning to celebrate the marriage of Rhéauna and Gabriel..." He reels off the usual patter that no one really listens to. The moment is nigh, it's about to happen, necks are craned, hands brought to hearts that beat too fast. Régina, Bebette, and Ti-Lou cannot imagine that the woman they are looking at from behind is the little girl they took in nine years earlier when she was crossing the country from west to east to come and join her mother in the city. They feel old and the tears that come to their eyes betray their dismay at the cruel passing of time as much as the emotion that weddings always elicit. The *curé* raises his arms, traces a sign of the cross and speaks to Gabriel. "You can take out the rings …" Édouard, Gabriel's young brother, all red, steps us, holding a paten. It's his great moment, he's been getting ready for it ever since Gabriel confided this important task to him. He's afraid of making a mistake despite the simplicity of his role, of tripping and falling full length at the foot of the high altar in front of everybody. He is standing too stiffly, feels absurd, wants to run away. He is convinced that he'll have nightmares about it for months. All the same he manages to hold out the paten to his brother before he walks away, trembling, certain that he's been ridiculous. Beside the two rings is a note folded in four. Gabriel takes it and hands it to Rhéauna. A few words in block letters: "I got the job." Rhéauna throws herself in Gabriel's arms, kisses his two cheeks through her veil. The cure startles, turns red. "It's not time, Mademoiselle, you aren't married yet …" Instead of speaking to him, Rhéauna turns to face the guests. "Excuse me. But I've just gotten the most wonderful wedding present imaginable …" Everyone applauds without knowing why, and the real ceremony can begin. At the back of the church stands a man looking with dismay at the one who has usurped his place next to his son. Later, when the priest declares, "I now pronounce you man and wife. You may kiss now, Madame and Monsieur Tremblay," applause even more exuberant rises up in the church while Rhéauna lifts her veil and Josaphat withdraws, angry. The mass is brief, without a sermon – that was Maria's request – it's hot in the church, the women are fanning themselves, the children are impatient, restless, bawling, the men wipe the sweat that's running down their necks. Quickly now, let it be over so the fun can begin! The ceremony ended, the newlyweds practically run down the central aisle, like children who want to go outside for air, and leave under a hail of confetti, happy cries, and congratulations. The organist tries a happy bit of Bach that's much too difficult for her, hits the wrong notes at the very beginning, and goes on quickly to something just as cheerful but easier to execute. The photo session is a hilarious confusion: the children run all over, the guests are rowdy, the men have already started making double entendres, and their wives castigate them with a look. It's a struggle, but the photographer manages to gather them up and just as he's about to take the first shot – the guests finally all together on the front steps in a tidy rectangular block – he realizes that the newlyweds are kissing in the shadow of the statue of the Sacré-Coeur. Ti-Lou is trying to be discreet but the eyes of all the men are on her. Those who don't know her wonder who that magnificent creature could be, those who do know imagine what they could do with her, where, how, and for how long. Once the photos are taken and the last bags of confetti are empty, Maria climbs to the top of the stairs to tell the guests that the reception is at her place, that it's nearby, a mere five-minute walk. The limousine rented by Fulgence Rambert is waiting for the newlyweds. Rhéauna refuses to get in, takes Gabriel's hand. "We'll walk too! It's more fun!" She winds her veil around her arms and takes the lead in the procession. A somewhat bedraggled parade of fifty or so crosses rue de la Visitation, turns onto Dorchester, then west, and finally, almost immediately, turning south onto rue Montcalm. The children up front, excited at the prospect of throwing themselves into an enormous meal where, for once, nothing will be forbidden even if it means they get sick; the women are hooting with laughter; some men are singing. A fat woman on Gabriel's side *turlutes*, warbling an old French song, and Rose thinks about weddings in Duhamel where everyone goes everywhere on foot because everyone lives close to the church and the *turlute* is on the menu from the church to the house where the reception will take place. Rose held Rhéauna against her heart, on the front steps of the church, wished for her a man like her own. The young bride didn't seem to understand and Rose didn't push it. After all, you don't find a Simon on the corner of every street ... Madame Desbaillets attends the wedding from Maria's balcony. She throws up her arms at the number of guests she'll have to take care of, welcomes them, and goes back inside shouting to the little boys from the neighbourhood who've been requisitioned to serve: "Get ready, here they come! They must be hungry, they took communion!" Access to the house was soon cut off because everyone wants to walk past the table with the wedding presents that had been set up in the living room, immediately left of the front door, to make sure that the torchère lamp, the set of dishes, the cutlery, the teakettle, or the decorative plates in cut glass or blown glass are prominently displayed. Those who are pleased because their gifts have been placed conspicuously linger, slowing down the flow of visitors, while those who are insulted because theirs are hard to see head immediately for the kitchen where one bar is already open. Bebette and Régina-Cœli want to grab the bride to gab with her for a while, they've come a long way and think they're entitled to spend a few minutes with her alone together, but they're narrowly beaten by Ti-Lou who, as soon as she's through the door, grabs Rhéauna's waist and pulls her into Théo's room, which is being used as a pantry and smells of sandwiches, ham or egg salad. Bebette wants to protest but Régina-Cœli holds her back. "Leave them alone. We'll talk later." Her sister turns her back, letting out a first *saperlipopette*. "It'll be too late later! She won't have time! We'll have come all this way just to see the bride go by like the queen of England and we won't see her up close!" Rhéauna and Ti-Lou have pushed aside the sandwiches and the cheese-stuffed celery sticks to make a little room for themselves on the bed. Ti-Lou takes the young bride's hand. "I didn't want to give you this in front of everybody and I didn't want to mail it either ..." She takes a small white envelope from her purse, holds it out to Rhéauna, who opens it. Two one-hundred-dollar bills slip out of a sheet of paper folded in two on which Rhéauna reads: "Waste this to my health." She drops the paper and the banknotes into her gown. "Come on, you can't give me that, it's a fortune!" Ti-Lou places her forefinger on her lips. "Don't say a word. Listen to me. I really do want you to waste that money. Part of it, anyway. The rest, use it to get off to a good start." "But it's way too much!" "To get off to a good start?" "Too much, period! I've never seen so much money at one time and I'm not sure I'm seeing it now!" "That's just it, allow yourself for once! I won't take that money to the grave, I have to do something with it ..." "Why are you saying that? Are you sick?" "No, no, no, I'm not sick ... Listen ... For supper, go to the Café Buade, it's not far from the Château Frontenac. Tell Henri, the maître d', that it's me who sent you, that we're related, you're on your honeymoon, and break your first hundred-dollar bill ... You'll eat well and you'll be treated like royalty. Québec City is full of good restaurants, take advantage of them while you're there ... The money that's left you'll use to start your married life ... Good luck!" Before Rhéauna has time to embrace her cousin, Maria comes practically running into the room. "Nana! Everybody's waiting for you!" Madame Desbaillets and her little helpers are racing all over because the guests are hungry and they're getting impatient. While the women lunge at the platters of assorted sandwiches and the plates of chicken à la king (everything served any old way and simultaneously), the men cluster around the kitchen table with two jugs of white wine, two jugs of red wine (which didn't draw many visitors), a number of forty-ouncers of Bols gin and countless cases of beer (much too popular). The women eat too quickly and gulp soft drinks to wash it all down, the men drink too fast and don't eat much. As for the children, they're over the moon: nothing is forbidden, they can stuff themselves as much as they want at a table set up just for them at the back of the yard. Théo has been anticipating this moment for weeks and he's taking advantage of it, just five minutes later he's smeared with white sauce and debris from egg salad. Édouard, a glutton who rarely has enough to eat, has built a pyramid of blue, green, and pink sandwiches and polished them off practically without chewing. Madeleine, his little sister, is playing with her food because there are green peas, which she hates, in the sauce with the chicken à la king. She dips into her brother's heap of sandwiches and he pushes her away, telling her with his mouth full to get her own. Little Ernest doesn't know which way to turn: stuff his face like the other children or walk around the yard to watch all the pretty ladies laugh and fan themselves, inhale their scent as his father does with his mother, but he's afraid of ending up with the lady who comes to visit them every year and fusses with him too much for his liking so he stays quietly in his chair. Victoire is sitting by herself in a corner and trying to hide her excitement at what she has piled up on her plate ... Don't eat too fast ... Don't make yourself sick ... Toasts are bellowed, shouting and laughter fill the yard as tempers rise and stomachs fill. The cake – white, three layers, shimmering with fake silver beads – had pride of place in the middle. No one dares to approach it yet. As she leaves the house, Rhéauna is greeted by a burst of applause. The women want to see her gown, the men to kiss her. She spends the first hour of the reception visiting all the tables to greet every one of the guests. Gabriel follows her, holding her by her waist. He doesn't participate in the conversation very much because he's not a chatterbox, but he smiles a lot and turns red every time someone, always a man, makes a double entendre. The bride sits for a good fifteen minutes with her great-aunts Bebette and Régina-Cœli, thanking them for having come from so far away, and who remind her with considerable detail, as if she hadn't lived it, of her stop in Regina and in Saint-Boniface nine years earlier. She reassures Victoire, promising to take good care of her son, and nearly brings tears to Rose – who suspects it's to make her happy that she claims her wedding wouldn't have been complete without her and her family. She speaks English with her aunt Alice, who appreciates it, and compliments her uncle Ernest on his imposing presence, which makes him swell his chest and straighten his back under the broad-brimmed hat he won't take off all day because a Mounted Policeman is never bareheaded. She promises Tititte and Teena to invite them as often as possible to play cards after she has thanked them – without irony – for helping her choose her wedding gown. Teena fans herself with her napkin all the time Rhéauna is speaking to her, and her sister, for once, doesn't bawl her out. Rhéauna has taken off her veil, her gloves, she has left her bouquet in the house until the moment near the end of the reception when she will throw it over her head to the unmarried girls. Théo follows her like a little dog, hardly ever breaking contact with her: he holds her hand, holds her by the sleeve, by the train. She eats a few sandwiches, drinks a glass of wine, laughs heartily at everything that's said to her. Édouard has approached his mother who has just served herself a healthy portion of chicken à la king. "When I get married, Moman, I want a gown just like that." Télesphore and Josaphat, who've been holding back since the night before, quickly dived into the *gros gin*. And they both stopped shaking. Josaphat felt his resentment gradually go numb, then go on to lodge like a closed fist in the area of his heart. Less than a pain and more than heartbreak. Télesphore, for his part, is relaxed, it's over, this happens to him often, to move from hostility to a gentle torpor, he's toned down, his urge to crush Josaphat has given way to a rather condescending pity for his wife's brother, a poor country fiddler when all's said and done, an uneducated failure he's wrong to be jealous of. And when his conscience starts to show him his own flaws, what his life has become on account of alcohol, in fact, what he makes his family put up with, then he drinks even more. Not to forget. He can't forget. To stun himself. Before long he feels an urgent need to go out on the balcony and launch into Lamartine's "Le lac" or Nelligan's "Le vaisseau d'or," but a look from his wife – she always sees everything – stops him. For now. During one of his numerous visits to the kitchen he meets Josaphat who is pouring himself a shot of gin, they exchange a look. Josaphat raises his glass. Télesphore does the same. Josaphat speaks first: "You think we oughta talk?" Télesphore shrugs. "Maybe." "So we talk?" "If you want …" They head for Maria's room, push aside the men's hats crowded on the bed, sit down side by side. Télesphore gulps his gin. "Go ahead. I don't think I got nothing to say. You know what I think about it all, that won't change." After knocking back his drink, Josaphat closes his eyes, clears his throat. "Gives you courage when you haven't got none …" "Yeah, and takes it away when you …" "As far as that …" "That's all you got to say?" "No. But what I got to say, it's tough … Listen … There's one thing you gotta understand. And if you don't understand, you gotta accept it anyway … What there is between Victoire and me, that's not gonna change either. It's there forever. We didn't want it, it happened, and it was wonderful.

And after all this time it's still wonderful. Threats are no good, punishments neither. You knew what you were getting involved in when you married Victoire, Télesphore, you're the one who wanted it ... We accepted it, her and me, for the good of our children, so they wouldn't be brought up like outcasts, so they'd have a normal life. I nearly died of a broken heart and I'm sure Victoire did too. She couldn't drink, I don't know what she did to get over it ... Me ... Me, I been drunk for twelve years, there's big parts of those twelve years that're like holes because I passed through them without living them ... Hopelessness tastes like gin, forgetting does too. Her, she hasn't even got that, she hasn't got the means to forget. She's a great woman, Télesphore, and us men compared with her, we're assholes." He runs his hand over his forehead, looks at the bottom of his glass, stands, faces Télesphore. "All that to say that your two children are from you, Télesphore, quit making up stories to tell yourself, forget about jealousy. Victoire and me, we're too honest, and maybe too stupid to get together on the sly. When we do see each other, which is fairly rare, it's to cry. Not even holding hands, we don't even allow ourselves that. We cry, the both of us, about the misery we lived together that maybe wasn't so bad when you think of it as the misery we're living now, apart. We're cut off from everything we loved, even the countryside, we're closed up in a city neither one of us can get used to and it seems to me like we don't deserve to be punished like we are. Not her, anyways. Love her, Télesphore, love her in my place. Respect her, she deserves it! Love the children that you made with her, they need it and she does too. The past can't be erased, true, but that's no reason to perpetuate it. I love Victoire and Victoire loves me, but we've never done a thing to betray the ties between you and her. You can hate me, I guess it's normal, but not her! Not her!" Télesphore gets up in turn, brings his face close to Josaphat's. "If I find you in my way one more time I'll kill you!" Josaphat raises his empty glass. "If you find me in your way one more time I give you permission to kill me." They bring their empty glasses to their lips. The door opens, Madame Desbaillets comes into the room. "Which one of the two of you is called Josaphat? Madame Rathier's looking for you, apparently it's time for the music ..." The two men follow her into the corridor that leads into the kitchen at the back of the house. The small upright piano that Madame Desbaillets had left in the apartment seven years earlier because none of her children – all of whom had gone off to make their living and were sick of the music lessons their mother had imposed on them since childhood – wanted to take care of it, had been transported to the back gallery by four pie-eyed men who'd nearly dropped it more than once. The chairs that blocked the veranda were crammed together, the piano pushed in front of the window so the pianist's back would be to the audience. Seeing these preparations, the guests have calmed down a little. The "artistic" part of a wedding is often deadly boring but out of sheer politeness you have to display a certain patience, put up with the pathetic or ridiculous numbers, wait for it to be over because usually the fun begins right after the *matantes* who sing the appropriately pious ditties and the sloshed *mononcles* who think they're Caruso. The talk isn't so loud, the chairs have been arranged. The women are sitting, heads turned towards the house. The men are still standing. Everyone, without exception, is holding a glass. Maria goes to join Régina-Cœli and Josaphat who are quietly waiting to be announced. They didn't know that there would be two of them making music and they're sizing each other up while they bow politely. Maria brings her hands up to silence the few guests who are still talking. "Nana's aunt Régina-Cœli came all the way from Saskatchewan, and Gabriel's uncle Josaphat, a great fiddler, have agreed to offer us a little concert before we bring out the gramophone so people can dance ..." She goes towards Régina-Cœli, already seated on the piano bench, places her hands on her shoulders. "I have to warn you, ma tante Régina, the piano hasn't been tuned for years ... Good luck anyway ..." Laughter. Some polite applause in the yard, Bebette declares to the company at large: "She plays good even when she plays out of tune!" Régina, red to the ears, runs her hands here and there over the keyboard. "True, it really is out of tune ... This won't be easy." Maria pats her shoulder. "It'll be nice anyway." Josaphat leans over to Régina. "D'you want to start?" She opens the music book she's just set down in front of her, smooths it with her hand as if to get rid of creases, though it's brand new. "As you wish." He sits down beside her. She moves over to make room for him. He looks over the score though he can't read it. "We could try and improvise a little something for two, if you want, instead of making music that's too serious…" "I've never improvised, Monsieur Josaphat, I learned everything in books, I just play classical…" "You'll see, it isn't hard… Just follow me… I'll start, then you join in when you want… I'm sure you can do it…" Getting no answer and ignoring the obvious panic that's just taken hold of Régina-Cœli, Josaphat stands up, faces the guests, offers a slight obeisance, lifts his bow. As usual, his first note, long, drawn-out, straight as an arrow, pierces the heart of each of the guests. No one is expecting it. Looks are exchanged, sensitive women bring their hands to their mouths. "That's so sad, will it be like that all the way through?" Régina-Cœli looks in Josaphat's direction. She can't accompany that, it's just one note. She crosses her arms on her chest, waits for something more to happen. Once the note is drained – you'd've sworn that it would never end – another one is added, shorter, not so languorous, then a third, clearly happier. He repeats them, mixes them, doubles, triples them, plays them in reverse, multiplies the combinations, and then, from that fusion of three notes, repeated differently every time, the interpretation shaded, is born what could be called a tune, still confused, an embryonic musical line, a promise, as if the musician were saying: listen, it's building, it's coming along… New notes are added, a suggestion of rhythm seeps in, Régina-Cœli thinks she recognizes what could be something like the rhythms of a waltz. She positions her hands on the keyboard and punctuates with notes, every one of them false, that give her instrument the rasping voice of a honky-tonk piano, which she thinks is Josaphat's attempt to improvise a waltz. He looks at her, winks. She gains confidence and of that meeting between a tune that has not yet found its final form and the accompanying figure that emphasizes the downbeats and upbeats is born, little by little, a genuine waltz. Bodies start to sway, they are following the rhythm, at last, something they can recognize! At the most beautiful part of the waltz, Gabriel approaches his bride, holds out his hand to her. She rises, a big smile on her lips, follows him to the middle of the yard, applauded by the guests. He takes her in his arms. They're awkward, they step on each other's toes, apologize, laughing, the dance steps they sketch have practically nothing to do with the waltz but they are clearly thrilled, they laugh, accompany the waltz by singing the tune that has finally taken its definitive form and that they will never forget. Monsieur Rambert and Maria join them. They are more experienced, they move fluidly, you sense that they've done it hundreds of times, down there in Providence, maybe, in disreputable cabarets at the harbour visited by jubilant sailors, or chic dance halls where you could win a bottle of champagne if you made it to the finals of the dance competition put on every Saturday night. They must have won some of those bottles because they cover the dance floor as if they were alone, nearly professional. They are applauded and bow gracefully even as they carry on with their waltz, turning and swirling faster and faster. Télesphore, not to be outdone, pulls Victoire into the middle of the yard. But they don't dance. Standing face to face they are content to take small steps, to the left, to the right, swaying in place. Victoire has closed her eyes. She hasn't danced with her husband since their wedding. Télesphore bends over her ear. "I promise I'll try to behave even if I haven't had anything to drink." When the waltz is over they give a big hand to the dancers and the musicians. Régina-Cœli gets up to speak to Josaphat. "You're right, it wasn't all that hard …" He gives her an ironic look. "Hang onto your tuque, now it's going to be hard!" He embarks on a frenzied rigadoon that has her rooted to the spot. It's fast, it's nearly violent, it's happy to the point of irritation, it puts pep in your shoes and excitement in the small of your back. In the yard everyone has got up and someone shouts: "I don't think we'll need your gramophone, Maria!" Régina-Cœli has gone back to her seat. "I've never played that, I don't know what to do …" Josaphat shouts at her: "Do like you did before, let yourself go!" "I've never let myself go to that kind of music …" "It's the same as the other one, you just have to like it!" She places her hands on the keyboard and draws on her memories of childhood, of family parties where the jig competed with the rigadoon and the reel, a melting pot of music from the old countries, from France, England, Ireland, Scotland, the shock of cultures their encounter had produced, their nuptials not always easy, their mutual influences. Her fingers grow excited, she's off to a bad start, she doesn't have the right rhythm, she's mad at herself, starts over. Josaphat has come and sat down beside her, encouraging her with his voice: "Go on, you can do it! If you can play Mozart you sure can play my reel. Think about where you come from Régina, and use it!" "I'm thinking about it, I am, that's what I'm doing!" And all at once, it unblocks. She has understood the complex simplicity of what Josaphat plays and her fingers start dancing on the notes, she guesses more than she plays, she plays straight, as if it were Bach, surprises herself thinking, "as if it were Bach!" Everyone is standing, couples have formed, they dance any old way, they jump in place, the children form a circle, pull too hard, fall, pick themselves up. Tititte can be seen tapping her feet and Teena fanning herself and laughing instead of complaining. Some guests have grabbed all the spoons their hands can hold and the clink of utensils rises into the sky over Montréal as it does into that over Duhamel or Sainte-Maria-de-Saskatchewan or Saint-Boniface or Regina. Someone, people realize quickly that it's Simon, takes out a harmonica and its acid sound is added to the tinny notes of the piano and the reeling tendrils of the fiddle. Aunt Alice raises her flask and shouts, in French, a toast to the newlyweds. Ernest looks elsewhere. Victoire and Télesphore, despite the music that buries everything, are deep in discussion. Josaphat spies them, closes his eyes, concentrates on the grand finale that is coming and that he wants to play as if it were the apotheosis of his love for his sister. Rhéauna approaches her mother and slips something that resembles a banknote into the pocket of her dress. "Don't look and see what it is till I've left…" Ti-Lou has seen her and smiles. She also picks up two spoons and makes them clink against her sore knee. Bebette, who has drunk more than usual, is at her one hundredth *saperlipopette*, louder than the others because for once it's expressing happiness rather than frustration. Béa and Alice dance, holding one another's hands even if it means that they'll have a shouting match as soon as the wedding is over. Rhéauna goes to join Gabriel who kisses her hands. Everyone is tapping their feet, the spoons make a sound like heavy rain on a tin roof, Régina-Cœli and Josaphat, in perfect harmony, outdo themselves and have the impression they are floating above the yard. The union of the two families is being accomplished in music. This piece, which Josaphat will play until the end of his days, alone or with others, and which will stay in the annals as one of the most beautiful reels ever composed, will have the title "The Grand Melee."

On the upstairs balcony of Madame Desbaillets's house next door, Rose, Violette, and Mauve are tapping their feet while they knit. Florence, their mother, eyes closed, is listening to the music rise up into the sky of Montréal.

*Key West and Montréal*
*January 3 to May 27, 2011*

Thanks to Louise Jobin and Jean-Claude Pepin
for their invaluable research on the year 1922.

—M.T.

NEXT IN MICHEL TREMBLAY'S
DESROSIERS DIASPORA SERIES

# TWISTS OF FATE

## IF BY CHANCE & DESTINATION PARADISE

In *If by Chance*, set in 1925, the great Ti-Lou, the famous She-Wolf of Ottawa, returns to Montréal. After a fruitful career in the royal suite at the Château Laurier, where she entertained diplomats and men of the world, politicians and men of the cloth alike, she packs up and sneaks off, her suitcases replete with savings. Unrepentant, always whimsical, Louise Wilson-Desrosiers was a proud, free, top-class courtesan ... But when she arrives in the hall of Windsor Station, five possible fates await her, each with their share of risks and opportunities. In any of these alternate lives, Ti-Lou will have to deal with more than mere chance, because awaiting her at the crossroads is the threat of loneliness and, worse still, the fear of allowing herself to be loved.

In *Destination Paradise*, we enter the Paradise Club on boulevard Saint-Laurent, one of the few establishments catering to middle-aged bachelors. It's where Édouard Tremblay – Ti-Lou's distant cousin – makes his entry into the "big world" of 1930s Montréal. Precocious despite his eighteen years of age, he is carried away by his double, the Duchess of Langeais, whose story he has just read in Balzac's eponymous novel. Readers of Tremblay's *Chronicles of the Plateau-Mont-Royal* will already know that Édouard will become the undisputed queen of the Montréal drag scene; but we knew less about Édouard's beginnings in life and about the inception of his stage character. *Destination Paradise* tenderly reveals Édouard's rite of passage.

## TRANSLATED BY LINDA GABORIAU

# ABOUT THE DESROSIERS DIASPORA SERIES

"Wanderers. All of them. All the Desrosiers, never satisfied, always searching elsewhere for something better..."

Renowned Québec author Michel Tremblay's *Desrosiers Diaspora* series spans the North American continent in the early years of the twentieth century. In nine linked books, this 1,400-page family saga provides the backstory for some of Tremblay's best-loved characters, particularly Rhéauna, known as Nana, who later becomes the eponymous character in Tremblay's award-winning first novel, *The Fat Woman Next Door Is Pregnant*, and who is based on Tremblay's own mother. The *Desrosiers Diaspora* follows Nana and the other remarkable Desrosiers women, including Nana's grandmother, Joséphine, and her mother and aunts, Maria, Teena, and Tittite, as they leave and return to the tiny village of Sainte-Maria-de-Saskatchewan, dispersing to Rhode Island, Montréal, Ottawa, and Duhamel in the Laurentians. In Tremblay's vivid, headlong prose, with its meticulously observed moments both large and small, the Desrosiers' tumultuous and entwined lives are revealed as occasionally happy, often cruel and impulsive.

The first five volumes of the *Desrosiers Diaspora* series have been translated into English by Sheila Fischman and Linda Gaboriau and published by Talonbooks. English translations of novels six through nine are forthcoming. The French originals were published by Leméac Éditeur and Actes Sud.

In the first volume, *Crossing the Continent*, we find Nana living with her two younger sisters, Béa and Alice, on her maternal grandparents' farm in Sainte-Maria-de-Saskatchewan, a francophone Catholic enclave of two hundred souls. At the age of ten, amid swaying fields of wheat under the idyllic prairie sky, Nana is suddenly called by her mother, Maria, whom she hasn't seen in five years and who now lives in Montréal, to come "home" and help take care of her new baby brother. So it is that Nana embarks alone on an epic train journey through Regina, Winnipeg, and Ottawa, on which she encounters a dizzying array of strangers and distant relatives, including Ti-Lou, the "she-wolf of Ottawa."

The story continues in *Crossing the City*, where we meet Maria as she leaves the city of Providence, Rhode Island, pregnant and alone; we also meet Nana in Montréal, two years later. Having crossed the continent from her grandparents' farm in Saskatchewan, Nana now traverses the city, alone, in an attempt to buy train tickets to reunite her family. *Crossing the City* includes vivid descriptions of Montréal's early-twentieth-century neighbourhoods, which Nana traverses as she makes her journey.

The third novel in the series, *A Crossing of Hearts*, opens during a stifling heat wave in Montréal in August 1915, as war rages in Europe. The three Desrosiers sisters – Tititte, Teena, and Maria – have been planning a vacation in the mountains, to do nothing but gossip, laugh, drink, and overeat while basking in the sun. Maria's children beg to come along. Reluctantly, Maria takes her children on the week-long trip to the Laurentians. As the reader views the journey through young Nana's eyes, we come to understand the impoverished circumstances they leave behind in Montréal, only to find poverty evermore present in the country. Yet it feels good to get out of town, and encounters with rural relatives crystallize young Nana's true feelings for her mother, as confidences and family secrets fuse day into night.

*Rite of Passage* finds Nana at the crossroads of the end of childhood, facing the passing of her adolescence and the arrival of new responsibilities as her grandmother Joséphine approaches her last hours. To calm the storm, Nana reads the enthralling tales of Josaphat-le-Violon – a returning character in Tremblay's *Chronicles of the Plateau-Mont-Royal*. Three of

Josaphat's fantastical stories contain revelations whose full influence in her own existence Nana cannot yet measure. In parallel, Nina's rebellious mother, Maria, languishes back in Montréal. She is torn between her desire to gather her young family around her and her deep uncertainty about being able to care for them properly.

**Sheila Fischman** is the award-winning translator of some two hundred works of contemporary fiction from Québec. *The Grand Melee* is her eighteenth translation of a Michel Tremblay book. Her other authors include Hubert Aquin, Anne Hébert, Gaétan Soucy, Marie-Claire Blais, François Gravel, Larry Tremblay, Christine Eddie, and more. She has been a finalist for the Governor General's Literary Award for French-to-English Translation fifteen times, and she has received the Molson Prize in the Arts. A Member of the Order of Canada and a Chevalière of the Ordre national du Québec, she lives in Montréal.

A major figure in Québec literature, **Michel Tremblay** has built an impressive body of work as a playwright, novelist, translator, and screenwriter. To date Tremblay's complete works include twenty-nine plays, thirty novels, six collections of autobiographical stories, a collection of tales, seven screenplays, forty-six translations and adaptations of works by foreign writers, nine plays and twelve stories printed in diverse publications, an opera libretto, a song cycle, a Symphonic Christmas Tale, and two musicals. His plays have been published and translated into forty languages and have garnered critical acclaim in Canada, the United States, and more than fifty countries around the world.